AMBUSHED!

Cheves was on the point of turning off when, from directly ahead of him, there came rolling through the forest the report of a gun, followed by a series of short, bouncing crashes. Cheves drew up, nerves on edge. It sounded like a hunter—possibly from Vincennes. But no, a hunter from the Fort would have small necessity of traveling so far afield for game. Perhaps, then, it was some independent British trapper.

The Virginian was about to step into the brush when a stir from behind whirled him about. He stopped, half turned. Twenty yards away stood a half-naked, paint-daubed Indian buck. Out of the corner of his eye Cheves saw another advance from the brush in front. He was trapped! For a moment the idea of resistance surged over him. A step and a shot and he would have at least one of them. But the idea passed swiftly. That rifle report meant a larger party nearby. He lowered his gun and threw up a hand in token of peace.

The Indians closed in, rifles advanced.

Other *Leisure* books by Ernest Haycox:
NEW HOPE

BURNT CREEK

Ernest Haycox

LEISURE BOOKS   NEW YORK CITY

A LEISURE BOOK®

November 2000

Published by special arrangement with Golden West Literary Agency.

Acknowledgements may be found at the end of the book.

Dorchester Publishing Co., Inc.
276 Fifth Avenue
New York, NY 10001

ISBN 0-8439-4798-5

BURNT CREEK

Ernest Haycox's parents were divorced when he was very young, and he attended almost a dozen different schools just getting an elementary education, spending his boyhood in logging camps, shingle mills, on ranches, and in numerous small towns in Oregon. Later, following his graduation from the University of Oregon, he spent part of 1924 and much of 1925 living in New York City, writing short stories for Street & Smith's *Western Story Magazine*. In 1926 he returned to Oregon where he spent the rest of his life. However, it was during his New York period that he fashioned his first series of interconnected stories, those set in and around Burnt Creek, a small crossroads town in Central Oregon. This was a region he knew well, and the characters in the stories are probably based on people he had met during his transient years. The stories proved very popular with readers, and at one time character actor, Guy Kibbee, hoped to have the stories adapted for the screen with himself in the rôle of the merchant, post master, and locator, Dave Budd. Taken together, and appearing now for the first time in book form, these stories do indeed form a picaresque novel, capturing indelibly the people and the land during the early years of this century when homesteaders were still coming to Oregon to make a new life.

I

"A BURNT CREEK YULETIDE"

By day the scooped-out clearing that formed Burnt Creek seemed rather bleak. The surrounding jack pines were drooped under a niggardly coat of snow, and the ground was a streaked white across which the Bend-Klamath Road straggled, taking brief respite from the forest. In truth, the first inch of snow in the desert country makes the land resemble nothing so much as a molting hen minus all but tail feathers.

As darkness closed down and Christmas Eve came, the snow drifted heavier and the kitchen lamp of the solitary crossroads store cast a mellow gleam through the window and upon the ground. Old man Budd, having attended to his night meal, stood on the front porch and watched the air grow dizzy with flakes — quite strange and quite beautiful to this lonesome storekeeper. He struck a match to his pipe and wrapped the Mackinaw tighter about him.

The lamplight managed to push its rays through the white flurry and faintly illumine the snow-encrusted branches of the dwarf pines. They looked ever so much like Christmas trees, and Budd, drawing sharply on the pipe, was aware of an old, old memory that would not be brushed aside. It was the sweet and mellow thought of his far-away boyhood home in a Pennsylvania village. On just such an eve as this they would be sleigh riding, and the windows of the neighboring houses would be warm with light and silhouetted with tinseled and glittering trees — pleasant, cheery houses. And he would fall asleep with the utter relaxation of youth in his own feather bed, to wake on Christmas morn with the church bells sounding across the frosty air. He had never cared much for those bells as a boy. Middle age, somehow, made their chimes infinitely peaceful, infinitely poignant.

He drew at the pipe with harsher strength. All day he had been plagued with depression, and now the night with its weird shadows and white silence caused him to move aimlessly up and down the porch. Emotion did not easily break through his strong, inscrutable face, so he stared at the drifting snow, at the dark outline of the pines, while the church bells of far-off Pennsylvania haunted his brain.

"Christmas evenin'," he murmured. "Just like another night, only there's a difference. Somethin' wrong with you, old-timer. Too much of your own company, I guess."

A flurry of snow obscured the pines entirely. Budd had the impression that someone was coming toward him from the Bend-Klamath Road. The impression was verified when horse and rider bulked through the white storm and approached the edge of the porch. Budd moved back. The rider slid from his saddle and under the roof's protection, beating the flakes from his coat and stamping heavy boots against the floor boards. It was entirely too dark to make out features, but the storekeeper, who knew every homesteader and cow hand for fifty miles around, welcomed this unknown visitor gladly. Here was companionship for Christmas Eve.

"Bad time to be out," he said. "Lead your horse in back

9

to the barn an' I'll throw up a little snack meanwhile. Who is it? My eyes ain't so good as they was once." He stared through the velvet shadows.

The newcomer leaned against one of the two-by-fours which supported the porch roof. For a moment he said nothing at all. Then a grunt of amusement, which was half a whine and half an essay at contempt, issued from him. "Never could see very well. Dunno your own son, I reckon. Bad egg rolled back to smell up the place for a bit."

Budd's head jerked up. "Dan?" he challenged.

"The same. An' I'm in a powerful hurry. Got somethin' to eat?"

The answer came as an explosion of temper. "Nothin' fer you, my lad! You wore out your welcome long ago! I told you to git away an' stay! You're no son of mine. Git off this porch!" He finished the declaration with a bellow, striding forward with a forbidding arm. The younger man was but a dwarf in front of the storekeeper's massive bulk and seemed even smaller when he huddled back against the two-by-four.

"Aw, cut it out," he growled, and again a whine tinged his words. "I didn't come because I wanted. They're after me, an' I ain't had a bite of grub since mornin'. Gimme that an' I'll leave right off."

"In trouble again, huh? Like a yellow dog you run for cover with your tail atween your legs. Well, I've given you my last boost. Ain't goin' to fish you out of any more scrapes. You made your bed. Now you sleep in it!"

"It wasn't my fault this time," protested his son. "The gang did it an' framed me! Honest . . . I'm clean. They framed me, I tell you. Sheriff's on the way here, too! Lemme have a bite of something and a cup of hot coffee! Fer heaven's sake, don't let a man freeze out here!"

Budd dropped his arm. Here was his wayward son come back to bring him sorrow on Christmas Eve. The boy had left five years before, choosing wilder company in spite of all that Budd might do to dissuade him. And so, after many bitter quarrels and much forgiveness, he had disowned him, had closed the last sober, belated chapter of what had once been — twenty-five years back — bright romance. No one ever mentioned Budd's son in his presence.

The younger man shifted, whimpering. "Aw, lemme in. It wasn't my fault. And I ain't askin' for protection. Just gimme something to eat, and I'll beat it." The apparent hopelessness of his request turned him to childish rage. "Who wants your protection, anyhow!" he shouted. "I don't! Don't want a thing you can give me! It's your fault. Maybe if you'd handled me like a white man when I was a kid, I'd been decent!"

All of a sudden those church bells began to ring again in the storekeeper's ear. Maybe the kid was right. Maybe it was partly his fault. It takes a mother to bring up children, and the kid had never had a mother but had grown piecemeal in the pines and on the desert while he, Budd, strove to make a living from the harsh land. This was Christmas. What was Christmas for but the giving of gifts? Not just packages wrapped in white tissue paper but other things. So the storekeeper, who knew his son to be worthless yet wished to believe there was in him a redeeming spark, moved aside.

"All right, Danny," he said in a gentler tone. "Go in."

The younger man brushed by, teeth chattering, and ran to the stove. "Shut the door!" he ordered sharply. "Don't be a fool! Sheriff might be lookin' from the road right now!"

Budd did as requested and walked into the kitchen. When his son turned around and faced the lamplight, the storekeeper was startled by the change he saw. Once there had been a certain youthfulness on Danny's face, a certain handsomeness to hide the petulant mouth and the greedy eyes. It was no longer present. An unwholesome wisdom was imprinted on the face now, broken by lines of reckless living. The mouth which formerly had curved in a too-frequent pout was set in a perpetual sneer. If he knew anything, the storekeeper told himself, he knew that his son was wholly bad. It took but a glance at the prematurely hardened face — Dan was twenty-five and looked ten years older — to reveal that.

And yet this was Christmas! Here was his prodigal son. For good or bad, he had come back. Budd's lonesome heart was eased at the thought. He went to the cupboard and took from there bits of food he had recently put away.

"What's wrong now?" he asked.

"Aw, it wouldn't be any use to tell," replied Danny. He saw that his trick had worked and, like some mongrel cur, grew bold and sullen. "Don't worry about it. Just pass out the grub."

A dish slammed on the table, followed by Budd's angry fist. "You snippet! Don't give me any of your tongue! I'm askin' you once more! What happened?"

Dan slid into a chair and attacked the victuals. Either from fear or hunger he would not raise his head, but between wolfish gulps he told his story. "Was playin' pool in Bend with Mike Reilly an' Toots' Billmire. . . ."

"Eghh! Herdin' with cow thieves now, huh?"

"Who can prove they're cow thieves?" cried Dan passionately. It seemed to touch a very raw spot, and he dared face his father. But the crafty eyes were not accustomed to so direct a meeting, and slid quickly away. "Anyhow we was playin' when Mike got in a fight with the house man, kicked the lights out, and pulled his gun. Mike was some drunk, I guess. There was a great ruckus. Then somebody donged me on the head and down I went. When the lights come on, there was the house man on the floor . . . dead. Mike did it, I swear. But the double crosser had clipped me in the dark and transferred guns. I saw it in a minute. The sheriff come on the run. Mike an' Toots starts for the rear. What was I to do, hold the sack? Not on your life! I couldn't explain those two empty shells. I dusted. Sheriff saw which way we went an' he knows where we'll be headin' for, I reckon."

Budd's eyes never left the furtive, pinched face. Every word he seemed to weigh, listening for that ring of truth which, though often very faint, accompanies the sincere at heart. He could not hear it and, after a dismal silence, shook his head.

"Dan, you're lyin' to me."

"I ain't!" yelled the son, white with rage. He kicked back the chair and stood up. "I tell you they framed me! Oh, I know I ain't no saint! It don't make no difference what I say, I guess. You never believed me, and nobody else ever has. I'll clear out now. You can go jump in the creek for all I care. Sweet father you've been!"

Budd was shaken mightily. This was a greater bitterness than he had ever heard in a man. Almost unreasoning. Perhaps he had misjudged. Perhaps he had been harsh. If there had only been a mother to care for his boy. Anyhow, this was Christmas, and those sweet, far-off bells mellowed his thoughts. He wanted to believe that Danny spoke the truth for once. He wanted to believe it more whole-heartedly than he had ever wanted to believe anything. A tenderness, strange and unfamiliar emotion, clutched his heart.

"All right, Dan, I ain't goin' to argue. I'll believe it. Now where you aim to go? This is a powerful bad night."

A greedy flash illumined the furtive eyes. "Across the line, I reckon. 'Tain't so far. But I'll need some money. Flat busted."

Budd was slouched over, his double chin rolling against the folds of the Mackinaw.

"If you only had a mother," he murmured, "things might have been different."

"Aw, cut that out!" rasped out Dan. "No more slush. I've heard it too many times."

"All right, Dan. Don't aim to quarrel. This is Christmas night."

"Christmas? Well, what about it? Just like any other night, 'cept it's a rotten cold desert to cross."

"Why, no," answered Budd, "that ain't all. It's a night they give things. Sort of a time to wipe out debts and mend the holes in the roof, you might say. Time to undo bad things, an'. . . ."

It was more than the younger man could endure, and his rat-like temper broke into a shrill squall. "Will you cut that crap? I ain't gonna stand it!" But he checked the rest of his turbulent objection; in his father's sober, lonesome face was the opportunity for which he had been waiting. "Gimme some money now, an'. . . ."

The snow, seen through the window, came down in a solid mass, a wind rattled the panes, and the sun-warped boards slatted boisterously. Beyond and above these sounds was another that swung Dan around like a cornered animal, arm raised instinctively to the front door. There was a voice, then another, subdued, followed by the scrape of feet on the porch.

"Sheriff," whispered Dan in a gust of fear. "I'll slide out the back. Put 'em off while I get clear."

A moment later he had disappeared while a heavy fist pounded at the front door. Budd passed a hand across his face as if waking from a stupor. For a few moments this fateful evening the load of care had left him, or at least he had forgotten it. Now it was back, bringing greater weight, greater depression. He fumbled with his pipe and walked toward the door. He hadn't reached it when Cal Emmons and a deputy broke through, strode past the littered counter, and shook the snow from their garments. The sheriff stopped on the kitchen threshold and shot a glance about the room. Budd waited gravely.

"It's a hard night," offered the sheriff, seeming embarrassed.

"That's right, Cal."

The sheriff thrust his finger toward the table where the empty dishes stood as witness to a recent diner. "You eat late, Dave."

Budd crossed his hands behind him and stared at the flaring stove grate. It seemed to him those mellow church bells chimed louder, more persistently. The sheriff turned to his deputy and muttered something in a low voice then began anew, obviously struggling after the appropriate words. He had been old man Budd's friend through twenty years, and the present mission held as much sorrow for him as for the storekeeper.

"That horse out in front . . . it ought to be stabled, Dave," he essayed. "Oh, by golly, there ain't no use in beatin' about the bush! Reckon you know what I'm after. It's an awful thing he did, Dave, an' I can't overlook it. You understand that, don't you?" Receiving no answer, he stumbled on. "But mebbe he's scooted already. Now, Dave, you speak up an' tell me. Is your son hidin' here, or ain't he? If he's gone, we'll not waste any more time. If he's here, why . . . why

15

I reckon we'll have to ask you to give him up, old-timer."

Budd drew at the cold pipe, tamping down the ashes with a finger that trembled slightly. "You ain't expectin' me to lie, Cal, so I guess mebbe I can't. Dan was here a mite ago. He went out the back way."

Emmons and his deputy strode toward the rear door while Budd watched, the pipe dipping between his clenched teeth, and a blaze of unexpected light shining from beneath his heavy brows. The sheriff reached the door first and put a hand to the knob. Simultaneously a draft of air struck them in the back and Dan's petulant voice issued warning. "Stay right there, gents. Claw air, *pronto*. Don't aim to fool with you people at all."

The officers swung around. Dan came through the front door, plucked their guns from the holsters, and tossed them behind a far counter.

"You two boobs sailed in here like you thought I was easy to take. Like I wouldn't make a fight. Don't you think it! When you take me, you'll know it." He appeared to be lashing himself into a rage. "Stand over in that corner. Now, Paw, I got to have some grub. That's why I come back. An' some money."

"Take what grub you want from the shelves," answered Budd. "There's a gunny sack on the counter. You'll find a little change in that tin box below the tobacco case." The storekeeper hardly moved a muscle of his face.

Dan worked swiftly.

"You're makin' a big mistake," warned the sheriff. "Better give in peaceable, Dan. I know your dad . . . else I wouldn't have walked in here so free an' easy. Better give up an' take what's comin'. We'll hunt you down if you don't."

He got no answer save a scornful laugh. The younger man was busy with the tin box.

"Leave a little of that money," said Budd. "Just take what you need." But this, too, invoked a malicious chuckle.

A moment later the fugitive was at the front door, gunny sack on his shoulder. "Don't you birds be in too much of a hurry," he advised. "As long as I'm in the clearin', you'll make good targets. I don't aim to be taken." The gust of wind struck them again, the door slammed, and he was gone.

Emmons stepped to the stove. The deputy rushed to the rear door. "I'll cut around the side of the house," he whispered.

The sheriff was surprisingly calm. "No. Never mind, Buck. He'll be gone, and there's a hundred places in the trees he could hide. It's pitch dark . . . and snowin' like blazes. The mornin's soon enough to follow. He won't get far." He looked toward Budd and clucked his tongue in sympathy. There was something so bitterly sorrowful on his friend's face. The storekeeper raised his head.

"It wasn't a trick, Cal," he protested. "I didn't know he was comin' back. Didn't think he'd have the nerve. But you couldn't expect me to take sides with you when he did come in. You couldn't expect that, could you, Cal? I'm his paw, and I could have walked up and took that gun right from him. But you wouldn't expect that . . . would you?"

"That's all right, Dave. I know how it is. Never mind that."

"I'm his paw. I couldn't do that," muttered Budd. His eyes caught sight of the tin box. He walked to it and stared. A shadow passed over his face, and he turned the receptacle open side down. There was nothing left.

"I told him to leave a little. And he didn't." A long minute later when he had moved back to the stove, he added slowly: "I don't begrudge it. The poor little fellow just ain't got the sand in him. But he didn't kill that fellow in the pool room,

Cal. He said he didn't, an' I believed him."

"That's mebbe what he told you," replied the sheriff. "It wasn't in no pool room. He an' Toots Billmire an' Mike Reilly held up a homesteader who was supposed to have a little money, twenty miles north of Bend. Homesteader put up a scrap, and Dan shot him, cold blooded. They got his money and pulled stakes. The poor devil lasted long enough to tell a passing neighbor. Cold blooded, Dave. I'm sorry, but it was that."

Budd's head came up, and the mildness forsook his face. "Then he lied? There was no fight in the pool room?"

"Dave, it was like I told you. Toots and Mike went south on the Prineville Road. I got a couple men scoutin' that a-way. I figger Dan'll join 'em tonight or tomorrow."

Still the storekeeper was unbelieving. He had placed a last faith in the boy, and he could not see it so abruptly shattered. He turned to question the deputy, but he saw no different story in that officer's face, and a shudder of distaste moved his big shoulders.

"Murder, was it? Out-an'-out murder. 'Thout givin' a man a chance to help himself? Oh, Cal!" And the storekeeper was utterly stricken, utterly ruined of spirit. A pinched, bleak look settled in his mouth; a misery inhabited his eyes. "A plain murderer!"

" 'Twa'n't your fault, Dave," protested the sheriff. But his friend would not be comforted.

"He is *my* son," he muttered. "My son. An' he did that."

The sheriff got up. "Well, we'll stay here overnight. Got some blankets extra, Dave? We'll flop by the stove."

"Take my bed."

"Oh, no. That'd put you out. Just give us a blanket an' we'll do fine."

"Take it," persisted Budd. "You think I could sleep, Cal?

18

Reckon I won't move from that chair tonight."

So the two officers turned in while the storekeeper stoked the stove, extinguished the light, and settled in his chair. The rising wind howled about the corners of the house. Through the window could be seen the relentless, diagonal sweep of the snow, increasing in fury each hour. It was very bleak, very cold out there, and the warm rays of the fire rendered it all the more uncomfortable to look upon. But such a storm, with blasts that were equally devastating, shook old man Budd's mind, drained the ruddy blood from his face, and left it very, very tired. From time to time his paw-like hands clutched the chair. Again he would lean forward, and the glare of the flames revealed lines that were savage, unrelenting. Once, during such a movement, he muttered: "I'll have to do it, so help me God." And thereafter he seemed to find a rest of spirit.

When morning came, the sheriff and deputy found breakfast before them, with Budd wrapped in his Mackinaw and smoking imperturbably.

"Two foot of snow on the ground," he announced. "But we can travel just the same."

The sheriff protested immediately. "Now don't be foolish, Dave. We'll do this alone. I promise we won't shoot him down. We'll bring him back."

"Aim to go," answered Budd. There was no more argument. They saddled and set off down the Bend-Klamath Road, toward the California line. There were, of course, no tracks left in the snow, but Emmons seemed quite sure of his way and pressed on. "Dan ain't goin' to turn back," he said. "He'll meet up with the others and scoot over the desert. Wouldn't be surprised if they'd holed up in some cabin overnight."

So they traveled for two hours or more, breaking a trail

in the crusted snow. The sun came out but brought no warmth. Dead silence pervaded the cold, crisp air. The earth seemed wrapped in peace; the men, when they spoke at all, hushed their words, conscious of the bell-like echo which floated in crystal clarity down the ribbon of road and rebounded from the pines. There was no place along the first part of the route, any lesser way or by-path, no break in the trees. But, around mid-morning, the glittering highway suddenly thrust two branches from its main course into a startled forest. The sheriff halted here to arrange his tactics.

"Main way is shortest to the border," he said. "If a man traveled alone, that'd be his path. But Toots an' Mike went by the Prineville Road an', if Dan aimed to meet them, he'd switch to the left here. Guess we'd better split. You go straight ahead, Buck. I'll take the left road. Dave, you do like you want."

"Take the right," said Budd. "If I find him . . . I ain't likely to shield him."

They split. Budd pursued the narrow, tortuous trail that was hardly wide enough to accommodate a wagon as it ran away from the central highway, lost vigor, and curved back again like a truant finally become afraid of its freedom. Budd went steadily for better than half an hour and at a fault in the trees struck to the left, leaving the road.

He seemed to have some plan or some knowledge which had been withheld from the officers for, when a few moments later he came to the main way, he was cautious enough to stop and sweep the vista with his shrewd eyes. The snow told of the deputy's already having passed by, and Budd urged his animal across the road and into the forest again, still maintaining his direction due east. This would bring him, in time, to the left fork of the Bend-Klamath Road and within shouting distance of Cal Emmons.

The pines grew smaller here, and the underbrush became very scanty. Budd picked his route without hesitation. He seemed on familiar ground.

Finally he stopped and dismounted, going on with remarkable celerity of movement for one possessed of so much avoirdupois. Within a hundred yards the pines gave way to a natural clearing fifty feet in circumference in the center of which huddled a small shanty. From and to the door of this place ran the fresh trail of men and horses. The forehoofs of one such horse was even then visible from a rear corner of the place.

Budd leaned against a sapling and drew his revolver. There had been a sort of rugged determination on his face all during the ride. It was, at this moment, even stronger, although he held the pistol in his hand for a long interval, staring at the dull metal very somberly. This was Christmas morn, the day on which men gave and received holiday greetings and presents — were happy. And he, Dave Budd, held a revolver in his hand and hunted his son.

A certain intuition had brought him to this cabin in the woods. Many years before he and his son had stopped overnight here on one of their camping trips. It had become a regular resting spot, and he knew that, if Dan had sought refuge in the storm, this would be the place. The footprints indicated more than one man, and it behooved the storekeeper to be watchful. He stepped forward, gun advanced, regarding the door.

He had gone ten feet when a shot broke the silence of the jack pines, coming from nearby on his right. The deputy, then, had met one of the desperadoes. A shout of pain followed at a close interval, and Budd stepped quickly forward. But, if he aimed at surprise, he was to be disappointed. The noise had been a warning. The door of the

21

shanty popped open, and Dan ran out, struggling into his Mackinaw. He was followed by a red-jowled fellow Budd knew as Mike Reilly. They saw him instantly. Dan, trapped by his half-donned Mackinaw, backed against the wall of the place and poured out a wealth of curses. Reilly put his arms behind him.

"Stay fast, both of you," ordered Budd. A gust of anger set his words on harsh edge, and then the pent-up feeling of the long night's vigil spilled over, like water rushing from a dam's floodgates, like lava erupting from a crater. "You dog!" he cried, leveling the gun at his son. "Thought you'd get away, eh? Kill a man in cold blood and then use me fer shelter! Bearin' my name an' actin' like a rattlesnake! You're no son of mine, an' I'll not have you runnin' loose to bring sorrow on me! Stand up, you cussed murderer, an' take what I'm goin' to give you!"

He leveled the gun directly at his son's breast.

So this was the result of the bitter night's travail of spirit. Old man Budd had meant to do the world's justice by his own hand — to show people that the skulking cur who bore his name held no bonds of affection from him. The pistol's muzzle slid toward the earth, following the young man who collapsed, inch by inch, from sheer terror. And at last the gun was aimed at the base of the shanty. Budd's face turned the color of dead ashes as he watched his son grovel and gibber for mercy, issuing words that could not, for charity's sake, be repeated. The words were so panic stricken that they carried no meaning, nothing but abject fear. The store-keeper's mouth quivered in disgust. Many years had he endured, but this last spectacle was the sharpest, most cruel experience of all his life.

"Get up!" he bellowed, breathing fast. "Get up, you yaller cur! Ain't there a mite of spunk in you? Get up, I say!"

Reilly had backed a little aside and was now on the store-keeper's left, nearly out of vision's range. Budd had no eyes for him, being bent on infusing a little of his own dogged fatalism into the corrupt clay that was his son. Dan crawled to his knees and thence upright, a sense of shame at last giving him ballast to face his father's wrath. The gun's muzzle came up. Budd's trigger finger crooked, drew back the hammer. Then, quite slowly, quite impotently the hammer slid back, and the gun wavered. Strength seemed to leave the big arm. It dropped.

He could not do this thing! Murder was murder, and he had meant that Danny Budd should fully expiate so terrible, so unmanly a crime. But at that last moment when the front sight of the gun stood against the white flesh of Dan's forehead in startling clearness, and Budd's eye met it evenly through the rear sight notch, the weakness of the blood was too great. It seemed to him that the crisp air was filled with the sweet resonance of church bells.

Was there a chance to save the soul of Dan? Even yet a chance? Something choked him, and a film covered his eyes.

"I can't do it!" he muttered. "I jest can't do it!"

Dan's cry ran across the clearing, and Budd jerked up his head in time to see Mike Reilly's hand streak for a gun. He had paid no attention to Mike. Now he swung a bit and waited a full breath. There was a double explosion which seemed to break the clear air into a million bits and send a great fury to the sky. His shoulder was punched back, the gun slid from his fingers, and he found himself sagging to the cold snow. Mike Reilly had strangely disappeared and, when he looked closer, he saw the man had fallen face downward.

Dan scurried up and stooped over his father. There was,

in his ratty face, a most curious look, an expression that might come to one who had seen and felt an unusual thing and labored mightily to understand it. Mechanically he kicked the pistol behind his father's reach. "Well," he grunted, almost dispassionately, "I never thought you was a gunfighter. Got him plumb center through the heart. Guess it was an accident. But you was goin' to kill me, wasn't you? And changed your mind. What for?"

Budd supported himself on one hand. "Go on," he said thickly. "Get away. I can't stop you, nor wouldn't. Go on now. Some day, mebbe, you'll have spunk to be a man . . . jest fer a minute or so before you die . . . a whole, grown man just fer a minute. Git out now."

There was a sound of a body crashing through the brush on the right. It might be the deputy or Toots Billmire. On the left, too, was a sound, fainter but coming up hurriedly. Dan moved uneasily, seeming unable to shake off the lethargy.

"It's mighty funny," he said. "Sure is funny."

"Get out!" roared Budd, and turned away. He no longer wished to see his son. After he had struggled to his feet, Dan had gone. The shanty door stood open, and the horse still was tethered behind. Tracks led across the fresh snow and disappeared in the pines. Budd groped for the pistol and got it just as the deputy ran into the clearing, with a smear of crimson running down one side of his face and a pistol swinging loosely in one hand.

"Where'd they go?" he shouted. "I got Billmire! Where's the others?"

Budd nodded to the east, and the deputy turned off. He hadn't reached the fringe of the pines before another blast of gunfire was flung in his face. Two shots that stung the eardrums, disturbing the balance of the forest, singing

24

sharply for an interval in echo then dying to a sinister silence. Budd charged after the deputy, regardless of wounded shoulder, regardless of whipping branches and shrubs that plucked at his legs. Fifty yards brought him to the left-hand road, and here he saw Dan crumpled in a heap with the sheriff bending over him. Budd ran on and, pushing the sheriff back, knelt beside Dan and raised him up with the one good arm. And there came from him at that moment the oldest, saddest cry in the human tongue.

"My son . . . Dan . . . sonny!"

Dan snuffled like a broken-spirited child and opened his eyes. A rack and a rumble welled in his throat, significant of the advancing tide of death. But the same surprised expression he had carried from his father was still on his face and a brief, weak phrase explained it. "Why, it ain't a bit hard to die, is it?"

"I guess not, son," muttered Budd. "I guess it ain't . . . fer a man."

"I'm a man," whispered Dan. "It's funny what come over me when Mike winged you. It's funny . . . I dunno . . . but I faced the sheriff fair an' square . . . dunno what made me do that . . . you ask him . . . Dad. . . ." And with that last inarticulate, futile cry, he died.

The sheriff bent down. "That's so, Dave. He come bustin' through the pines just as I ran up the road. He saw me and figgered he was cornered. I called fer him to give in, but he said he guessed not. Queer, too, the way he said it, straightenin' and facin' me like he aimed to make a good target. He sort of drew a hand across his face like he was dizzy. Then he says: 'I'll count three an' draw.' Danged if he didn't. I beat him to it."

Budd's face turned to stone. "He fought fair, then? He stood an' faced it?"

25

"He sure did, Dave. Like I told you. Never flinched."

"Thank heaven," said Budd very softly, and laid an arm affectionately across the boy's grimed forehead. A single tragic tear sparkled in his eye and fell. Peace had come to Danny Budd, and he had given his father, in departing, the greatest of gifts. He had died in a man's way. The erratic heart might never have had the same fair impulse again, but some inexplicable emotion carried him to the high limit of his courage, and at that moment fate had chosen to fashion a crisis. And Danny Budd had faced it like a man.

"Thank heaven," said Budd. It seemed to him that the bells were filling the air with a resonant beauty, a swelling glory. There was a great sorrow in those sweet chimes, but greater than sorrow was the promise of enduring peace.

II

"BUDD DABBLES IN HOMESTEADS"

Time passed, and now Burnt Creek — three frame out-houses and one general merchandise store — simmered under the midday heat. Old man Budd sat on the porch of the store, his bulk welded to the chair, and watched the successive atmospheric waves dance across the Bend-Klamath Road and evaporate in the jack pine forest. "Must be a hundred 'n' ten degrees in that brush," he commented to himself. A laggard drone accompanied the heat. From the highway came the red-hot puff of air which funneled the sand and struck the porch. Budd closed his eyes and endured it with stoic gravity. "Scorch, dang ye. I'm seasoned."

He opened his eyes and found company. Sim Meeker rode a slattern horse through the jack pines, wilted in the saddle. Budd clucked his tongue and moved a foot back from the sun. He'd heard rumors of Meeker's being in trouble. The newcomer got down, tied his animal on the shady end of the porch, and walked up.

" 'Lo, Sim."

" 'Lo, Dave. Kinda warmish."

"So it be, Sim. What's made you travel this a-way at noon?"

Meeker's sun-blackened face draped itself into wrinkles of bitterness. He was a tall man, very thin, and passing into middle age. His hands were lumpish, his shoulders rugged, indicative of many years' hard work; the sharp rebellion in his eyes, however, was witness to the fact that no prosperity or happiness had come of all that toil. "Why," he said, "I thought I'd like to talk a mite with you, Dave. Fact is, I'm about to be thrown off my ranch."

It was a startling announcement to Budd. He closed his eyes again and gently scratched his chin. "What fer?"

"Foreclosed mortgage," was the laconic answer.

"What in time! How'd that come?"

"Needed money last year fer seed an' some tools. So I borrowed four hundred 'n' fifty dollars on the place. Thought I could pull out this season an' pay it off. But I'm like all the rest. Wheat burned to cinders an' my few cows ain't worth shippin'."

"What you worryin' about?" queried Budd. "We're all in the same wagon. Ain't anybody in a hundred miles out of debt. But no bank's goin' to freeze you out. They can't afford to. They got to stick with the crowd, else they go bust."

"I couldn't get the loan from a bank," confessed Meeker. "Aaron Bixby lent it me." The last phrase was an angry shout. "At nine per cent! You understandin'? And he warned me he wa'n't givin' no extensions, either. That's like him, but I couldn't help myself. Had to take it."

Old man Budd wrinkled his face. All the genial humor faded. Long ago some grateful homesteader had labeled this noncommittal storekeeper the "shepherd of southern Deschutes County." It was a title he took pride in, and he had quaintly boasted that, if he were to press collection of all the money due him from farmers, half the county would be his property. "Share an' share alike's my motto," he had always said. "When water comes, we'll all be rich. Ain't but one soul in fifty miles I wouldn't trust."

Aaron Bixby, all knew, was the exception, a shrewd, avaricious creature whose house resembled a swine pen, whose horses were half starved, and whose fences were forever on the verge of decay. The man was never known to release a cent without a scowl, and he was worth, reputedly, more than twenty of his neighbors put together. A dozen tales of close dealing and actual injustice were attached to his name, and yet in hard times people trafficked with him out of sheer necessity. He always stood ready to exact his penalty in the bad years on the homesteaders and, like a buzzard, always seemed on hand for these occasions.

Budd's displeasure grew more pronounced. "Sure walked into trouble, didn't you?" he grumbled. "Nine per cent! That's worse'n Shylock. Got any papers with you?"

Meeker was in the depths of misery, and Budd had to repeat the question. Finally the man drew out duplicate mortgage papers and passed them over. The storekeeper went through the clauses word by word, his lips pursing in greater dissatisfaction as he proceeded. "Huh," he said. "Air tight, rain proof, an' iron clad . . . fer Aaron Bixby. Son of a gun! Whyn't you come to me when you needed help? Ain't my money good enough?" His pride had been touched.

Meeker found an embarrassed answer. "Well, I figgered there'd be others wantin' help from you, an' I didn't want to bother. Everybody seems to come to you."

"So they do. But I could've spared that money last year."

Meeker's face mirrored sudden hope. "Could you do it now, Dave? I been to the bankers again. Nothin' doin'. Bixby's holdin' the watch over me. Money by tomorrow night or

29

out I go." The thought of it made him groan. "You don't know what that means, Dave."

Old man Budd shook his head. "Sim, I can't do it now. My credit's no good. Was the President of the United States to come to Bend he couldn't borrow a nickel from anybody. It's that bad."

Meeker dropped his chin and turned his face away. By and by he thrust forward his callused hands. "Look at 'em! Ten years I spent on that place. Worked like a field slave. Up before light and out to dark. Dog tired all the time an' just breakin' even. No fun, no knickknacks, no shows . . . nothin'. Barely keepin' above the surface an' hopin' water'd come some day and make us well off."

" 'Twill," interrupted Budd, with unshakable conviction.

"What good will it do me?" cried Meeker in a fury. "Ten years outa my life and Ethel's life . . . then we lose it and there ain't a cent . . . not a red cent . . . to show!" The heat beat against the porch and took the energy from him. "Oh, well, I guess I can manage," he added dully. "Always have. But it's nigh killin' Ethel. She's been the one to bear the most. Most of her health an' spirit's buried on that land."

Budd reached for a cigar and chewed distractedly. "Poor kid," he muttered.

"Guess I'll go to Bend an' get a job in the woods," continued Meeker. "Back where I started from ten years ago."

Budd shook his pendulous chin. "Poor Ethel." He bit the cigar in twain. "That two-footed hog! Now you listen, Sim. 'Member that place Steve Ordway forfeited to me . . . 'twas his own fault? It's beyond your land a quarter mile toward the Paulina Mountains. There's a house an' well. You just up stakes an' move into it while I see what we can do with Bixby."

"Too late," answered Meeker. "It ain't no use. You can't

move him after he forecloses. He's gettin' a bargain."

"Never mind," interrupted Budd testily. "You do as I say. There's more'n one way to skin a skunk." A bit of his offended pride rose. " 'Course, mebbe I ain't his equal in brains, but I'll stand it somehow. Get along now an' do that. I'll be travelin' to Bend right off an' see what I can figger."

Meeker got to his feet. "You're a square gent," he said, and walked toward the horse.

"Hold up," ordered Budd. "You folks ain't had any grub from the store fer a long spell."

"No money for grub," answered the other, keeping his face averted.

Budd exploded. "Who said anything about money? Cuss my hide! Get in that store an' fill a gunny sack afore I bust!"

Meeker did as requested and, when he left the clearing, provisions across the pommel, old man Budd called wistfully after him: "You give my regards to Ethel, Sim." The homesteader turned in the saddle, his gray eyes blinking. "All right, Dave."

The storekeeper watched his friend bend under the wilting heat and disappear into the oven-like forest. Then, rising, he went through the darkened store to a bachelor kitchen and poured himself a glass of lemonade. It eased him, and presently he was in a deep study. Aaron Bixby, he told himself, was such a character as would estimate values to the fraction of a penny. Once in possession of the Meeker place, no amount of sentiment would move him to consider disposal of it at less than his own figure, which certainly would be more than four hundred and fifty dollars. In these stringent times money was very, very hard. Land was worth nothing at all. But a prosperous year would increase the price tenfold. And Bixby could afford to wait.

Budd drank another glass of lemonade, staring thoughtfully into the depths of the liquid. The cussed, two-footed hog! There was no crime equal to that of dispossessing a man of his land, even when a mortgage fell due. They must all work together in this country. There could be no strict accountability in seasons when the bottom fell away from the market, and the desert sun burned men's hopes to a blackened shred. In all the southern end of the county, only Bixby failed to respond to common decency. Legally right, he possessed no moral justification for his action in the storekeeper's mind. To shoot a man was less injury than to take away his home, wherein had been placed so many hopes, so many dreams. And there was Ethel!

Budd looked out the door at the fluttering heat mirage — and it seemed like he could see there the corn-colored hair of Ethel and her clear, sweet face. That was many years ago when both had loved her. Budd dropped his eyes from the intolerable glare. "The penny-pinchin' hog!" The lemonade was gone and, with it, peace. He rose and went to the barn. A half hour later he was driving toward Bend, the store wide open, and a scrawled invitation to **Help Yourself** on the door.

"One thing about Bixby," he said two hours later, as the town popped out of the plain, "the smell of a nickel makes him cautious, but ten dollars goes to his head. All curmudgeons're like that. We'll think it over."

He had a great deal of business to transact in the small Central Oregon town. All the afternoon and evening was spent in seeing men and soliciting money. It was a forlorn venture, as his better judgment told him, and at last he gave it up and late in the evening called a small party in his room where he held earnest counsel.

Early morning found him bound back toward his own country via the Prineville Road. As far as the eye might reach, there was nothing save the uneven roll of the land, with the heat beating down and refracting from it. Budd lolled in the buckboard and passively suffered, breaking his silence only when a homesteader's shanty varied the monotony of the bare horizon. Then, at the end of two or three hours, he turned off the road and journeyed cross country. Presently he was at Bixby's place. He would have gone by, but the miser came from the house and waved a hand. Budd drew rein out of common courtesy.

"Whut yuh travelin' around here fur?" demanded Bixby. The voice was a thready whine, mixed with a wavering contempt. It fitted well with the thin, stubbled face and the close-set, avaricious eyes. The man wore clothes that were ragged. He stood in a yard littered with trash, articles he had collected from the countryside in the hope of profit. The fences were broken down, and the house was a slattern thing, scarcely to be called a shelter. Around the corner limped a horse with prominent ribs and a beaten look.

"A mite of business," answered Budd. It had always been a mystery to him how such a man could make money.

"Heard yuh was goin' to let Meeker stay in Ordway's old place," said Bixby. "That so?"

"Aim to."

"Free?" screeched the miser. He saw Budd nod and broke into enraged protest. "Coddlin' people won't get yuh no profit! It ain't right. Make 'em pay . . . it'll teach 'em to stand on their own feet! Now I was goin' to let Meeker stay on his ranch at ten dollars a month, me sharin' crops. What'd yuh butt in for? Can't let a man make a little money?"

Budd squinted over the land. A quarter mile along stood the deserted Ordway place, with the rise of the Paulina Mountains behind. In another quarter of the horizon, just visible, was the Meeker ranch. "Business," he grunted. A chuckle of satisfaction escaped him when he saw the miser's futile rage. "Meeker'll sort of fix up the house and barn so's it'll be worth somethin'," he continued. "I aim to sell it as soon's I can find a buyer."

This was shrewdness Bixby could understand. A sly grin flitted across his parsimonious mouth. "Guess you ain't so much of a saint as people think."

"Oh, I make a nickel when I can," agreed Budd. He gathered the reins. "If you hear of anyone wantin' to buy land, let me know. Giddap, Toby." Farther down the road he exclaimed: "Cussed swine!"

When he reached the Meeker ranch, he found the family and their belongings packed in a wagon. Sim's discouraged droop left him as he saw the storekeeper, and he asked the inevitable question. "Could you fix it, Dave?"

Budd said no, eyes fastened on Ethel Meeker. Ten years of labor in the desert had left its mark, but still she retained a spark of youthful beauty and even time, it seemed to him, could not dim the luster of her corn-colored hair. She, too, looked eagerly for some happy bit of news, all the heartbreaking disappointment confined in her blue eyes. Budd felt a sudden reverence and removed his hat. "No," he repeated. "I'm sorry, folks, but I couldn't fix it."

The woman gripped the seat, and her lips set to trembling. The hurt of this last dead, forlorn hope was almost too great for her to bear. But the man broke into a bitter tirade, flinging a hand to the place that had been his home. "There's a fool's reward!" he cried. "Worked like a field slave . . . and get kicked out with just the clothes on our backs! Without a penny!" He turned to the reins, face lowered. "What's the use? Dave, you should have married Ethel ten years ago. You could have provided at least."

"Sim!" protested the woman. "What have I done to deserve that? Shame on you!"

"Guess I'm crazy," he admitted. "But it hurts to be a failure."

"I haven't complained," she said and put a hand to his shoulder. "We'll get along." Then, conscious that she was showing her affection, she dropped the hand. "Dave, we're glad to have such a . . . a friend."

"Shucks!" growled out Budd. "Shucks! You people get along now. Fust forty years are always the hardest. An' you can live right comfortably in Ordway's house. Call on me for grub an' seed at any time. Everybody else does. We're all in the same wagon this year! 'Tain't no disgrace to be broke. Fact is, a man's queer if he has got any spare change. People'd suspect he wa'n't honest."

They drove down the road. Budd continued on his journey homeward. "I'm gettin' to be a regular cry baby, Toby. Son of a gun! That cussed, mean swine!"

He passed Ralph Olmstead's place and started into the jack pines. As he left the open land, he saw on the right two horsemen angle toward the Prineville Road. The heat waves fluttered and rose like a curtain, obscuring them, and Budd was satisfied with a long gaze, after which he plunged into the stifling shade. "Son of a gun!" he muttered. "But there's more'n one way to skin a skunk."

The two horsemen he had noticed continued across the open land. They passed the deserted Meeker home, and one of the two, the younger, stopped. "This it, Bill?"

"Nope, Bixby lives in the next rancho, I think. We'll amble on."

When they drew up in front of the latter's piece-meal structure, the miser walked around the yard and met them.

"Howdy," he grunted.

"Looking for a place to board," said the one called Bill. "Could you put us up for a few days?"

Bixby's suspicious eyes followed them from head to toe. They were dressed in light khaki and carried what appeared to be surveying instruments. "Guess so," he decided. "But it'll cost yuh somethin'. Times is hard an' I'm a poor man. Two bits a meal an' two fer bed."

"That's fair enough."

"Apiece," he added swiftly.

"Sure. If it's not too much trouble. Otherwise we'll just go on to that other place," he said, pointing to the Ordway house.

"No . . . no," said Bixby. "They're just movin' in. I'll take yuh. Come in. What might yuhr business be?"

They dismounted and walked to the door, not answering the question. On the threshold Bill got a view of the interior and stepped back. "Maybe it'd be just as well, Johnny, if we did go on to the other place."

Bixby raised a quick objection. "I'll feed yuh well here. Lot of grub an' a good feather bed to sleep in. What'd yuh say yuhr business was?"

They were young men but evidently bent on keeping their own counsel. Bill turned to the horses. "We'll stay, I guess. There's still time to work, Johnny. I think we'll run a piece of line westward." He turned to Bixby again. "If you want to make a few dollars, go cut us some stakes, about a foot high and pointed on one end. Quite a few."

Bixby disappeared in the woodshed. When he came back a quarter of an hour later with an armful of such stakes, the surveyors were at work down and beyond the road. Bill was busy at his transit, sighting along a fold of the Paulina Mountains.

"Take the pegs down to Johnny," he ordered.

Bixby trudged through the sand, his curiosity at fever heat by this air of secrecy. He had secured no answer from Bill, but Johnny seemed younger, and therefore it might be easier to get information. He dumped the pegs nearby and watched the young fellow adjust a high measuring stick on the ground.

"Say," he spoke up, smitten by a fearful idea. "Yuh're on my land. If yuh're a dummed county surveyor tryin' to shave my claim, yuh get off right now!"

"Left!" bellowed Bill from the distance. The measuring stick edged toward the road, stopped, edged again, and finally was beyond Bixby's land into government entry stuff. "That's good," yelled Bill. "Set 'er!"

Johnny beckoned. "Your name's Bixby, ain't it? Well, drive a peg right here, Bixby, and follow me."

Bixby obeyed and ran after this man who by now had shouldered the instrument and was still farther down the road. The rising curiosity could not be stifled. "What'd yuh say yuhr business was?" ventured the miser.

Johnny accelerated his pace. Bixby followed and repeated his query.

"Why, we're running a line," said Johnny vaguely. He was a sorrel-topped youth and had a jovial eye.

"What fer?" persisted Bixby.

Johnny threw a glance over his shoulder and spoke confidentially. "Can you keep a secret? I suppose you'll know sooner or later, seeing as we're working near your place. But keep in under your hat . . . there's a railroad coming across the country."

"Jerusalem!" Bixby's eyes sparkled. "A railroad! That means money." Immediately he became suspicious. "Say, young fella, what'd be the use of a road through here? There

37

ain't no towns, an' the country's dog poor."

Johnny set his instrument, and again the peg-setting formula was repeated. Bixby, squinting along the line, saw that they were headed straight for the Ordway place; moreover, they would strike the house into which the Meekers had just moved. He chuckled at the thought.

"Towns?" repeated Johnny. "Who cares for towns? This is a cut-off from the main line out of Huntington. It's to get California traffic around Portland and save ten hours. To speed up through freight. That's what."

"Jerusalem! That means money. They pay well fer right of way." Right there disaster broke over his head, and he screeched like a frightened owl. "But say, ain't yuh goin' across my land?"

Johnny jiggled his instrument. "Drive a peg. Where's the corner of your land?"

Bixby pointed to the road. The young man shook his head. "Nope, we miss you by two hundred yards. You're lucky. Right of way cuts farms into messy strips."

"Lucky?" shouted Bixby. "The devil, that land ain't good fer anything but road beds." He had for a moment seen a fat check in his pocket, accrued from sale of right of way. There would always be adjoining land to farm on, land to be had dirt cheap, but there would only be one road bed. The sight of fleeing dollars made him frantic. The thought that the Ordway place — Budd's property — would be used made him still worse. "Say," he whined, "why can't yuh shove this line over to my proputy? Few yards wouldn't make no difference."

Johnny gave him a cold eye and marched ahead. "You're no surveyor. Shut up."

"I'd make it valuable fer yuh." He made a reckless offer. "Twenty dollars."

Johnny planted his standard. "Shut up, I say. One more crack like that and I'll turn you end for end."

Bixby subsided, trailing through the blistering sun. As the rows of pegs advanced straight upon the Ordway place, his small eyes flickered with rage. Who was Budd to profit by this while he was passed by? But the storekeeper had declared his intention to sell, evidently not knowing of the forthcoming road. Bixby's colorless lips snapped, and he permitted a dry grin to waver across his face.

"That's all for today!" yelled Bill. They returned to the house. Bixby got supper, and watched the two men eat. "Reckon that was half a day's work fer me," he announced. "It'll cost yuh three dollars."

Bill grinned. "All right, you pirate. It's not my money."

"I got to go away tomorrow," added Bixby. "But I'll cut the pegs an' scatter 'em along the line tonight. That's a day's wages, too. Six dollars."

"Correct, Shylock. Why waste your talents in this wilderness?"

So Aaron Bixby performed his chores while the others slept. At dawn he cooked their breakfast, saddled his horse, and with a purse bulging in his pocket crossed the desert toward Burnt Creek. When he reached the store, old man Budd had gone, leaving a note on the door. **In Bend. Help Yourself.**

"Jerusalem!" panted Bixby in a panic. "I got to ketch him afore he sells to anybody else." He was in a tremendous hurry, and yet the bent of his nature would not be denied. Going into the store, he took a can of coffee and some lesser articles from a shelf. "That'll teach him a lesson," he grunted. He was not a very robust thief, and stared furtively around as he stuffed the plunder in his saddlebags. Then he urged the horse along the Bend-Klamath Road. "I got

39

to ketch him," he murmured.

Old man Budd was having a peaceful dinner at the Bend Eating House when Bixby found him. The trip had not improved the miser's temper, and the sight of the larger man's serenity caused him to bark like some ungrateful lap dog. "Whyn't yuh home tendin' to business? Snakes, I can't see how yuh make any money!"

"Whose business . . . mine or yourn?"

"Yuh'll learn better when yuh're broke," warned Bixby, taking a chair. He attempted a smoother manner. "Wanted to see yuh. Figgered I might take that Ordway proputy if yuh wa'n't onreasonable."

"Aim to please," said Budd mildly. "What need have you got fer more land?"

"Well, now, I figgered on tryin' cattle next year, an' that takes a lot of space. Yuhr place an' the government land atween . . . which I can use free . . . will just about be what I need."

"So it will," agreed Budd. "Cows'll be as good as gold, some day. What's your offer?"

Bixby's face took on a bargaining cast. The storekeeper had a reputation for being an easy man to deal with, and he meant to take advantage of it. "Well, now," he whined, "I'm a poor man, an' I know yuh'll be easy. That Meeker place . . . I ain't got a bit of use fer it. Too far away. But it's shipshape, good house, well, nice barn, fences tight. Tell yuh what, I'll trade even up."

Budd's fork clattered on the dishes. "Gosh almighty, Aaron! What ails you? I ain't Santy Claus. Son of a gun!"

"Meeker's place is twice as good," Bixby defended. "It's cultivated. Ordway's ain't."

"Ordway's place is twicet as big," countered the storekeeper. He recovered sufficiently to partake of his beefsteak.

"No, I guess you 'n' I can't dicker. Ain't got any use fer more land, anyhow. Need hard money. There's a fella made me an offer this mornin'. Think I'll take it, hook an' sinker."

"How much yuh want fer it?"

Budd balanced a potato on his knife. "Well, land ain't worth nothin' now. I'm pinched an' got to sell. A thousan' dollars. That's givin' it away, too."

Bixby was horrified. "I could buy Deschutes County fer that!" he yelled. "I won't pay it!"

"All right, don't." Bud was serene about it, and the miser, after half rising, fell back. He detested this gross, easy man with all the passion of his small body. He wanted to emit the whole load of his scorn, wanted to sneer, but these things he dared not do yet. Choking back his rage, he made another offer. "I'll trade farms an' give yuh a hundred to boot."

"Chicken feed, Aaron. Now here's what. Trade farms an' five hundred. No more, no less. Take it or leave it."

The miser protested again and made an offer of half the sum. Budd seemed not to hear. "Three-fifty," urged Bixby. And still the storekeeper was deaf. It left Bixby greatly perplexed. He had not expected to bid so high, and each hundred extra caused a revolt of his conscience. Yet the right of way should bring him a good profit and leave him a large piece of land near his original place, a piece twice as big as the one traded. It would be good business. He thrust away the last silent objection, cursed Budd under his breath, and gave in. "All right, I'll take it."

The storekeeper seemed unpleasantly surprised. "You do? Shucks, Aaron, I didn't think you was serious. I can get more from the other fella."

"I took yuhr offer!" raged Bixby. "Yuh can't back down! There's the money." He threw the purse on the table. Budd was silent, plainly unsatisfied. "Yuh got to take it," con-

41

tinued the money lender.

"Spoils my meal," complained Budd. "I reckon I'm caught. I gave my word an' I'll 'bide by it. I warn you, though. You might be disappointed in that land."

A malicious grin spread over Bixby's face. "I ain't to be talked out of it. We'll sign an' seal right off."

He was visibly anxious to have the deal consummated and impatient of Budd's elephantine pace. He attempted to hurry the journey down the street but found himself alone. Budd had stopped to talk with a shopkeeper. "Dang!" snarled out Bixby. "I can't be kept all day! Time's money. It's a wondeh yuh ain't stone poor!"

They reached the office of Budd's attorney and there transacted the deal. Budd signed with reluctance, further warning Bixby. "Never say I didn't tell you, now." The miser counted the gold pieces from the purse, pinching each eagle as if he could not release it. He took the deed, when it was tendered to him, and stuffed it in his pocket with a leer of triumph. "I heard tell yuh was a smart man, Budd. I doubt so."

They came to the street, and Budd turned from his companion. But Bixby could not let him go without a taunt. The stored malice would not be longer repressed. "Smart!" he cackled. "Heh! Yuh know why I bought this land? I wouldn't pay five hundred fer ten thousand acres just to farm. I bought this," — and he yelled the phrase at the top of his voice, his small eyes squinting their pleasure — " 'cause there's a railroad comin' through, an' it hits dead across the Ordway place. Surveyors told me!"

Budd's cheeks flushed red. So far he had endured the miser, retaining his serenity in face of all the petty malice Bixby had used. But the exultation over this shrewd piece of business was more than he could bear. It recalled to his

mind the discouraging case of the Meekers, and of a sudden
the wrath broke upon Bixby's head as a prairie storm, un-
announced and in full fury.

"You cussed, two-footed swine!" roared Budd. His voice
boomed down the street and brought people from the stores.
A doubled fist wavered under the miser's nose. "There ain't
no animal that travels in a lower track than you! Somebody
ought to get you a rattle an' make a regular snake of you!
The kind of man that'd throw Sim Meeker off his place in
a year like this is the meanest, dirtiest skunk as ever
breathed! There ain't no place in Deschutes County for such
trash an', if you ever cross my trail in five miles, I'll tie
a rope around you and drag a trail clear to the Californy
line. Now you get to the devil outta my sight afore I lose
my temper an' shoot! Go on, git! You shifty-eyed rat! I'm
'most tempted to kick you!" He had relapsed to cow-hand
idiom in his wrath. The crowd had gathered around at a
discreet distance, and Bixby, face yellowed with fear, ap-
pealed mutely to them. There was no one to answer such
an appeal. Old man Budd was not a character to side against
at this moment.

"Yuh . . . ," stuttered Bixby.

"Get out! If I see you in ten minutes, you'll wish you was
dead." The irate storekeeper advanced, a lane opened
through the crowd, and Bixby shot down it like a hunted
rabbit. Budd watched him go to the hitching rack, jump
a saddle, and tear through the sultry haze along the
Prineville Road. Then he reached for his bandanna to wipe
away the perspiration, and the rosy complexion deepened
to a look of shame. Old man Budd always suffered for the
loss of his serenity.

The sheriff walked up to him. "What in time did he do
to bring down all that?"

43

"Oh, gosh!" moaned Budd. "Did *you* hear it, Cal? I oughta be kicked clean back to Burnt Creek! Me a-losin' my temper like that. I ain't goin' to feel right fer a month. Oh, gosh, what did I say, Cal? Anything bad?"

They could not console him. Downcast and miserable, he climbed into his buckboard and rode away through the late afternoon glow. He scarcely moved in all the trip, save once to shake his head and mutter, "I sure deserve to be shot fer such a ruckus."

But when, in the first of the dusk, he came upon the Ordway house and saw Ethel Meeker and her husband on the porch, he felt greatly cheered. He paused for a moment to tell the news that would please them, omitting the part about the railroad. "So," he concluded, "me bein' owner now, you move back. In a few days we'll fix up fresh mortgage papers an' you'll be ready to start all over."

He would not stop to hear a crowded, uncertain sentence from Ethel Meeker. "Giddap, Toby," he said, and his eyes were blinking, and he seemed to see the woman's corn-colored hair beside him. Then he started to find the two surveyors, Bill and Johnny, on horseback by the side of the buckboard.

"Did it work?" asked Bill.

"Sure did," agreed Budd. He chuckled softly. "We traded farms an' got a little to boot, which is more'n I expected. There's a saying, boys, that you want to remember: 'A penny makes a miser wise, but a dollar goes to his head.' "

Johnny grinned. "It was easy, Mister Budd, except for sleepin' in Bixby's house. I wouldn't do it again. But I guess we made a good imitation of two young surveyors. Say, honest, do you ever think there'll be a railroad through this country?"

"In about thirty years," replied Budd, chuckling again. "So

44

long, boys. You'll find your pay in town."

He gave the horse free rein to follow the homeward trail. On the horizon stood the black line of the jack pine forest merging with the dark, star-scattered sky. A heavier shadow formed on his right, and it seemed to Budd as if it were a tree advanced beyond the ranks of its kind. He leaned forward and stared. The shadow dissolved to nothing. That, he thought, was like his own hard-spent forty-five years, full of illusions until he peered at them with the eyes of experience. Then the illusions dissolved, and there was only the reality left — hard reality.

A gust of chill desert wind brought up the clack of crickets and the pungent odor of sage. Budd lifted his heavy chin. "But reality's better'n illusions," he grunted. "Dang, I love this country . . . an' all that's in it. Git along, git along, Toby."

III

"WHEN MONEY WENT
TO HIS HEAD"

It was mid-afternoon in Burnt Creek, and the three frame outhouses and one general merchandise store baked under the heat, cracked and weathered. It was a desiccated town site slit in the jack pine forest as an initial carved from the bark of a tree. A sultry, sand-ridden place, dying for want of water like all the rest of Central Oregon at that time. Old man Budd was lumped in a chair on the porch of his store, the sole witness of life.

Ralph Olmstead came out of the jack pines from the Bend-Klamath Road and urged his horse to the hitching rack in front of the store. "You ain't moved out of that chair since last Friday," said Ralph.

"Too hot."

Ralph came up the steps. He was a compact young man, red of hair and scorched of features. Homesteading had left its mark on him. He had the bitter expression of one pushed to the limit of endurance. "Well, I need a sack of Durham and a can of coffee."

"Tobacco in the case. Coffee somewheres on the top shelf. Find 'em yourself."

46

Ralph walked into the small store and rummaged through the cluttered shelves. All commodities were indiscriminately mixed and all alike were covered with a thin film of sand. He found what he needed and, obeying the immemorial custom of the ranchers, scratched his name and the articles on a slip of paper, transfixing it to a spike. This was old man Budd's charge system.

"Mail in the box fer Lewis," grunted Budd.

Ralph came out finally with his packages and the letter, scowling more than usual. A tremor of amusement disturbed Budd's vast frame. "Seems like you ain't so pleased with carryin' mail to Grace Lewis like you once was. Gosh, don't you look like a rattler bit you. She was your girl, wa'n't she?"

"She choses her own company. After this she can chose her own letter carriers."

Old man Budd made a shrewd guess. "Scrappin' ag'in. Cats an' dogs couldn't be worse. You two oughta have more sense. The trouble is, you're both on edge with the heat an' so forth. This ain't no country or time to git your back up."

Ralph scowled again. "The trouble is, a man comes into this country with the cards stacked against him. There ain't a chance to win. Not once chance in a million. Here I've hung on for three years, scorched in summer an' near froze stiff in winter. My crops come up good . . . an' then the heat ruins 'em. An' if I did become lucky and harvested a little extra hay, what'd I do with it? Who'd buy it? Here I need a new horse, need barb wire for my fence, the roof of my shanty has to be tar papered before fall sets in, and I owe you for six months' groceries. That's homesteadin'!"

"Son, you ain't tellin' me anything I ain't heard before,"

said Budd. "Everybody fer forty miles owes me a year's grocery bill. We're all busted. What's the difference? I ain't seen any hard money since McKinley was President. Wouldn't know what to do with it if I did git some."

"If Congress would only pass that bill, we might get a little courage to fight it out!" exclaimed Ralph. "But there won't be an ounce of water in the country until they do pass it . . . and they wait and wait and wait!"

"Reclamation projects're always kinda slow," said Budd. "It'll come some day." He turned his head. "Speakin' of money, there's a chance fer you to make five hundred dollars. Read the sign over on the wall."

Ralph turned to a notice tacked on the rough boards and saw this announcement:

FIVE HUNDRED DOLLARS REWARD

For information leading to the arrest of the three masked men who held up the Bend-Klamath mail stage four miles north of Burnt Creek, June 1, 1904.

"Day before yesterday," said Ralph. "Road agents, huh? An' we ain't had any trouble for a couple of years now." Then he read further:

Said three masked men bound and gagged driver of the stage, broke into an Endicott Express Co. chest, and took gold and paper coin amounting to thirty-five hundred dollars. Bandits were of medium height, weighed about one hundred and fifty pounds each, and wore corduroy pants, olive-drab army shirts, and Stetson hats. Leader of the trio heavier than the rest

and had light-blue eyes. Any information should be given to the Endicott Express office, Bend, Oregon.

Old man Budd's voice lost a measure of its serenity. "When a rattlesnake sticks to its own rock, there ain't no fuss to be made. But a varmint's to be shot when it starts runnin' wild. I didn't think they'd have nerve to do it."

"Who?" asked Ralph. Old man Budd's mind held many shrewd bits of knowledge, and it paid to listen.

But the storekeeper had given one hint and would offer no more. "This country's hard, but it's sweet an' clean," he said. "Ain't no room for desperadoes. They ought to be shot down like coyotes."

"Got to find them first," replied Ralph.

"Just you remember this," warned Budd. "There's danged few people can stand prosperity. A little money goes to the head mighty fast. Somebody'll spill the beans. There's three of 'em with more'n a thousand dollars each. It'll burn their hands. Watch."

Another horseman appeared from the jack pines and rode up. Ralph's mouth, habitually set, grew still thinner. Elvy Dakin was not his friend nor his kind; the lowering, saturnine face marked the bully too plainly. The cold, blue eyes held their unsavory secrets.

"Need some chuck, old man," said Dakin, giving an unfriendly glance to Ralph. He fetched an empty gunny sack from the pommel and stalked into the store. Budd and Ralph stared out upon the sand until Dakin came back to the porch with the gunny sack half filled. He flipped a coin into Budd's lap. The storekeeper held it forward in his palm with a grunt of surprise.

"Gold piece. Heard tell they still coined 'em, but didn't believe it. Thought the government had decided money

49

wa'n't any use to us Westerners. How d'you expect me to change this?"

"Reckon I owe you that much," replied Dakin carelessly. "It don't make any difference." He tied the gunny sack to the saddle.

Ralph shook his head, and he could not avoid expressing some measure of resentment. He had worked hard and honestly, with nothing to show for it save the memory of bitter struggle. "Kind of reckless with your money, ain't you, Elvy? Seems strange to throw gold pieces around like that."

Dakin's blue eyes glittered as he met Ralph's sober face. Then the need for explanation evidently occurred to him. "Farmin' ain't the only way to make money," he said. "People still have thirsts."

"Moonshinin'!" exclaimed Ralph in disgust.

"I don't like your tone an' I don't like your manner," flared Dakin. "Don't try to put on airs. *You* ain't got nerve enough or brains enough to beat the law."

Ralph's fist came up. "Once a crook, always a crook. Maybe I haven't got any brains . . . sometimes I doubt it fer stickin' to this country . . . but I can beat you to a pulp if you open that ugly mouth at me again. Now you get out of here before we have war."

Elvy Dakin glowered and twitched his nose. Perhaps he would have accepted the challenge if old man Budd's conciliatory voice had not interrupted. "What ails you boys, anyway? It's too hot to fight. Git on your horse, Elvy, an' pull out."

The man did so, very slowly. When he was ready to depart, he flung a warning at Ralph. "Next time you spring that stuff on me, old-timer, we'll do battle. An' it won't be just fists, either." With that he turned toward the Bend-Klamath Road and, although the day was stifling, he

50

urged his horse to a lope.

There was a long silence. Ralph stared at the jack pines, still ridden by the discouragement. Presently old man Budd spoke again, apropos of nothing at all. "Yes, sir, a varmint's to be killed when it gets the rabies. No mercy to be shown. Did you say you was interested in that five hundred dollars, Ralph?"

"I'm no manhunter. Against my grain to snoop after other people and their affairs."

"Just you remember what I said about varmints. An' don't fergit about people not bein' able to stand prosperity. Just remember those things, Ralph. Think 'em over. Five hundred dollars is a lot of money."

Ralph got his package of coffee and swung into the saddle. "If somethin' don't come my way pretty soon," he said, "I'll blow up an' bust. Everything I turn a hand to goes wrong."

Old man Budd's voice came after him, but he did not hear it. The Bend-Klamath Road, the intolerable heat, and the stifling sand engulfed him. His own temper was short enough to cause him many weary moments of self-discipline. Now, as he had put it, he was on the verge of a blow-up.

He plunged into the jack pines and gave the horse free rein to follow the narrow, rutted road. Old man Budd's cryptic sentences kept recurring, no matter how he turned his mind. Five hundred dollars. Why, five hundred dollars would be like a gift from the skies! It would give him heart to go on, heart to continue the weary, unequal fight for prosperity. It meant horses, fences, buildings, and seed. It meant self respect. It meant he might even ask Grace Lewis. . . .

"Oh, no, it don't," he said. "That little lady picks her own company, an' I ain't going to butt in any more. She shut the gate, and I'll be danged if I open it."

Of a sudden his eyes picked up a diverging trail of hoofprints ahead, hoofprints that swung from the main road to a narrow path leading into the deeper shade of the forest. Ralph's dissatisfaction was given more fuel. "There goes Elvy Dakin to his shanty and his cronies and moonshine still!"

Then, simultaneously, his mind grasped three loose ends of information and made a strand of fact. The leader of the masked bandits was, according to the express company notice, above medium height, heavy set, and had blue eyes. And old man Budd had repeated his mysterious comment twice: *"Varmints out of their preserve . . . they won't stand prosperity very long. Somebody'll spill the beans . . . I didn't think they had nerve enough to do it."* The storekeeper quite evidently had some particular gang in mind. And perhaps it was more than a coincidence that Elvy Dakin had blue eyes and was above the ordinary height. Moreover, Elvy had partners who made the unsavory shack in the jack pines their headquarters. Several shiftless, ratty men who made and peddled white mule. They were lacking in backbone, save when drunk, but they would follow Elvy, and he had always been a restless, unpleasant character.

"So that was what the old man drove at," murmured Ralph. "I was a bonehead not to see it."

If he could get some proof, he would be the possessor of five hundred dollars. Five hundred dollars! Then the small hint of pleasure died away from his face. "I'm no manhunter. It ain't exactly fair . . . unless I give him warning that I'm out-and-out against him."

Thus thinking, he rode through the forest while the afternoon sun sank lower and lower. Somewhere beyond six o'clock he emerged to a vast prairie, and in another half hour arrived at his shanty, perched on a quarter section of land. In the distance was the huddle of another frame house — the Lewis place. Ralph made a short supper and in the twilight set across the country toward the far ranch with the letter he had brought from Burnt Creek.

He saw, presently, that there were people in front of the house. When he came closer, he recognized Grace Lewis and Elvy Dakin. His arm fell across the pommel of the saddle with an impatient slap, but he rode up through the graying dusk and joined them with a sober face. Dakin thrust out his arrogant chin and growled: "Nobody invited you over here."

"Them's certainly true words," agreed Ralph. "Truer than you know. But I don't always need an invitation, being in that respect like some other people."

He slid off the horse and walked to the girl with the letter extended. "There was this for you, and I thought I might as well bring it . . . this time."

She was a small, sturdy lass, and even in the dusk a glow of pink stood on her cheeks, visible to Ralph. The barren land of the West is no respecter of persons, and its toll is usually callused hands, roughened skin, and abraded beauty; but Grace Lewis seemed to have been excepted from that toll. Her eyes were dark to match her hair. A scent of rose perfume was on her clothes, the touch of gentleness unforgotten in a homestead shack. She took the letter with a faint thanks, returning his sober gaze with a slight air of confusion and defiance.

"Here Rover, there Rover," said Dakin sneeringly. "You fetch an' carry well."

The girl turned on him as if to protest, and her eyes snapped. Then she dropped her head and was mute.

"You're getting funnier and funnier," observed Ralph somberly. The rankling sense of thwarted labor came again to him, and presently he was thinking of the five hundred dollars that meant security and self-respect. "By the way, Elvy, I'm looking for five hundred dollars. You ain't seen anything of it, have you?"

"Haw! That's a good one, old-timer. You ain't ever had five hundred dollars, and you won't ever have five hundred dollars."

"No, but I'm lookin' for it."

Some of the amusement died out of Elvy Dakin's face and left him puzzled. The girl, too, watched Ralph closely. "What're you talkin' about?" demanded Elvy.

"Why, the reward for information regardin' the holdup day before yesterday. I just said to myself, 'I need that money,' so I'm looking around. I thought I'd ask you . . . so you'd know what I was doing. Just so you'd know, Elvy."

Dakin stepped back a pace, and his arm dropped toward a rear pocket. He was breathing fast, and a blaze of anger leaped into his hard, blue eyes. "What's that mean?" he demanded harshly.

"Nothing in particular and everything in general. Take your hand away from your hip pocket, Elvy. I can beat you to the draw. You ought to know better. Fan out of here now. And if you see anything of that five hundred, just let me know."

The two men stood face to face in the dusk, swaying slightly toward each other. Dakin's fingers twitched against his trousers leg, and every predatory bit of his nature rose to the surface and was visible. A rasp of emotion came out of his throat but no intelligible word. Ralph laughed.

"You'd like to fight it out now, Elvy, but you ain't got the crust. Go home and drink some of your moonshine, and you'll feel more like a lion."

The girl stepped between them. "Stop this quarreling. It's

ridiculous that two grown men must fight just like children."

Dakin turned away and climbed into the saddle. "All right, old-timer," he said, looking straight at Ralph. "I get you, but you won't ever make any use of what you think. See?" Then he spoke to the girl. "Sorry our little evenin's entertainment was interrupted. Better luck next time. An' mebbe you'd better think over what I said." A moment later he was lost in the thickening dusk.

"What'd he mean, 'think it over?' " growled out Ralph.

"There's no reason why I should tell you my private affairs, Ralph Olmstead," she returned defiantly. "You're not my guardian."

Ralph curled his fist at the thought of how the insolence of Elvy Dakin might have made Grace equally insolent toward him, and the girl, seeing it, was suddenly angry. "There you go, doubling up your fist! Just like everything and everybody else in this damned old country! Force, force, force . . . that's all people can think of. I'm sick and tired of it!"

Old man Budd's shrewd guess was correct. Both of these young, upright people were gripped by the heat and the rawness of their surroundings. Both were on edge, needing the impact of some exciting event to jar them back to normal behavior. Ralph turned to his horse and without a word got into the saddle and gathered the reins.

The girl stood undecided, the anger dying away. "Well, aren't you going to say something? I'm expecting to hear that terrible temper break out."

"Them days," said Ralph sadly, "are gone forever. Guess we don't do anything but quarrel. That's getting kinda monotonous. There's a little business I got to look after tonight, so I'll just travel on. Won't bother you any more."

"Wait," she commanded and came closer. "I . . . I heard

55

you say something to him that sounded like a warning. What was it? Where are you going?"

"Well, now, I can't just tell you," he answered. "It's a matter of business." He rode away, leaving the girl by the gate. She called after him. "Ralph, don't you be foolish and go into the jack pines tonight. Do you hear me? There might be trouble."

He refused to answer, riding on. But he had gone only a few yards when he heard a sound that set every nerve on edge. He dug his heels into the flanks of the horse and raced away. "Crying, she was!" he muttered. "Well, I won't ever give her reason to cry any more. But how did she know what I was going to do?"

Women, he decided, were possessed by an uncanny sense of events. Somehow she had learned of Dakin and his gang in the jack pines. Of course, it was no especial secret, and yet there was nothing tangible against these men. Then he thought of Dakin's insolent attitude toward the girl, and it turned him into a cold rage. "It's got to be settled right now!" he said to himself.

He came to his shanty and stopped only long enough to get additional shells for his revolver and to throw a lariat over the saddle pommel. This was by way of preparation for the unexpected. "If I'm going to do it right, I've got to force the issue. That gang may be getting all their gold pieces from moonshinin', but somehow it don't seem likely. And Dakin took up my hint too quick. If there's any booty, it'll be around the cabin somewhere. Here goes."

The dusk had turned to full-shadowed night. Above, in a clear, cold sky, a thin rind of moon let down a filter of light. Ralph urged his horse out of a walk and crossed the prairie. Turning in the saddle, he looked back and saw his shack setting in a desolate huddle. Farther away he observed some black, moving shadows against the sky line, but he paid no attention. Night riders were frequent enough in this country to attract scant notice. A few minutes later he plunged into the abysmal gloom of the pines and for a time was utterly blinded. Then his eyes became accustomed, and he saw the way ahead.

He was bound for the sinister cabin in the woods, something like a quarter mile farther along, and three or four hundred yards deeper in the brush. As he traveled, a rough plan formed in his head. He would leave the horse in the road and creep through to the shanty. It was early enough in the evening, and they would doubtless be playing cards or busy with the moonshine still. In either case, they would be together, and he would have almost an even break in the fight that would probably come.

He turned a bend of the road, and the horse picked up his head and shied to one side. Ralph came alert, but neither gun shot nor voice broke the night, and he relaxed again. "Don't be so skittish," he said. "Get along."

The next moment he was brought to a sharp halt. A shadowed figure stepped from the thicket. The crackling of brush behind told of other men closing in. The sullen voice of Elvy Dakin challenged him. "That hoss has more sense than you got. I thought mebbe you'd put your head into the trap. Give a fool enough rope an' he'll always hang himself."

"Ain't it the truth," agreed Ralph, sparring for time. He could not reach for his gun without precipitating a shower of lead, and he was too plain a target to afford that at this instant.

"Now," snarled out Dakin, "get down from that horse. I'm goin' to beat the sap outa you. When we're finished, you won't be able to talk about that five hundred dollars. Keep your hands up!"

Ralph slipped down. The horse's body shielded him from the men behind, and Dakin had not drawn his gun. He made a leap forward but, with all his planning, was not quick enough. Dakin was upon him like a tiger, beating his face and body with savage fists. There was no time, it seemed, to ward off blows. The horse reared up, turned around, and bolted up the road. The attackers closed in, and Ralph was struck a glancing blow on the temple. He went down, half paralyzed, and in the confusion of feet he took hold of a pair of boots and pulled with all his might. A body crashed on top of him.

"Clear away," panted one of the gang. "Gimme a chance to shoot!"

Ralph gripped his man while the fog cleared from his head. They were all around him, standing slightly off, and waiting for a chance to put in a bullet. His unwilling captive grunted like a bear in a trap and rolled in the sand. It carried them toward the brush, and Ralph, conceiving a better plan, let go and shoved his opponent away with his feet. They rose almost together.

"It's the man on the right!" cried a voice. "Let him have it!"

"No!" screamed Ralph's opponent, weaving as if drunk. Then it was too late. The woods thundered, and two orange blotches splayed out against the velvet darkness. There was a grunt, a cough and, as Elvy turned with his revolver, the man beside him fell heavily. Down the road echoed the patter of hoofs. "Outa here!" ordered Dakin. "We got to beat it! Come on, Bill."

They ran through the thicket toward the shanty. Ralph made a swift calculation. They still believed they had killed him. The scream of protest was too full of frenzy to sound like any particular person. It was such a cry as anyone might make who felt the imminence of death. The pound of the hoofs sounded clearer.

"Come on, Bill!" bellowed Dakin, retreating farther into the brush. "We're goin' out the other trail."

Ralph took his cue and lunged into the thicket after them. He found a narrow pathway and redoubled his speed. The others were strung out in front, and one of the two had reached the shanty. The door slammed against the outer wall, and feet thumped across the flooring. Ralph arrived in front of the place five paces behind the last man. He approached the open doorway and waited. It was pitch dark in the shanty.

"There's somebody on the road," said Dakin. "I'm goin' to light just one match while you get your stuff. Then we got to clear away. It'll be four hours before they gather a posse, an' that'll put us clean out of the country. Bert, did you saddle the horses like I told you?"

"Sure. Hurry an' light that match."

"That cussed Olmstead made an awful noise. Gives me the willies. Hurry up!"

Ralph gripped the sill of the door. A match scratched across wood and flared to a dim light, revealing Dakin's face, lined with dirt and perspiration. "Bill, where are you?" he called, and turned the match toward Ralph. The latter raised his revolver.

"Up . . . put 'em up . . . all of you. Hold that match, Elvy, and don't move."

The lesser member of the gang stopped as if carved of granite. "It was Bill we shot, then!" he breathed softly. But Dakin was of more durable substance. The arm holding the match swept down, and the light snapped out. Ralph jumped aside as the shanty trembled from floor to beams with Dakin's shot. The mushroom of flame gave him a point

59

at which to aim. He took another step to the side, raised his weapon, and fired. The other man had taken advantage of the pitch blackness to come into play, and the roar of another explosion beat upon Ralph's eardrums with terrific force. He moved again and came to the corner of the room, waiting in absolute silence. The acrid odor of gunpowder brought tears to his eyes. A cough broke from someone in the opposite corner, was repeated, and followed by a ragged, weakening voice. "I'm done for!" It was Dakin's voice. A chair tipped and fell, a body sprawled to the floor with an irregular impact, and a gun clattered sharply on the boards.

With the chief down and the false courage of moonshine ebbing fast away, the other one was bereft of support, and the nasal voice of the ferret-faced man whined out a surrender. Ralph clutched the wall of the shanty. "You ain't got a mite of spunk," he said in a drowsy voice. "Drop your gun. All right . . . now light the lamp. You sure must have had a lot of hooch in your system to rob a mail stage. Or else Elvy kicked you into the idea. Hurry up!"

Out on the road there was the stir of a horse, and the swish of brush. The lamp wick spurted a flame. The ferret-faced one affixed the globe and backed against the wall. His face was chalk white. "We got Bill!" he reiterated.

"Shut up," commanded Ralph in the same drowsy voice. The pistol wavered in his hand, and he found it unexpectedly hard to maintain himself upright.

Dakin was stretched awkwardly on the floor, one arm reaching outward for his revolver, and the other tangled in the fallen chair. The mattress of one bunk was dragged half from the frame, and Ralph saw the hint of a canvas bag in the boards. That, he decided, was the loot these men had taken from the mail stage.

He caught his breath. A sharp pain ran across his chest

and, try as he did, the strength left his legs, and the gun would not stay up to level.

The ferret-faced one took a step forward, his eyes glittering with a sudden hope. "Winged you, huh? Mebbe you'll sing another song, after all." His arms came down, and a malicious grin covered the ashen complexion. He made a tentative step toward his fallen weapon.

"Stay back!" commanded Ralph angrily. He tried to bring the gun up again, but his fingers were as pieces of ice and entirely bereft of strength. He made a last effort to stand, then the wall refused to support him longer, and he dropped like a sack of meal. The ferret-faced one gave a shout and dived for his gun.

"Stop it!"

The ferret-faced one rolled away from the weapon as if it had been a coiled snake. In the door stood Grace Lewis, holding a rifle on the two outlaws. "Ralph, did they get you?"

"Good . . . girl!" he murmured. "I'm . . . all . . . right. But . . . no strength in my legs. Turn around, you. Hand me that gun, Grace, then take that piece of rope and tie him up. See what's happened to Elvy."

She did as requested, trussing the arms of the man. A hasty inspection of Dakin revealed a welt along the neck. "Knocked out more than anything else," she observed.

Ralph said: "He'll come around soon enough. Tie him, too. We'll leave him here."

The girl bent over Ralph and opened his shirt front. "Ralph, the bullet just missed your lungs! Oh, I knew you'd come here. I saw it in your face. That's why I followed. I heard the shooting, and then saw the light in the window. What would have happened!" She shuddered. "Ralph . . . I . . . I won't lose my temper again!"

"Huh?" It seemed as if he reached a new reservoir of strength. He ripped off a piece of the shirt and made, with the girl's help, a rough dressing to stop the flow of blood. Then he managed to get to his feet and superintend operations.

From beneath the fallen mattress he picked up the canvas bag and found therein a packet of fresh five and ten dollar bills. Beneath Dakin's mattress was a second bag with gold pieces. Ralph explained the robbery to Grace then drove the prisoner out of the shanty and to the road. The girl had found Ralph's horse and brought it back with her. Both mounted, and with the prisoner trudging before them, tethered by the rope, they started toward Burnt Creek.

"We'll call the sheriff on the phone and have him down here in no time. He can come after Elvy and. . . ."

"And the dead man," finished the girl, shuddering again. "I saw him in the road."

"Poor Bill didn't get a square break," observed Ralph. "But the rest of them will pay for it."

The two horses came together, and Ralph had strength enough to lean over and capture a kiss from the girl. "Say, honey, what's been ailin' us, anyway? There's too much work for us to do without fighting each other."

"We'll never do it again, Ralph."

"Well . . . not too much," he amended, with the semblance of a grin. Then, later, he had another pleasing thought. "Five hundred dollars' reward. Say, that'll put us on Easy Street. And when water comes into the country, we'll be fixed for life. Ain't this a great land?"

IV

"STUBBORN PEOPLE"

Old man Budd sat on the porch of his Burnt Creek store, watching the shimmering heat waves that rose out of the jack pine forest and trailed across the small sand-floored clearing. A lazy drone pervaded the air, broken by the snapping of myriad insects and the impalpable, shutter-like beat of the blazing atmosphere.

He had a habit of reflecting on life. Every act in a man's life, he reflected now, was affected by every other act. There was no beginning and no end. Just an everlasting onward march. Take Jim Hunter, for example.

Budd's impassive face lightened. "Think of the devil an' he's sure to pop up." From the north leg of the Bend-Klamath Road rode Jim Hunter, a tall and supple fellow who, even in the saddle, seemed unable to bend his shoulders.

"Stubborn as a mule," reflected Budd in admiration. He waited until Hunter had reached the porch and led the horse into an ineffectual patch of shade before vouchsafing welcome. "You'd save a lot of energy, young fella, if you'd just slouch in the saddle when you're ridin'. That's advice from a broken-down cowpuncher. This ain't no parade."

Hunter stepped up on the porch. The effect of his stature

was heightened by the way he carried himself and the seasoned leanness of his body. The struggle on homestead land had definitely left its impression. With some men the abrasion of weather and work affects only a general hardening of features. In Jim Hunter it brought out the original tenacity of his nature and left decisive lines on the berry-colored face. A flash of humor widened his eyes.

"There's no use trying to save me trouble, Budd. Takes fire to burn a fool. I need some coffee and beans."

"Huh." The storekeeper hoisted himself from the chair and ambled into the dark building. "There's a letter. Mebbe you'll want it afore the beans."

Hunter took it with unrestrained eagerness. The gravity dropped from him like a mantle. It seemed he could not tear away the envelope quickly enough. Dave Budd, sharply watching, saw the young man's eyes race down the written page with actual avidity, but as quickly the face turned expressionless again. Presently he crumpled the page in his fist, scowling — so bitter and unforgiving a scowl that the storekeeper clucked his tongue and dumped the provisions on the counter softly.

"Anything else?" he asked.

"No! There isn't anything else," muttered Hunter. "There never is." He stared out of the door upon the sun-scorched clearing. His mind was far from Burnt Creek.

"I mean in the line of grub," added Budd dryly.

That brought the young man back. "You old goat, quit reading my mind."

"I been called a lot of things in my time, but I pause at the term goat," grumbled the storekeeper. "I figger some day I'm a-goin' to quit tendin' store fer a bunch of sassy homesteaders. Take your grub and git."

Hunter stalked to the porch, dumped the grub in his saddlebags, and climbed into the saddle.

"If a man was in his right mind, he'd never come to this god-forsaken land."

"Road's plumb open. You ain't tied to that land. If you don't admire it, why'n't you just sashay out?"

"Same reason you've stuck to this dump for twenty-five years," retorted Hunter.

The two traded sober glances. Budd nodded. "Guess you're right, son. We're sort of spellbound. Gets in the blood, I reckon."

Hunter turned his horse to the road. In a moment he had disappeared through the jack pines. Budd settled in his chair after securing a fresh cigar and reverted to his original line of thought. Jim Hunter now had been a homesteader three years and wore the same hard-bitten look that they all carried. It was partly the result of fighting the land, but it wasn't wholly so. Jim had come from Portland with the same tight lips and the same stubborn carriage of body. Three years had done a great deal in seasoning and tempering the body and wearing away all softness. The essentials remained untouched. Regularly he came to Burnt Creek for supplies and mail. Regularly he received a letter in the same feminine handwriting, which he opened always with a brightening of face and crumpled later with a scowl that seemed to cover hurt pride and forlorn hope. Those letters, evidently, demanded something he would not give, for he never sent an answer through Budd's little post office.

The storekeeper reluctantly left the chair and wandered back to his kitchen. The sun blazed up in the sky, intolerably scorching. Budd viewed an empty pitcher and set to work at making a supply of lemonade against the greater heat of the long afternoon. A few beans, some hard bread, and a dish of canned peaches served for dinner. Then, with a fresh cigar and the lemonade at hand, he settled himself in the sultry shade. All things in Dave Budd's philosophy came to those who waited — provided the waiting was mixed with a little judicious assistance.

The afternoon was not to be lonely. He had just started on the lemonade when the sputter of the Bend-Klamath stage motor reached him. The vehicle swayed out of the forest, climbed the ruts of the road, skidded perilously amid a shower of sand, and brought a boiling radiator nose to nose with the porch. The driver had a passenger this trip. A woman it was, veiled against the dirt and sun. Teddy Hanson climbed away from the wheel and helped her to the porch.

"Aw," he said, "now what's the good of stoppin' at a horrible hole like this, ma'am? Gosh, think how lonely I'll be all the way to Klamath."

"Flattery," said the girl. She drew back the veil, and Budd, greatly puzzled by this visit, found himself looking at an extremely pretty mouth and a pair of hazel eyes that could, when they pleased, be very friendly. Some shade of dark hair strayed pleasantly down a white temple. "Is this Mister Budd?" she asked.

"That's him," growled out the driver. "There's a lot of circumferance, you see. He gets it sittin' on the porch of this so-called store."

"I wouldn't listen to such slander," replied Budd. "It's the heat makes him that way. But I mistrust you've got to the wrong place. Ain't hardly anything here you could stop off for. It must be Klamath you mean." He could not help noting that it was not the friendly eyes nor the pretty mouth which most attracted him, as it was a firm little chin with the dab of freckle on it and an Irish nose. *She'll be wantin' her own way,* he silently prophesied.

"No," she answered. "It's Burnt Creek."

Teddy Hanson boosted the girl's trunk onto the porch, obviously disinclined to leave. She settled the matter by paying him. "Thank you." The inflection was as much as a dismissal. Teddy shot a glance of envy toward Budd and climbed into his seat.

"It's a wonder you wouldn't fix the road in front of your shack," he shouted above the clatter of the engine.

"That sand flea can burrow where it won't climb," retorted Budd. A cloud of sand shot from the wheels and, when the dust settled, the stage was gone.

"I dunno how that thing sticks together," he said. "It drinks sand an' runs on grasshoppers. They's a hundred dollars' worth of bailin' wire in it." He saw that she had lost spirit and was staring wistfully at the road. "What'd you say you were after, ma'am?"

"They told me in Bend that you'd help me. I . . . I'm looking for a homestead here."

"A homestead, ma'am?"

"Never mind how I look!" she cried. "And don't try to argue me out of it! I've argued all the way from Portland, and it's settled. If you won't help me, I'll have to get someone else. I want a homestead near Burnt Creek."

"Why near Burnt Creek, ma'am?"

"For . . . for reasons."

There was metal in her. She wore clothes that stamped her as a refined city woman, and her hands and clear skin were plain enough witnesses that she had never trafficked much with spade and bucket. Still, Budd did not make the mistake of arguing. He saw her determined little chin with the dab of a freckle on it. She was another of those stubborn people . . . such as made good in this country. They never knew when they were licked.

"Why, sure, I'll help you, ma'am," he agreed affably. "Most everybody comes to me sooner or later, around here leastwise. But it's powerful hot right now. Come in an' have some lemonade."

It was a great deal later, when the courtesies were dispensed with and the subject of land well talked over, that Budd thought of the Hazen place. "I been thinkin'," he said, spoiling a new cigar, "that you'll be all by yourself. It's a hard life any way you take it an', if you could get near other folks, it'd be a great boost. I've located durn near every other family in these parts, an' it strikes me there's a nice section about an hour's ride from here, adjoinin' Jim Hunter's place."

Her head came up of a sudden, and a sparkle of triumph set her blue eyes to shining. "That's the place I want!" she cried.

It staggered Budd. "Why, ma'am, how do you know? Mebbe you wouldn't like it at all. Better wait till you see it."

"I do know! Is there a house on it?"

"Ordinarily the government don't furnish houses," said Budd with the suggestion of dryness. "But it so happens old man Hazen took this up an' got plumb discouraged. He went to Bend. You can take up the rights fer next to nothin'. I'll see about that. There's a house, well, an' barn on it."

She sprang from the chair. "Mister Budd, can't we go right over and move in now? I want to get started."

Her face was tinted with a pink excitement and her mouth, which Budd decided was about as kissable a one as he had ever seen, was puckered in determination. She was finding a great satisfaction in something. The puzzled storekeeper watched her. "Why, I reckon you could, but. . . ."

"But!" she exclaimed. "That's the only word I've heard lately! I don't want to hear any more of it. I want you to

help me file the necessary things and help me move. Whatever it's worth, I'll pay you. But you've got to help. Can't we start right now?"

The storekeeper found things moving too fast, and he promptly vetoed the suggestion.

"We ain't goin' no place at two o'clock in the afternoon. Why, ma'am, people don't travel through them jack pines this time of day unless it's powerful necessary. Terrible hot. 'Bout four-thirty we'll start. Meanwhile, we'll be collectin' some grub an' tools."

She seemed to acquire more and more energy. The delay fretted her, and she moved restlessly around the store, choosing what she needed from the shelves. There were sundry implements of which she knew nothing at all, and Budd explained them. She listened quite carefully, a wry expression now and then tempering the determination. Budd was compelled to admire the way in which she accepted his picture of homestead life. None too rosy did he paint that picture, either. He wanted recruits for the land, but he wanted them to be disillusioned before they started residence. Once she stopped him.

"You're trying to discourage me," she said.

"Huh. I been here in this country twenty-five years, an' I'm tellin' you as straight as I can. The land grows on them as can stand it. For the rest, it kills or drives out."

"It won't scare me. What others do, I can do."

He silently applauded. "You can go out an' live on the place without hindrance while I sort of fix up things with Hazen an' the land office. You can go to Bend later."

The sun blazed downward, and after four o'clock Budd ventured from the store, hitched his buggy, loaded on the trunk and duffel, and began the journey through the jack pines with his passenger. He watched her from his heavy-lidded eyes, waiting for some sign of weakness. In the dwarf forest the heat scorched them, and the sand rose out of the road and cascaded from the branches. It was a dismal entrance to a hard land. However, if the girl felt any discouragement, she kept it well to herself, hands folded in her lap and sitting erect in the swaying seat. So Budd turned to casual topics, directing her attention in his kindly way to the things she must do and expect.

"Ma'am," he said finally, "if I ain't too personal, just what makes you do this?"

It struck tinder. He saw a spark flash. "Because I want to show him . . . people . . . that I'm no butterfly! That's why! And I *will* do it!"

There was, then, a man involved. Budd, seeing partial light, moved away from the subject. They drove in silence while the rutted highway wound slowly through the heart of the pines, passed sundry trails, and came at last to a vast open plain over which the sun shed a blood-colored glow.

"Purty, ain't it?" asked Budd, wistful pride in his voice. "See yonder house? That'll be your nearest neighbor, Jim Hunter. A mighty fine boy. You'll do well to know Jim."

"H'm."

"Yes, sir. Jim's the stubborn kind. Hard as nails an' never says much, but that's the only breed who'll survive this country. He'll help you."

The buggy turned off the road and went bumping over the flat land. They passed a corner fence and in time drew up at the door of Hunter's house. Budd called out: "Hey, Jim."

The girl seemed to become very still, and the storekeeper, turning, found a flutter of excitement again in her eyes. Jim walked from his place, stooping slightly to

70

pass the upper sill.

"You're goin' to have a neighbor, Jim. I'm locatin' her on the next place. You'll kinda watch. . . ."

He got no further and found himself thrust completely out of the picture. Hunter strode toward the buggy, the soberness quite gone from his face.

"Why, Mary, what on earth . . . ?"

"Don't make any mistake," she broke in. "I've come for that apology."

Budd raised a hand to a sorely puzzled head. The girl was sitting like a statue, her fingers interlaced in her lap, her chin held a little higher than usual, the delicate pink spreading slowly. The excitement was gone. Budd had the idea that it was suppressed only by an effort. Hunter stopped dead. "What?"

"I said I've come for that apology, Jim."

"Now why," he said angrily, "did you come all the way out to this hot and dusty place? Budd, you ought to have more sense."

"I asked him to bring me." She stamped a foot against the buggy floor. "Jim Hunter, don't you boss me. The time's past for that. I'm going to make you take back what you said that time if it takes me ten years! If writing letters won't do it, then I'll try farming. You might at least have answered my letters out of courtesy."

"What's all this foolishness about her living on the next place?" demanded Hunter, turning on Budd with a scowl. "Have you lost your mind? Great Scott, a woman can't fight this desert, and you of all men ought to know it!"

Budd made an ineffectual gesture with his hand. There had been no preliminary warning to all this. The girl's mouth was puckered together, and she seemed on the point of crying from sheer anger. Budd was about to mention the former Grace Lewis when Mary burst out: "Oh, if I were a man, I'd make you apologize right now! You can't bully me, Jim Hunter! I'll not stand for it, you hear? And I'll show you if I'm a butterfly! Go on, Mister Budd."

The storekeeper was only too glad to escape. The end of the reins smartly thwacked the horse's rump, and they bumped over the uneven ground toward the Hazen place a quarter mile on. Budd threw a quick glance behind him and saw Jim Hunter rooted in the same spot, arms akimbo, face furrowed. If he knew anything about it, Budd reflected, there was a young man who would soon wish a strong interview.

He discretely held his peace and, when they reached the house, began the job of packing the trunk and various tools and utensils inside. When he had finished, he found the girl seated on the trunk, surveying the walls with plain dismay. Truly, it was a sight to discourage a mortal woman. A bachelor originally had lived here, a bachelor who had found the job of keeping up externals too great, let alone the niceties of housekeeping. The floor was littered with dirt; the walls and ceilings were bare and unpleasant. A stove was half dismantled. A chair and table were overturned and partly broken. A bunk had once stood against a wall but now had parted company from itself.

"Well," said the girl, taking off her jacket, "the first thing's to sweep."

The storekeeper was ready to shout. Spunk! She had more of it than a dozen men. Heretofore he had nourished misgivings, but now he moved solidly to her support. Those nice clothes and white hands didn't mean anything.

"Yes, ma'am," he agreed. "We need a new deal. You just take a bucket and go out back fer some water in the well. Meanwhile I'll tackle the broom, it bein' a dirty job."

Broom and water, hammer and nails, elbow grease and much talk — by these means and two or three hours' time Budd and the girl transformed the place into a passable shelter. There had been some wood left. Budd built a fire and cooked a meal while the girl added a touch here and there to the bare walls. It was after dark when Budd climbed into his buggy and started for home.

"Well, I reckon you're dog tired. It's easy to sleep out here. An' that gun I give you will scare away most anything that walks or crawls. Ain't nothin' to be afeerd of, anyhow. In case anything should happen, you. . . ."

"I'm not asking him for any favors!"

He suppressed a grin and continued as if there had been no interruption. "In a few days I'll bring you a collie dog an' a hoss. Then you'll be fixed. Meanwhile you just set tight an' git organized. I'll see Hazen an' the land office. G'night."

He drove away, bent for the pines and Burnt Creek. But if he thought to avoid Jim Hunter, he was mistaken. The young man was camped outside his house, and Budd saw him move through the dark toward the buggy. The storekeeper sighed a little and came to a halt.

"All right," he acquiesced wearily. "Go on now an' say what's been burnin' you."

"Of all the old fools!" rasped out Jim Hunter. "You know very well she can't stay out here! It's impossible. What can a woman do? Here I work my head off and just break even. How do you expect her to get by? Just because she's bent on. . . ."

"What should I have done?" asked Budd gently.

"Told her to go home, of course. Discourage her from such a crazy idea."

"Huh. No wonder you 'n' she quarreled. Don't you s'pose

I did some arguin'? Huh? It was like talkin' to myself. If I hadn't brought her, she'd've up an' walked out on the darn desert by herself. Got to handle her another way. She's as stubborn as you."

Hunter groaned. "I know it. She's always been like that. If she gets her mind set, nothing short of an act of God can change it. But she can't stay!"

"I wouldn't be so durned certain," snapped out Budd. The late hour and the prior excitement had put him a little out of humor. "She seems plumb able to take care of herself. I've seen women get by on this desert. Grace Lewis did quite well for herself till she married a man just like her! A woman can beat a man all hollow fer endurin' things."

"It's not only that," broke in Hunter. "It's not safe. All sorts of queer ducks roam these places. A lone woman just invites trouble. There's Bottle-Nose Henderson, for example. Great Scott!"

Budd scratched his stubbled chin. He, too, had thought of Bottle-Nose. It was a prickling thought that remained in the rear of his head, vaguely disturbing. Yet here was Jim within a short distance of Mary. If she called for help, he'd be over in a jiffy. "Ain't nothin' to worry about. Giddap, Toby. You people fight it out atween you."

"There's not going to be any fight . . . or anything else!" bellowed Jim.

Budd had no answer for that, but a mile later, when the pines swallowed him, one small phrase came out of all the wonderment: "Son of a gun, just look what's happened to us today!" The peace — and the monotony — which had enfolded him during the last hot summer month was gone. Life was just one dog-goned problem after another. That's what made living endurable. "Giddap, Toby. We got to figger around this somehow. There's a couple plumb in love with

74

each other an' wantin' to make up. But they'd die afore they'd admit it. Got to fix that."

He found as the week went along that all ordinary conciliatory means had no effect. The quarrel had gone too far, endured too long. The battle had arrived at a stage of siege. It worried him, for the robust storekeeper was not a man to stand by and watch the tide carry his people downstream. Faith had made him the prophet and leader of the homesteaders. He loved them and fought for them, took an unreasoning interest in their small affairs, argued with them, cursed them, and at the last word, when it seemed they could no longer struggle against the eternal hardships, gave his own time and money to keep the small flame of courage in their hearts. They were all, Budd believed, in a common brotherhood, striving for a common happiness, and every sorrow and discouragement they suffered was sure to find its way eventually to his own big heart.

He had no means of knowing the nature of the quarrel, but still he worked shrewdly to dispel it. The day after the girl had settled on the homestead, Budd saddled the gentlest horse of his lot and sent it over to her by Slivers Gilstrap, a passing cow hand.

"You tell her, Slivers, that I'll be over after a while with the necessary filin' doodads, an' that she'd better ask Jim Hunter to fix that lock on the door."

Late that night Slivers came back with blood in his eye. "Say, you old galoot, what'd you go an' tell me to tell her that for? Minute I says it she flies off'n the handle an' says she ain't askin' Jim fer nuthin'. I thought mebbe he'd insulted her an', bein' a gentleman, offers to shoot him er hog tie him, er anything. Dog-goned if she didn't larrup me, then."

Thereupon Budd went to Bend and rode back to the girl's

place with filing papers, another sage move up his sleeve. But he had no chance to act upon it. Mary, dressed in some kind of old clothes and already freckled by the sun, met him with fire in her eyes.

"Mister Budd, I wish you'd go over and tell Jim Hunter I forbid him coming on my land! He's been here twice trying to browbeat me. You tell him I don't want but one thing from him, and that's an apology. Otherwise I'll use this pistol. I will!"

She flourished the heavy weapon in her hand, and the storekeeper, suppressing a chuckle, noted that she used both hands to raise it. It would have been disastrous to offer advice then.

"Mebbe," he gravely offered, "I'd better notify the sheriff to arrest him fer trespassin'."

"No, oh, no! I wouldn't do that. But you tell him what I said, will you?"

So Budd, inwardly chuckling, went to Hunter's place, only to be motioned away. "Get out of here, you old goat. I won't listen to any more of your ideas. You're the cause of all this."

"The most ungrateful thing in the world," opined the store-keeper, returning to Burnt Creek, "is mixin' in family troubles. Men've been killed fer less. But if I'm to be hung, I might as well be hung fer somethin' good. Patch that up somehow."

Man and woman were crowded from his mind in the succeeding weeks. Events in the sparse Central Oregon country move with the same irregular frequency as elsewhere. Out of a serene sky broke seven kinds of trouble into which Budd was directly or indirectly drawn. For one thing, threshing season was on full blast, and every able-bodied man gave his services. This was communal law. Then the road commissioners in a frenzy of economy — just before election — decided to leave unimproved a more or less impassable stretch of the Bend-Klamath Road. The storekeeper, being apprised of it, rode to town in a fury and shocked those commissioners out of their economic resolutions. He fought for his people and his land ruthlessly and, being a power in his own right, won. Hardly had this subsided when the shadow of Bottle-Nose Henderson fell across the land.

Bottle-Nose was one of those derelicts for whom society has no honored place. In a more highly organized community he would have been sent to an asylum. Deschutes County tolerated him because he stuck to the open spaces and left people alone. But somewhere on this lone trail the last remaining fiber of reason snapped, and he reverted to the law of the jungle. He ran amuck, terrorizing the edges of the county, and sent unprotected families into gusts of fear. No one seem safe from his swift attack. The sheriff sent out a posse, and they traced his course southward toward the Burnt Creek region by three pilfered houses and several frightened women. This trail was all the posse found. Bottle-Nose had become elusive as well as a highly dangerous character.

It was from him that the storekeeper conceived what seemed to be a sound idea one late summer evening as he jogged homeward. Toby, plodding along in dignified weariness, was startled to feel his master shake as if from ague, something that passed as a chuckle issued from Budd's barrel-like chest.

"If I got caught, I'd sure be hamstrung," mused the storekeeper. "Would lose all my reputation if I got caught an' mebbe git a dose of lead poisonin'. But it certainly oughta bring results."

And results were all that mattered to Budd. At any rate

the idea took possession of him. His chin fell forward, and Toby, unchecked, picked a faster pace toward Burnt Creek, viewing doubtless the measure of oats in the stall. A wise horse was Toby, but this time sentenced to a grievous disappointment. On reaching the store Budd went in and returned with his revolver.

"Giddap, Toby, we've got to hustle. Dog-gone it, quit your balkin'! I feed an' pamper you too much, that's what. Git now! Ain't to be fooled with."

After a short argument the sad Toby walked into the jack pines, bound for the desert. Leaving his horse to find the way, Budd relapsed into that reverie which years of solitude had acquainted him. Nor did he raise his head until the last dwarf pine was passed, and he stood against the gloom of the open land.

It was near nine o'clock. The moon displayed a thin, lifeless rind in the sky; the countless stars blinked down without dispelling the shadows. Across the open ground winked two lights, one from Jim Hunter's kitchen and the other from the girl's house, both cheerfully beckoning. Budd clucked his tongue and struck across the open, passed Hunter's place at a good distance and, on arriving within a few yards of the Hazen house, climbed out of his buggy.

"Now, you gol-durned animal," he whispered, "stay put. When I come back, it'll be a-foggin'."

He took the revolver from the holster and, under the impulse of an unusual kind of excitement, drew the hammer part way back and turned the cylinder with a thumb. Ten feet away Toby and buggy dissolved into an indistinguishable blur. Budd took a mental line from his horse to both lights.

"Got to place that dog-goned critter," he murmured, advancing.

A heavy boot toe struck a projecting rock, and he balanced wildly, failed to right himself, and fell to the ground. The impact seemed to shake him loose in a dozen vital spots. An immense grunt escaped him that seemed as if it exploded in the air, but that was only imagination. He crawled painfully to his feet and went on until the light from the girl's kitchen window was quite clear. He could see inside the small room but failed to locate her.

"Gosh, I got to see where she is afore I shoot."

He angled aside to get a better sweep of the room. It occurred to him then that he was more or less in the position of a Peeping Tom, and a rod of ice smote his back. "Fer a nickel I'd quit this fool stunt," he said to himself. Then the light was eclipsed for a moment as the girl moved to the front of the room. "That'd be the corner the stove's in. She's safe." He raised the revolver and aimed at the window.

It was not the best idea in the world. Budd began to suspect that earlier in the evening. But his self-defense was adequate enough. Both the girl and the man were too obstinate to listen to reason, and summary methods had to be employed for their own good. They were just like two fighters who struggled long after the original injury had been dead and buried. Now the only thing a man could do with stubborn pride was blast it. What he meant to do was put a bullet through that window and shatter a pane of glass. That would give the girl a much-needed scare, sort of shake her confidence in her own strength. If, on hearing that shot, Jim Hunter didn't rush over to her house he, Dave Budd, would be greatly mistaken in his man. And if that threat of danger, always a welding influence, didn't change their relations, he'd be mighty disappointed. He brought the gun down on the bright window, taking care that the shot would break a pane and bury itself in the sill.

There was, of a sudden, a pad-pad of feet on the ground, an alarming rush of body that went past him, wheeled like a football player, and bore down. Budd's revolver arm fell. A low figure hurtled from the shadows, struck him amidships, closed about him, and knocked him over with the savageness of a hungry cinnamon bear. The storekeeper's teeth rattled. He bit his chin and choked in the sand. A rock struck his head and nearly put him to sleep. Quite instinctively he put up both huge arms — he had dropped the gun — and pushed his assailant off; but before he could take advantage the man had thrown himself back again. A fist smacked against his temple, and a familiar voice reached his half-buried ears.

"You sneaking coyote! Thought you'd raise the devil in another lonely house, eh? Thought you'd scare another woman half to death! I've been laying for you. Next time maybe you'll be more careful in sneaking up on a place. I'm just about going to kill you, you Bottle-Nose skunk!"

It was Jim Hunter on the warpath, mistaking him for Bottle-Nose Henderson. Budd's mind worked in circles, amid a confusion of blows, a ton of sand, and smarting eyes. He had to get out of here in a hurry, no mistake. It wouldn't do for Jim to discover his identity. Jim wouldn't consider him in any better light, wouldn't understand. He had overlooked the fact that the young man would patrol the girl's home after dark and, in patrolling, might see him. The thing now was to make an exit and call it a bad venture.

He stifled a groan of protest. It was a darned good thing Jim had never seen Bottle-Nose and noted the man's skinny shape. The storekeeper raised hands and feet, throwing Hunter back like a blanket, got up, and dashed toward Toby.

By golly, but this was a mess. Look where he'd got himself in trying to do a good deed!

Hunter was on him like a wild cat and down to earth they went, rolling, clawing, fighting, with no words at all to waste. Budd flung the lighter man off, got up again, ran a yard, and was pulled down. Somehow Jim's fists found their mark. Budd felt his nose ache with resentment. In turn he traded blows and heard them land solidly. There was a burly strength in the storekeeper's shoulder, a power which once in the older days had made him top hand of the county. Right now he spared none of it to get clear. But it didn't matter how many times he threw Hunter away, the man was back again, pinning him to earth like a clothes dummy. Each fall hurt the corpulent Dave Budd more than he cared to admit.

"I got to quit smokin'," he said to himself. "Wind ain't no good."

Toby, nearby, snorted. They rolled beneath his very feet, and he moved uneasily. Budd dragged himself and Hunter upward toward the buggy. "No you don't!" panted Jim. "Come back here." Budd, falling, had his face turned toward the girl's house, and he saw a shaft of light spring out of the opening doorway. Somebody stood on the threshold. He wondered if this was actually so or whether the little sky-rockets in his head caused the illusion. He was soon enough put to rest about it; for a shrill, terrified scream shattered the air. Hunter's aggressiveness instantly ebbed, and a gasp broke from his hard-pressed lungs.

"What's that?"

Budd's mind attained an unprecedented nimbleness. Somebody had come across the desert from an opposite direction and gone into the house while they were fighting the silent battle. Bottle-Nose Henderson, then! The man was somewhere in the Burnt Creek region.

"Huh," he grunted, "I thought you were tryin' to put somethin' over on me. Thought you was Bottle-Nose. Been trailin' him all day. Leggo, you darned scorpion! This dog-goned darkness! I thought I had him pinned down."

Together they ran across the prairie and reached the open door. Hunter was the faster, and he made a single stride to the far corner where the girl, back to the wall, faced a thin, nondescript creature whose crimson, bulbous nose and slack mouth gave him a particularly vicious expression.

Hunter flung himself upon the man and threw him against the wall so hard as to make the small place shake from rafter to floor. Budd, near done up, was content to watch them fight. Hunter was a veritable wild cat. He beat down the invader's defense and, like a boy who has found pleasure in throwing things, swept his man across the room and slammed him against another wall, overturning a chair and table on the way.

It was soon over. Bottle-Nose collapsed with a sigh of defeat, slid to the floor, and whined for mercy. Jim Hunter strode over to the girl, looking as one just emerged from a mob attack. His shirt hung in ribbons about his gangling arms. There were sundry cuts over his face, and his hair was ground with sand. But nothing could conceal the flare in his eyes.

"Honey!" he cried. "I'll kill that skunk if he's hurt you!"

"Jimmy, what *has* happened?"

Budd turned his broad back and wryly moved his nose. There was a more or less incoherent explanation and questioning from both and out of it, unexpectedly, came: "Jimmy . . . I won't ask that apology if you don't want to give it."

"I'm a bum. I give it, Mary. I'm just a stubborn bum."

"You give it! Jimmy! I'll never ask another. And I take back everything."

A great and ponderous silence ensued, broken by the impatient Budd. "Here I trail this fella all day long and then you dog-gone wild cat . . . look what you done to me."

It was not a very strong story, but Jim Hunter was too preoccupied to pick flaws.

"I'll take Bottle-Nose back with me," continued Budd. "Say, just what was this quarrel about, anyway? Seein's I got so durned involved in it, might as well tell me."

"He called me a useless butterfly, and I had to show him I wasn't."

"Which was after she told me I couldn't do anything worth while."

"For gosh sake," stuttered the storekeeper. "Was *that* all?" It was certainly queer what small things set people at a tangent. Stubborn people, chiefly. But what great fighters they made. Just the kind to populate this sturdy, harsh land. He fell gloomily to another thought. "Suppose now you'll make up an' go back to town."

"Not on your life," declared Jim. "It's the only place I'm worth anything. Why, I'm happy here!"

"So'm I," added the girl. "That settles it."

Budd was forced to a rare smile and looked like the cat who had swallowed the canary.

"Well, I'm sure sorry my little peace efforts didn't work. Took Bottle-Nose to turn the trick. So long, folks."

It was later, entering the dark forest with his prisoner, that he lifted his face to the dim, star-scattered sky and gave thanks. Some day this country would blossom under the hands of these vigorous and clean-chosen people. Some day!

V

"FALSE FACE"

"Now listen, you gol-durned, slab-footed curmudgeon," exclaimed Sheriff Cal Emmons, "you're goin' to take the deppity star I give you! Don't want to hear no more objections. It's my duty an' privilege to draft an' swear in whomsoever I choose. You ain't got no right to stand there an' tell me you feel disinclined to serve yore county. It's a downright perversion of public spirit, and I'm not a-goin' to stand fer it."

"Don't want nuthin' to do with it," repeated Dave Budd with a still greater vehemence. "Ain't goin' to go around with that hunk o' tin on my shirt lookin' like a dumb fool."

"Fool?" roared Cal Emmons. "I take it I look like a fool fer carryin' my star, then?"

"You're a duly elected sheriff," explained Budd. "People wanted you to serve, or they wouldn't have voted you in. As fer me, I'm a fat, old man, and my fightin' days are plumb past. Git yoreself some young and spry feller that likes to ride saddle all night long, or live on a slice of bacon four days runnin'. Me, I got to have more comfort in my old age, Cal."

The sheriff neatly strung together a series of strong words. "Why, you idiot, you're no older'n me! Call forty-eight old?

Howsomever, I ain't askin' you to track no criminals across the desert. You don't have to. Yore word is pretty much law in these parts, anyhow."

"Well, that bein' so," replied Budd, "why should I have to wear a gol-durned piece of soldered tin on my shirt? Now, you listen to me, old-timer. I got my own ways of dispensin' sech justice as these parts need. It don't have anything to do with totin' a badge around, either. Why, that'd set all my folks ag'in' me, Cal. No, sir, you let me be. We're real peaceful at this end of the county and don't need no deppities. When somethin' outrageous happens, you git here soon enough, anyhow."

Emmons opened the clasp of the deputy's badge and got hold of Budd's dusty vest. "Ain't listenin' to no more palaver," he said, snorting. "I'm a-goin' to brand you right now, critter. There, Deppity Budd, you're a handsome-lookin' peace officer."

The storekeeper's huge face was wreathed in a scowl as he stared at the trinket of authority on his vest. "It's all terrible foolish," he said. "What'm I to look after? Jack rabbits and coyotes?"

"You old maverick," said the sheriff in placating tones, "I been lettin' you alone fer a good while, but now's time fer some serious work. Jest take a look out in yore front pasture, and I reckon you'll know what I'm deppitizin' you for."

Budd had no need to glance through his front door. The invasion had descended upon him a week ago in the form of broken down farm wagons, old-time schooners, buggies, pack mules, and solitary riders on every shade and size of horse. Mostly it was a family affair; the clearing in front of the store was dotted with tents and lean-tos and stray baggage and fires. Men clustered in groups, speaking guardedly, or else in heated discussion, while the women bustled about the flames and prepared the night meal. Even as the storekeeper scanned the group, he heard the creaking of fresh wagons through the trees.

They came from every corner of the state and from adjoining states, rough people and refined, all eager to share in a new prospect of comfort and prosperity. The cause of this boom was a mere rumor, a thin, unsubstantiated report that the government, long idle in this part of Central Oregon, was about to dam a distant river in the hills and construct great main canals to irrigate the land. Budd shook his head solemnly. *It was,* he repeated to himself, *only a rumor* — and rumors had ugly ways of dying out, never again to be heard. Nevertheless these hopeful people came, camped in his clearing, while preliminary scouts were sent out to find land that had not been homesteaded and then vanished through the jack pines, bound for their new El Dorado, somewhere beyond the open country.

"Reminds me of the old days in Oklahoma," said Budd. "Dang me if there wasn't a rush fer the Indian lands. I can still hear the bugles sound for the sign we could cross in. By golly! Reckon I was younger then."

"Never mind that sad extemporizin'," interrupted the sheriff. "Jest foller my ideas a spell. You see that red-headed young man with the scowl on his face? I want you should keep an eye on him, Budd. Folks have been complainin' about losin' money and valuables from their wagons and sleepin' places durin' the night. Well, now, he's a reckless-lookin' son of a gun, and he's been hangin' 'round these diggin's fer a week, ain't he?"

Budd chuckled. "Huh, it's a girl that keeps him glued here, not money."

"Powerful suspicious lookin' to me, Dave. You keep an eye

on him. I been sizin' the whole crowd up, and he's the only one I'd figger to watch."

"All right, all right," agreed the storekeeper, turning morose again. "Got to be a cussed bloodhound, have I?"

The red-headed young man evidently had something on his mind. He fished through his pockets and fumbled among the few effects piled on the ground by his saddle. Rising empty handed, he turned toward the store. The sheriff clapped on his sombrero and started out.

"I'll vamoose, Dave, and let you alone until next week."

He climbed into the saddle as the young man swung to the porch. The sheriff's horse, catching sight of a skittering sheet of white paper, reared and snorted, plunged against a porch column, knocked a board off with his feet, and drummed out of the clearing.

"Hey!" exclaimed the young man. "What's he aimin' to do, make a fence jumper out of that cayuse?"

"Horse is jest a mite skittish," said Budd mildly. He opened a fresh box of tomatoes and began packing the cans to the shelf. Half way he stopped to observe. "Horses are plumb like women that a-way. Purty, but skittish."

"Yeah," said the young man, suddenly looking harassed. "Ain't it the solemn an' miserable truth?"

He took off his Stetson and scratched his flaming thatch. By no means could he be called handsome, with his pugnacious chin and nose, his slate-gray eyes, and his gaunt, weather-worn frame. It seemed as if he might have been recently subjected to an illness, for he seemed a little nervous and finely drawn. "Yeah," he muttered, "I'll tell a man it's so. First you're it, and then you ain't." His eyes were fixed on a couple that moved in and out of the trees.

Budd chuckled at the tomato cans and calmly asked, "What'd you say, Bill?"

"First you're it, and the next thing the earth ain't big enough to hold you." He wrinkled his nose in surprise. "How'd you know my first moniker?"

"Heard a gal call you by it," said Budd.

"Well, you won't hear her callin' me that no more. Oh, no, she don't know I'm a human bein' these days." He was talking as if half to himself, still keeping his slate-gray eyes fixed on the couple. They had advanced from the main road and were twining around the wagons and fires — a sturdy girl and a tall man in chaps. "Huh," he muttered. Then again: "Huh. Gimme a sack of tobacco, Budd. What road do I take out of this country? South, I mean?"

"Leavin'?" queried Budd. "Well, jest keep to the main way and you'll strike Klamath by 'n' by."

"Uhuh," said Bill. He rolled a cigarette, licked it, and reached for a match. "Thanks."

He leaned against the counter and drew a mouthful of smoke. Budd saw his face turn perfectly bland and cheerful. There was a gay burst of laughter and a man's short speech. The couple came in the door. The girl, foremost, stopped short at sight of Bill, looked at him and through him; her smile disappeared and a color came to her cheeks. Bill drew a deep draft of smoke and spoke to Budd as if continuing the conversation.

"Yeah, first thing in the mornin', I guess. This country don't strike me so much. Guess you'd better lay aside a can of them tomatoes and some bacon. I'll be back for the duffel later."

"Don't let me interfere with your business," said the girl haughtily. "Sam and I are only visiting."

"Oh, no," said Bill in sprightly tones, "there ain't room enough for all of us in such a small place." He walked by her and approached Sam. He had to look up a little to meet

88

Sam's eyes. The man was tall. His accouterments were neat, and his clothes well kept. He had a face that, to the genial and shrewd Budd, seemed as uncommunicative as any man could boast. It rarely smiled, and it rarely displayed emotion. To cap off the expression, Sam was exceedingly sparing of his words. Bill ground his cigarette on the floor and spoke shortly but to the point.

"So Sam's the moniker, huh?"

"Yeah."

"Don't open yore mouth too wide, Sam, or you'll show a tooth. Shucks, they named you wrong. It ought to be 'Paralyzed.' "

"Yeah?"

"Yeah," affirmed Bill.

He stepped back a trifle, teetered on his heels and swung his arms idly, the slate-gray eyes boring into the big fellow. Sam remained unconcerned; his face was perfectly impassive. It irked Bill. He snorted once, twice, and moved out of the door humming a tune to show his perfect indifference.

"Oh!" exclaimed the girl. "Did you ever see such an overbearing man?" She looked at her escort a little curiously. "What did you think?"

Sam seemed to ponder. "Didn't want to hit him," he said lazily. "Might hurt him."

"Yes," responded the girl. Budd, keeping his own counsel as to that eventuality, thought he heard a minor chord of doubt in the girl's voice. "Well," she said, "I think we'd better run along and let Mister Budd alone. It's getting dark. Supper's ready."

Budd watched them go across the clearing, the girl waving her hand here and there to friends, the man bending a little under his height and moving as if he had all the time in creation. Finally they parted and disappeared in the shadows. The storekeeper set his shelves in order and cruised to the kitchen to make supper. It was not a complex operation, consisting of slicing a few potatoes into a pan and dropping several strips of bacon alongside to lard the frying. For the main part Budd's mind ran along its habitual channels, prying a little here and pondering a little there.

What kind of a man was this wooden-faced Sam, anyway? No, not wooden faced, corrected Budd — poker faced was the better term. It was not the ordinary thing for a man to value his emotions and expressions so highly that he turned himself into a sphinx. You never could tell about those fellows — whether they wanted to give you a present or sink a slug of lead into you. Budd stirred his coffee and chuckled. Now, Bill was a fellow that wasn't made to conceal much of anything. He had a fighting face and, to judge from his last speech with Sam, he had a fighting heart. Certainly, he was badly taken with the girl, and she hadn't found him so distasteful until the last day or two, at which period Sam had ridden onto the scene. No, Bill had seemed to be the favored one until a quarrel blew up. What it was about Budd didn't know — or care. He had seen many such spring up — and die away.

He ate his meal, washed down a good many cups of coffee, and treated himself to a cigar from the shelves. In striking the match his hands came upon the metal of the deputy's badge, and he snorted in plain disgust.

"Shucks! Goin' to be a gol-darned snooper. Dave Budd, I'm plumb ashamed of yore unhandsome behavior. Paradin' around like a monkey on a stick."

It was in his mind to pin the thing inside his vest but, having once taken the obligation, he found himself unable to hedge. He stepped down the porch and sauntered forward.

The fires veered and danced in the late twilight. A fog had descended over the treetops, bringing with it a clammy touch. For the most part the people had finished with their suppers and were now lying around, spinning yarns and weaving dreams. It was a time for babies to be cooing in the wagons, half asleep, and for the younger boys and girls to be out among the shadows playing hide and seek. One darted up to Budd and used the storekeeper's vast bulk for a momentary refuge. A guitar strummed, and a couple intoned a song about "Sweet Genevieve." It struck directly to the hearts of all the middle-aged in that particular circle, and voices died away. Budd moved on with a feeling of compassion. These were his people, his kind of men and women. Then he saw Bill squatting, Indian fashion, before a solitary blaze.

"No company?" asked Budd.

Bill nodded his head to the group ten yards beyond. "Sam's there tellin' the gol-darndest stories. I don't need no company when I can listen in on them yarns."

Sam was, indeed, relaxing from his taciturnity. He sat with his feet crossed and illustrated his yarn with a jerky motion of his fingers and arms, greatly resembling Indian sign language. The girl sat across from him, her chin cupped in a palm, sometimes looking to him and sometimes away. Budd wondered if she had deliberately put her back to Bill. *'Spect so,* he thought, chuckling, and went on.

His last glimpse was of her staring somberly into the fire. He paid his compliments here and there, answered a question or two, and returned to the house. It was pretty late, and he had worked rather hard. In ten minutes he had found his bed and was fast asleep.

Budd's manner of slumber was an inheritance from early range days. No matter how exhausted, he had trained himself to wake at the least untoward sound. So it was that an unusual commotion out among the wagons around midnight brought him up instantly. A moment later he was diving into his clothes upon hearing the repeated bark of a revolver. A man's voice lashed out in the night, calling down all the wrath of heaven. A dog began to howl dismally, and a woman screamed. Budd, forging to the porch, saw the glimmer of a newly lighted lantern and heard the mumble of a gathering crowd. He walked over to the scene where a dozen sleepy men had gathered. The lantern, held high, revealed an irate and whiskered citizen waving a gun.

"I'll get the ornery sneak!" he shouted "Come right into my wagon, by gollus! Snuck the wallet from under my coat." He saw Budd and reiterated his charge. "You got to do somethin' about this, Mister Budd! Took four hundred an' ten dollars right from under my nose, by gollus! Jest stuck his hand through the canvas and helped himself."

A murmur ran through the group. Four hundred dollars was a large sum of money, and the manner of taking it had been audacious. The thief had obviously threaded his way around sleeping bodies until he found the wagon. Equally obvious was it that he must have spent some few days in observing the robbed man's habits.

"That's a purty tidy sum of money," ventured one. Budd's vast presence seemed to absorb responsibility like a blotter. To a man they turned their attention his way. He walked to the wagon. "Stuck his arm through here?" he asked. On affirmation he plunged his own burly hand through the slit. "Put yore coat right where it was when the money was took."

The man climbed inside and did as requested. Budd pawed around the wagon bed. "You shore that's where you had it?"

"By gollus, don't I know? Sure."

92

Budd shoved the weight of his body against the canvas and by dint of an extra lunge his fingers touched the coat. He said to himself: *That feller's arm was right long to do things so quick and quiet.* He turned. "What kind of wallet? How'd you have the money?"

"One of these twice-fold-over dinguses. It was black leather. My wife give it to me as a present nine years ago. Nine, wasn't it, Carrie? Yep, shore. Four hundred an' ten dollars in greenbacks. Sixteen twenties and the rest tens." He sat down weakly and ran a hand over his head. "By gollus, I . . . I don't know what to do about it. Powerful lot of money to lose."

The crowd moved again. Sam's tall, impassive presence stood forth. "This ain't the first time," he added significantly. "Stealin's been goin' on for three days. Jest little things."

Other lanterns arrived, and the circle became fairly well illuminated. Budd swept the faces, and for the first time made out Bill and his flaming red thatch standing silently and speculatively with his slate-gray eyes fixed on Sam.

"Got to stop," continued Sam. "What I say is . . . search every man here an' search his duffel."

There was a dubious approval. Men bent their minds to the feasibility of it. A voice murmured: "Sounds kinda severe, but I'd be willin'."

"Only way," asserted Sam. "Got to stop it now. Any man to object should be considered guilty."

A dry answer met this. Bill rubbed his red crest and stuck out his chin. "Go lay down, Paralyzed. Yore voice makes me tired. Moreover, yore idea is plumb foolish. Search the whole camp? Shucks, the man that got this money ain't an entire fool. He's cached it away by now."

"Mean to say," countered Sam in the same, inexpressive drawl, "you're unwillin'?"

"Yore brain does you credit. I said that an' I mean that. Don't care about a lot of loose fingers pokin' through my war bag." The chin seemed to advance a little farther. Those slate-gray eyes fired a plain challenge at the big man. But Bill had reckoned without the sudden, unanimous spirit that sometimes takes hold of a crowd. A pair of arms pinioned him around the waist, and the circle closed in like a rubber band. "See about that, young fella!" cried one.

The few women withdrew quickly. Budd, still a spectator, saw the girl's troubled face by the lantern's gleam. Then she was gone. Somebody took upon himself the task of inspecting Bill's clothes and for his pains found nothing. Sam's curiously disinterested voice pointed the search in another direction. "His war bag, boys. Better look there."

Two or three left the circle with a lantern. Budd, waiting, found time to study Sam's face again and was compelled to reflect admiringly: *Ain't that a poker expression, though?* Bill was plainly outraged and bucked in his captor's arms. "Boys, you better hold tight. Dad gum my soul, somebody's goin' to dance fer this!"

"Hi! Boys, here's the wallet all right! Take a look, fella. That it?" The crowd moved over, the robbed one identified his wallet with a brightening eye, and the crowd turned upon Bill with a satisfied sigh.

"Now, Bill, you're in poor company. Better cough up the money, or we'll get plumb mad."

Bill stared around him in plain disgust. His gaze fell upon the cool and aloof Sam. "Paralyzed, I shore give you credit for bein' the little detective." Then he grew sober. "Oh, go home, you galoots, and get a night's sleep. I got nobody's money. Can't you see it was planted? That's terrible old stuff. Gamblers used to pull that in Montana when I was a little boy."

They were all silent and ominous. Someone spoke the popular opinion. "Talkin' ain't helpin' yore case at all, Bill. Figger you'd like to dance a jig in the cold night air? Don't be foolish. Where's the man's money?"

Bill snorted in anger. "Money? I tell you I ain't got the money! Was sleepin' peaceful-like when some ornery maverick stepped in my face and hollered there was a wallet missin'."

Once again silence and finally a slow, hesitant suggestion. "Mebbe a rope'd help things out considerable, boys."

Budd elected to become active. He put out his two arms and moved a half dozen men out of his path in the manner of one shoving aside the branches of a tree. "Reckon the talk is gettin' a leetle wild, friends. When a gent says 'rope,' the time's come for a mite of mature reflection. Speakin' as deppity sheriff, I guess I'll jest take the boy in hand. Mebbe a few hours' thought'll change his mind."

"Don't need no reflection," muttered somebody. "Need rope. Ain't goin' to be sidetracked this a-way. The measly cuss stole a man's hard-earned money, and it ain't to be tolerated in these parts. I'm fer summary justice."

"Ain't carin' what you're for," stated Budd in flat finality. "Anybody wishin' to doubt my authority?"

Somehow in the lantern light the man had become as a mountain of purpose. His face, which in daylight looked bland and cherubic, was rock hard. He spoke easily, and his movements were deliberate, but there was no single man to raise a voice in farther protest.

"Bill, you just march in front of me to the store. Rest of you night birds walk around a while and cool off. Don't get no queer ideas about rope and tree limbs. I don't aim to tolerate foolishness. We'll stick to plain law."

He marched Bill into the storeroom, shut the door, and

put his lantern on the counter. "Regardless of circumstances and greenback bills," he said, "I reckon I'll have to tie you up for the night. Don't aim to make it any harder on you than I have to. There's blankets on the floor. Git down on 'em, young feller. I'll bundle you up so's it won't bind you."

"This," said Bill in a kind of restrained fury, "is plumb unreasonable and aggravatin'. First I get my face stepped on, and next they want to lynch me. Now I got to be wound up like a roll of fence wire."

Budd clucked his tongue. "Shore is enough to make a man swear. Git down, Bill. Now take it easy. Sometimes certain moves lead to certain other moves."

Bill submitted to the operation. "Yeah, ain't that as clear as mud? First you put out yore right foot and then yore left. But, if I never do anything else in my life, I'm shore goin' to change that waddy, Sam's, complexion. I shore am." He rested finally with his arms and legs more or less tightly bound.

Budd had done the trussing cleverly enough to allow the prisoner a certain comfort on his hard bed. He strung the free end of the rope through the kitchen door and tied it to a leg of the range. "Reckon if you go to threshing around too much," he observed, "I'll hear the stove creakin'. Now I aim to finish off a little business of six hours' sleep."

Bill surveyed his bonds and cast a candid eye upon his captor. "Now listen, *hombre,* if a man wanted to wiggle out of this . . . ?"

Budd looked him in the eye. "You dang fool," he muttered, "you dang fool."

The captive closed his mouth and opened his eyes a little wider. After a few moments silence he muttered, "Oh."

Then he turned his back to the big storekeeper and fell silent. Budd was as inscrutable as a Chinese idol. He picked up the lantern, went back to his bedroom, and blew out the light. *Feel a lot easier in the conscience,* he thought, *if I didn't have this cussed piece of tin.*

He stared at the ceiling and presently was asleep. No more strange sounds from the wagons awoke him that night and, if the kitchen range creaked, he gave no notice that he was aware of it. Yet he seemed fated to be wakened by another noisy event. When gray dawn seeped into the clearing, a file of excited men trooped through the house, banged at his door, and brought him up from the pillow with one trenchant question.

"Whar's yore prisoner?"

Budd yawned and reached for his pipe. "Guess you'll find him sleepin' behind the counter where I tied him."

A sarcastic rumble greeted this. "Yes we will! Of all the fool ideas! He shucked himself out of that rope and vamoosed."

The storekeeper's heavy lids drooped. He fumbled with his tobacco pouch and muttered: "Y' don't say."

Then he slid into his clothes and led the impromptu committee back to the storeroom. Sure enough, his bird had fled. The free end of the rope still was tied around a stove leg, but the rest of it was slit in a dozen places. The cheese knife, which ordinarily rested on the counter, was stuck in the floor boards, mute witness of Bill's manner of passage. Budd ruefully clucked his tongue. "Slick an' clean. There's a damn' good six-dollar piece of rope made wuthless."

"Huh . . . you're a sweet deppity! Should've let well enough alone last night. Now what're you goin' to do?"

Budd picked up the knife and sliced himself a piece of the cheese. "Well, now, first I aim to eat. Then I aim to take care of the store. Then mebbe I'll do a little figgerin'. Might even send word to Sheriff Emmons to keep a lookout at his end of the county. Come back later an' I'll tell you the rest."

"Meanwhile," stated one of the committee, "he's scootin' with four hundred dollars of this man's hard-earned money. Terrible!"

They conferred among themselves, found Budd strangely imperturbable, and went out dissatisfied. The storekeeper cruised back and got his morning meal.

As the day wore on, he found part of his duty performed for him. The more determined of the landseekers organized a posse and galloped up the road toward Bend. Around noon they came back with nothing for their efforts. A few beat into the jack pines a half mile or so and returned empty handed. Budd, standing on his porch, gave them a few choice words of advice. "Takes an experienced hand to find anything in the brush. Not much good in yore tactics." They chose not to give up the pursuit and after dinner again scoured the road, this time to the south. Budd was not much interested in these movements. Such time as he spent on the porch was used to keep a shrewd watch over the girl and Sam. The latter had not elected to go with the posse, but at one point in the afternoon he picked up his gun and, seeming to have a plan of his own, marched directly into the pines and was lost for the best part of an hour. The girl, who had been idling around her wagon, watched him go and after a short interval vanished up the road. She was back in a little while, coming directly to the store.

"Mister Budd, this is dreadful! Do you suppose anyone will find him? If they do, they'll be sure to shoot."

"That's the portion of thieves, ain't it?"

"But he's not a thief!" Then she seemed to collect herself, and a color rose in her cheeks. "No, I don't believe he did it. I don't believe it."

"Thought you didn't think so much of him?"

"Oh that! We may have been quarreling, but . . . but I know him to be an honest man."

"How long've you known him?"

"Why, we met on the road about a week ago." She saw a question in the storekeeper's face and flushed again. "It doesn't take a woman forever to judge, you know. If Bill chooses to run off, I'm sure I have no reason to worry about his affairs." She spoke it primly, unaware that her eyes told another story. "But I'm quite sure he'd not be a sneak thief."

The girl changed the subject abruptly and asked a question about homesteading. Budd turned to one of his never-failing stories and kept drawling away until he saw Sam duck into the clearing and make for the store. He sighed, fingered the deputy's star on his vest, and turned toward the cigar box which served as his cash till. "Storekeepin' used to be a nice quiet trade until this boom hit me. Now I got to be a regular bookkeeper." He was shuffling a pile of paper bills on the counter when Sam came in.

"Yore prisoner," he said in the same lazy voice, "is a slick one. Got plumb clean."

"Twenty-five, thirty, forty-five," counted Budd, thumbing the bills. "You been chasing him, too?"

"Thought I had a scent, but it petered out." Sam's eyes followed Budd's pile of money. "He's ducked. What I can't see is why he didn't make a stab to get his duffel and horse."

"Eighty-nine dollars and fifty-three cents," tabulated Budd, rumbling to himself. He made a few weird scratches with a stub pencil and thrust the money carelessly back in the cigar box. Sam watched the operation with his poker face, patently disinterested. "Well," continued Budd, "he'll be caught sooner or later. They always are. Never saw a crook git far yet."

"That's right," assented Sam. He turned to the girl. "Care to amble around and scare up an appetite?"

"Yes," she said.

Her eyes were likewise fixed on the cigar box. A swift look went to Budd. He was slivering off another piece of cheese, intent on the process. So the two walked out and circled around the wagons.

The storekeeper put the cigar box on the counter, ransacked the shelves for writing paper, and sat down to compose a rather long letter. He was not a rapid penman and, before he had finished, night once more was upon the clearing with the fires sending their veering tongues of flame to the black sky. He went back to the kitchen, got something to eat, and sat down for a long, dark study over the tip of his cigar. Alternately he chuckled and frowned.

"That girl," he said, "is shore a case. Been playin' Sam ag'in' Bill to even up a quarrel, and now she's terrible sorry. Jest like what a woman'd do." He looked down at the star and was acutely displeased. *This thing shore sets on my mind. If I was jest an ordinary citizen, it wouldn't be sech a risky experiment. Bein' an officer makes my conscience troubled, and that's a fact.*

He went to the front door and swung his lantern idly to and fro, passing a glance at the wagons in which most of the landseekers were now asleep. Then he turned back, still swinging the light so that any one looking through the open portal might see him, and passed to the kitchen. There he blew out the lantern, turned about, and tiptoed to the front room. He took up the blanket, wrapped it around him, and sat down behind the counter with his back to the shelves and his revolver in his hand. Presently he dozed off and dreamed of his boyhood in Pennsylvania.

He seemed, after a time, to have trouble with his dream. It was winter, and he was skating with his young companions on the ice. There was a crack in the middle of the pond and a danger sign pointing from it. But he felt as if he could safely dare that sign, so he skated to the very edge and turned away. He had been too bold. There was a sharp cracking of the ice and — he woke with both eyes fixed upward. The illusion of cracking ice had been made by a loose board creaking under a weight. Budd took a firmer grip on his gun and breathed softly. Again the board registered protest, not a loud sound but enough to tell the storekeeper that the bait in his trap found a willing stalker. Something very slight swept over the counter surface and struck the cigar box with an audible tick. Budd made out a dark, moving shadow in the gloom. He hoisted his body with surprising celerity and quickly snapped the revolver forward.

"Freeze right in yore tracks," he commanded. "Hands above yore haid. Hurry now!"

The command was not obeyed. Budd, peering closely, saw the intruder's weapon arm streak downward. He moved aside and shook his head under the stunning crash of gunfire. A little finger of orange-blue momentarily flashed in his face. He jumped, and again the room shook under heavy echoes. The intruder let out a great breath of air as if he had been punched in the stomach, pawed at the counter, and seemed to dissolve. First the gun struck the floor, then the body collapsed, muttering, "Got me, you sly old fox."

All was still. Then the wagons came to life, and a few landseekers ran up to the store. A lantern swung and winked.

Budd lighted his own lantern and bent over the intruder.

It was the man he had supposed — Sam, his long body sprawled awkwardly on the boards, his face white and wholly without expression, staring toward the storekeeper. He was dead. In falling, he had pulled the cigar box with him whose contents of greenbacks were now scattered over the floor.

The landseekers crowded into the room, and the assembled lanterns made a great light. It was a story too plain to need explanation, and in the silence Budd ventured his mild explanation.

"I knew it was this feller all the time, and not Bill," he said. "But I wasn't plumb shore. So I arranged to let Bill escape and baited my trap with the money in the cigar box. Sam saw it and sprung the trap, shore enough."

"Why'd you let the other fella go?" inquired one.

Budd smiled and pushed through to the porch. He expanded his lungs and bellowed at the pine trees. "Oh, Bill! She's all settled!" Then he made further explanations. "I don't *know* that he's hereabouts, but I'm figgerin' so. He ain't the kind to run off without tryin' to clear his name, and I guessed he'd try to catch Sam in the act of cachin' the money somewheres in the woods or else raisin' the cache."

Footsteps thumped on the porch, and Bill, drenched with the night dew and tousle-haired, came up. "You old son of a gun," he said. "You're purty shrewd. I figgered you'd make a play like that. Saw it in yore face last night." He held out his hand for a cigarette. "When mornin' comes, I'll show you where Sam hid the four hundred dollars. I was in the brush an' saw him go to the place this afternoon. That's when all the boys were threshin' the thicket for me. Shucks, don't you know it's a hard job to ketch an old hand in the brush?"

There was a call from the porch, a woman's urgent command. "Bill!"

Bill grinned. "Reckon she's been tryin' to clear me, too. Tried to foller Sam this afternoon but got lost and ran plumb into me."

"Still mad, is she?" asked Budd.

Bill passed him a wink and elbowed his way out of the room.

VI

"ROCK-BOUND HONESTY"

At first sight, Old Man Cruze looked as spry and cheery as a cricket. His eyes were that kind of snapping black which mirrors the peppery, forthright spirit. He had other features, too, that fitted well with such a picture — a small sharp nose, leathery cheeks, and a stubborn chin well flanked by the drooping ends of a once-white mustache. Moreover, when he moved in the buckboard seat or raised his mittened hand, it was with a sudden, jerky gesture. All things put together, no one could mistake him for anything but a picturesque character, even in a land of picturesque characters. As such he was known, and had been known, for twenty years throughout the length and breadth of the country.

But Old Man Cruze was not his normal self on this wintry day. Always before, on his semi-monthly visits to Dave Budd's Burnt Creek store, he would emerge from the dense thicket of jack pines, lash his horse to a gallop, and bring the ancient buckboard up to the store porch in a perilous, careening semicircle, meanwhile emitting a long, quavering whoop such as the native Indians once had sent forth in blood-curdling accent through the dark underbrush. Invariably it brought Budd out to greet his crony with an answering bellow.

On this day there were no such antics. The horse, ears laid back in astonishment, plodded alongside the porch and stopped. Old Man Cruze tied the reins around the whipstock, fished a gunny sack from the bed of the vehicle, and silently stepped to the porch. He sighed a little as he straightened his small, wiry figure, and his free arm went exploring tentatively around toward his backbone.

"I guess," he said, "it's lumbago. If 'tain't that, then it shore is the rheumaticks. Curse sech infernal pains."

He kicked open the door and entered unceremoniously to find himself confronted by a gross, towering figure of a man who easily might have made two Cruzes and still have had bulk left over. Dave Budd surveyed his friend in profound surprise — or with as much of that emotion as could find a place on his cherubic, inscrutable face. "Am I gettin' hard of hearin'?" he asked, "or mebbe you figgered your wreck of a buckboard too old to come up like she used to?"

"Guess it's a man's privilege to travel any way he pleases, ain't it?" replied Cruze testily.

"Why, shore," said Budd, more amazed. "Now what's eatin' your miserable old self?"

"Nawthin'. Nawthin' whatsoever. When you git through askin' fool questions, mebbe you'll find some time to gimme half a sack of spuds, ten cans of beans, some bacon, and some flour."

The storekeeper went silently behind the battered counter and pulled down the bean cans. Old Man Cruze eyed them speculatively and finally qualified his order. "Come to think, Dave, I reckon I'll only take six of them cans. You put the rest back."

"Won't last you two weeks," said Budd. "Better take the

same amount you allus has."

"Who's buying this truck?" shouted Cruze in irascible accents. "You er me?"

"Why, you poisonous reptile!" grumbled Budd. He sliced the bacon and filled the gunny sack half up with potatoes. "Ain't needin' no eatin' tobacco?" he pursued.

"No."

"Dang me, you must shore be off your feed. Mebbe your shack needs patchin'. Won't do to let it git too drafty. Man ketches cold mighty easy these days."

"No."

"Waal," ventured Budd, not without some hesitation, "I shore hope you ain't sick."

"No!" Then Old Man Cruze weakened. "Tell you what, Dave, I *don't* feel so pert as allus. Reckon I'm beginnin' to feel my age. That's it."

"Old granny's talk. You're jest a-fumin' fer spring to come down among these cold flats. That's all."

But Old Man Cruze shook his head and shouldered his sack of potatoes. He opened the door, stowed the provisions in the buckboard, and dropped into the seat, unwinding the reins from the whipstock.

"Say," said Budd, "ain't you stayin' a while to gossip like allus?"

"No," replied Cruze. "Ain't got time for foolishness. Giddap, Pinto." And off the buckboard creaked.

"I hope," shouted Budd, "you bite yourself and ketch hydrophoby! Cussed curmudgeon!"

Old Man Cruze vanished into the jack pines. The twilight of a short afternoon descended around him as the buckboard moved, and the sharp wind scoured along the tunnel-like road with greater velocity. A coyote dodged out of the underbrush and loped a hundred yards or more in front of the buckboard, then sat unconcernedly on his haunches. To all this the man seemed unaware. He had given the wise horse plenty of rein. His head was tipped forward on his chest, and the snapping black eyes were a study in far-off speculation.

Suddenly he reached into his pocket and drew forth a soiled and wrinkled bit of paper which, from numerous finger prints upon it, appeared to have been read many times before. Evidently it still possessed interest. He raised it closer to his eyes and slowly scanned the words, written in a fine, delicate script:

Portland, December 31st.

Dear Pop:

The doc. says there isn't so much awful much wrong with me, but thinks I ought to be operated on, to save trouble from coming up later. It will cost fifty dollars more, Pop, than I've got. Can you spare it? If you can't, we'll tell old sawbones to be satisfied with what he's made off me already, but if you can afford it, it'll be a terrible relief to get things all over with now. My music studies were coming along fine until this bobbed up. And I had to quit my job. Heaven knows just when I'll be able to find another.

Your loving daughter,
Elize

So here was the problem that gnawed at Cruze's heart and robbed him of his accustomed cheer. "Dang me," he muttered, "where in creation can I git fifty dollars?"

The longer he studied — and he had racked his mind three days with the problem — the surer became the distressing knowledge that an old desert rat commanded little credit and no earning power in so wide and barren a country. Food and bed — he scraped that much from his piece of land and from an occasional bit of bounty money on the hide of some legally outcast animal. But he had no savings. His generation didn't know about nest eggs. They just lived from hand to mouth. Their training had given them a magnificent assurance of ability to get along somehow. Rugged health, ingenuity, and a rifle had always managed for Old Man Cruze's kind — not a savings bank. Perhaps times in the West had changed, but Cruze had not.

"Jest got to fetch that sum out of the air, I guess," he soliloquized.

His pride was bruised; his parental instinct outraged. It had been three years since Elize had set out from a motherless home for the city, bent on making her own way in music. Never once — until now — had she called for assistance. The sturdy, independent Cruze blood had seen her through. While she studied, she worked in lunch counters, as a maid in hotels, or at any single thing which might carry her on. Now, in distress, she fell back on her father. Cruze groaned and slapped the rump of the horse with the reins.

"Git on, you old rep!"

He had never felt old until now, had never been aware of any aches until now. This was the sort of thing that made people feel old and useless. Elize had called on her old pop, and he could not answer.

"Whoa."

From long habit he stopped the buckboard and got down.

All along the darkening way was a litter of dead limbs and fallen trees. The old man set methodically to breaking and gathering this fuel by the arm load, piling it in the back of the buckboard. When the bottom of the vehicle was full, he set out afoot in the road, the horse following after him. Within five minutes they arrived at the edge of the jack pines and commanded the view of a vast prairie upon which a mysterious blue haze had fast settled. Not far out upon the prairie loomed a house and barn toward which the troubled man directed his steps. By the end of a half hour he had stabled his horse and was preparing his own frugal meal over a battered, rusty iron stove.

It was no great meal. From the manner he debated over it, one might have thought him a great chef calculating some Epicurean feast, but that, too, was just one of the many idiosyncrasies that helped to pass the long, lonely stretches of time. At first he sliced three pieces of bacon and laid them in the pan, only to mutter an inaudible phrase to himself and pull one slice out. A brace of hard biscuits, a cup of ink-black coffee, and a few spoons of cold beans complemented the bacon. He perched on a stool in front of the stove and ate.

"Got to be a mite more savin' of grub," he said aloud to himself. "Ain't much an old codger can do any more. Elize, gal, your old pop is shore on hard times. Curse sech days when a man ain't fitten to help his own kind on the johnny spot!"

He set the coffee cup down carefully and, with a swift expression of interest on his face, turned toward the door. A drumming of hoofs became audible, growing clearer at every pace. Even before Cruze got around the corner of the table, half way to the shanty's solitary window, the furious rider was sliding to a stop. Cruze was hailed in a gruff, impatient voice. Within the count of five the door burst open and a tall youth, flashing a pair of hot, restless eyes around the room, catapulted in without so much as a by your leave. Cruze, summoning his long knowledge of Western character, classified the man at once as one of those itinerant cattle hands who made his way from ranch to ranch, never staying long on one job and never leaving behind any great record for sobriety or ability.

"Pardner," said the young man, gulping down his words in haste, "I smelled coffee, an' I'm next to dyin' of hunger."

Cruze waved a hand toward the coffee pot. "Help yourself to what you see. Sech as I got you're welcome to share."

The young man thrust a spoon into the beans and freighted down a cargo, without superfluous motion or unnecessary etiquette. He whisked the coffee pot from the stove and filled the cup, which a moment before had been emptied by Cruze, to the brim. A spare biscuit caught his eye and, in a twinkling, had vanished. All this took place without the formality of taking a seat, or offering conversation. Time seemed to press him hard. Once he raised his head as if trying to catch distant echoes. Cruze, likewise listening, heard nothing, but it appeared to be otherwise with the youth. He swallowed the rest of the coffee in still greater haste.

Cruze rolled a cigarette, tamped it, crimped the ends, and sought for a match, all the while showing a short and knowing smile. "Son," he said, finding his match, "you ain't the first fella I've fed, and you ain't the first that's come acrost these prairies as if old Joe himself was close behind, but I swear you shore are the most impatient of the bunch. Looks as if you felt some one blowin' hot an' cold on your neck. I reckon the road you want leads direct toward Burnt

Creek. Yeah?"

The young man was spending one of his precious moments in sizing up his host. "Say, ain't you Old Man Cruze?"

"That be the handle I've had ever since I struck this cussed land of desolation," agreed Cruze, not without a touch of pride.

"Uhuh. Heard of you before. Reckon you got the reputation of bein' square as a Swede's head in these parts. Yeah, so they tell me."

"Aim to treat my fellow man right, so long as he ain't no more ornery than me."

The youth cocked his head sidewise and listened again for whatever the night seemed to bear upon the soft wind. "Say," said he in the manner of one taking a turn of mind, "I'm bein' follered by the sheriff . . . it bein' none of your business why."

"Ain't asked any questions, have I?" broke in Cruze tartly. "Seen men runnin' this way afore you was born, and it ain't nawthin' new. I expects more men have been chased by the front of my shanty than they is residents in the county. It's a real popular road."

"They got my trail," explained the youth. "Ain't more'n a half hour behind. Curse that bloodhound of a sheriff!"

"Then," returned Cruze imperturbably, "you better be goin'. The sheriff's a bad man to play tag with."

"But he'll take your word," returned the youth significantly.

"What's my word got to do with it?"

"Lemme hide in your barn. When the sheriff comes up, you tell him you heard a horse go poundin' across the desert. He'll take your word without question and foller. That'll gimme a chance to cut back and git into the jack pines."

"No," said Cruze, "you're barkin' up the wrong tree. I ain't

111

a liar, and I don't conduct no stable fer them that's been foolish with their words or their actions. At my time of life it's plumb bad policy to change habits."

The youth's face turned color. He made a gesture toward the gun sagging on his hip. "Now, you old curmudgeon, I ain't listenin' to no goody-goody lectures. You're a-goin' to do jest as I tell you, or it'll be disastrous. I ain't in no humor to be fooled with a-tall."

Cruze dropped his cigarette and snorted contemptuously. "You ain't in a position to do much of anything. So keep your head. I been hearin' too many threats to git skeered by that bluff. 'Tain't as if I never saw the business end of a Colt before, sonny."

The youth changed his tactics. "All right, Dad, you win. But here's my offer. I'll give you a hundred dollars fer the use of your barn." To accompany the assertion he plucked a handful of bank notes from a bulging pocket and skimmed a finger over their tops. "What say?"

"No!" roared Cruze, thoroughly outraged. "I ain't no bribe taker, and I ain't shieldin' no thieves."

"Two hundred dollars, Dad. It ain't goin' to hurt your repitation a bit. What nobody knows is nobody's business, see?"

Suddenly Cruze's fingers passed over the letter in his pocket, and the glow of anger died from his face. Two hundred dollars? Why, that would settle the question of Elize's doctor bill. It would prove to his girl that her old pop still was capable of answering her needs as he had been in earlier years. It would quell that uneasiness as to her safety. It would restore a measure of his old spirit, and perhaps with this gnawing difficulty out of the way he could forget those cursed lumbago pains in his back.

A faint trembling of hoofs arrived at the shanty and set the loose glass panes to quivering slightly. The youth stretched out his hands with the money. There was the pallor of anxiety on his face. "Say something, Dad! I'm offerin' you three hundred bucks jest for a minute's protection!"

Old Man Cruze sighed. "Hustle into the barn and leave the rest to me."

"Fine!" The outstretched money dropped into Cruze's palm.

The fugitive youth was out of the room and running toward the barn with his horse in a few fleeting moments. He wasn't any too soon. While the barn door screeched, the sound of those pursuing hoofs swelled rapidly. Cruze stared at the money with a kind of fascination, stuffed it into his pocket, and moved over to the table, turning up the lamp wick. He was engaged in washing his supper dishes when the sheriff and posse hailed him from outside. Walking over, Old Man Cruze opened the door with great deliberation. Four mounted figures loomed against the black night, and the sheriff's genial voice boomed out a question.

"Say, Cruze, you seen or heard of anybody passin' this a way lately?"

Cruze reached for his cigarette papers and seemed to ponder. "Ain't been home more'n a half hour myself," he mused. "But I did hear *somebody* go lickety-larrup acrost the prairie, about twenty minutes back."

"Yeah, that'd be him," said another member of the posse. "Which way?"

"Sounded like he was bound fer Burnt Creek," said Cruze. "Anyhow, he was goin' in some hurry."

"Yeah, on a mighty tired hoss, too. Oh, we'll ketch him afore long."

"What's the gent gone an' did?" asked Cruze with a mild curiosity.

"Son of a gun took a thousand dollars from the post office at Tule Lake. Mighty slick. I never. . . ."

The sheriff checked his talkative deputy. "Yeah, but this ain't no legislative session. Come on, boys, we'll see if we can't turn him afore he reaches the lower range of the Bar T Bar." The party spurred into the darkness, sending back a final word. "Thanks, Cruze. There's a reward out too of two hundred dollars."

Cruze listened a while as the sound of the posse grew fainter and fainter. By and by he whistled softly. The barn door screeched again, and presently the fugitive youth rode up. "Much obliged, old-timer. That's shore saved my scalp, and you're welcome to the money. Now I'll jest cut back to the jack pines and bunk at the old trapper's cabin fer the night."

Cruze fished in his pockets and sorted out the money by the lamplight. He handed part of it up to the youth. "Here, I only want fifty dollars."

"Say, I offered the whole works," said the youth. "Keep it. Mebbe I'm crooked, but I ain't no cheap skate."

"Take it," insisted Cruze. The youth laughed and reached down. "All right, it ain't goin' to hurt my pockets none. So long, Dad. You're shore a soft-minded old cuss."

He galloped away. Cruze stood for a moment, peering into the dark, then retreated and closed the door. He seemed a little undecided as to his next move. Usually the evenings were spent over a glowing pipe bowl and a pack of greasy cards, with occasionally a dip into a paper that might be a week or a month old. But though the cards were on the table, he made no move to take them up. Rather, like a man perplexed, he lit his pipe — having thrown away the recently made cigarette — cast the bank notes on the table and fell to studying them from corner to corner and side

114

to side. He folded and unfolded them, picked them up and laid them down, with tobacco smoke all the while wreathing and curling around his face. He sighed tremendously and then, finding a pencil and bit of paper, sat down to labor out the following brief lines:

Lize,
Everything here o. k. with your pop. I send fifty dollars, if it ain't enough, write and I'll try to get more. Been cold here, but can hope there's going to be an early spring.
Your loving
Pop

He folded the money inside the note and put the missive inside his shirt pocket. Tomorrow he'd go back to Budd's store, borrow an envelope, and mail it. He banked the fire in the stove, drew off his boots, extinguished the lamp, and crawled into bed. Another day was done, and another problem had been solved, rough-and-ready fashion.

But the sleep which had always so swiftly and sweetly carried him through the dark hours refused on this night to come. He shut his eyes and saw the clear vision of the stolen money as it lay folded in his hand. Opening his eyes, he saw a picture of his friend, Sheriff Cal Emmons, looking reproachfully out at him. The echo of his own voice plagued him with the lie he had uttered. *Heard hoofs go lickety-larrup acrost toward Burnt Creek.* With that he fell into a fitful sort of condition that was neither sleep nor wakefulness. For the first time in years Old Man Cruze had a nightmare.

Somewhere around the middle of a black morning he woke to find himself bolt upright in bed, staring desolately through the darkness. The fire had long turned to cold ashes, and the wintry wind seeped through the many loose boards of the place. Yet it was not the coldness that had stirred him. It was a swift conviction that seemed to have burst its fetters from a deep recess of his mind, upsetting the whole routine of his life. He rose and groped for the lamp. A match sputtered and revealed him, a tousle-haired, hollow-eyed old man with a grim expression of distaste on his sharp features. He carried the lamp to a corner where a cracked and badly scratched looking-glass hung, and he stared at his dimly reflected features with a grimace.

"You ornery, miserable skunk, you low-down, double-crossin' sheep eater. Why, you ain't good enough to associate with a cattle rustler. Your friends oughta ketch you by the neck an' swing your carcass in the breeze. Whatever possessed you to do sech a terrible, terrible thing?"

The tirade seemed to relieve his mind. At the same moment it evidently crystallized a decision, for he put the lamp on the table and slid into his shoes. According to his watch it was three-thirty — a good two hours until dawn. The fact caused him apparent satisfaction. "Said he'd bunk up at the old trapper's cabin. I reckon I'll jest make it."

He put on his coat and, pulling out the note which he had written a few hours earlier, tore it to bits. The fifty dollars he carefully restored to the pocket. Then he blew out the light and trudged through the chilly air to the barn. Fifteen minutes later he was riding as rapidly toward the jack pines as an indignant mount would go, a rifle cradled across the saddle.

No, sir, he kept thinking to himself, *I got to find another way. This ain't goin' to do at all. Poor 'Lize!*

He reached the jack pines and plunged into still blacker shadows, with only now and then a glimpse of an ever-paling moon to guide him. But he was too well versed in the territory to grope aimlessly. Following the main road for the better part of an hour, he turned sharply toward the left. After some little threshing he met a much smaller trail that the horse seemed to know well. It took them around a hundred sudden curves, over countless mounds of earth, and once across an ice-fringed stream. The farther they advanced, the less impenetrable did the curtain of night become. Old Man Cruze looked skyward and reassured himself. *Jest about time.*

Urging the horse to more speed, he kept up a steady clucking of tongue. Presently the road led him around a wide detour. Morning broke in the pale, frosty sky, and the horse and rider came face to face with a small clearing in the center of which squatted a small log cabin half fallen in, and minus door and windows. A horse moved slowly in the clearing, hobbled. Cruze brought the rifle muzzle well to the front and slipped quietly to the ground. A dozen cautious steps brought him to the doorsill, and a quick glance revealed the fugitive youth sound asleep on a littered floor with one Army blanket rolled around him. Cruze cleared his throat and spoke conversationally.

"Rise up, cowboy, hands first, an' greet the mornin'."

The youth started, opened his eyes, and began a swift unwinding movement to free himself of the blanket.

"Careful now," warned Cruze. "Keep them hands clear up. That's right. Now, back toward me." The old man's free arm jerked the youth's gun from the holster. Together they emerged from the cabin. The youth turned, saw his captor clearly, and began a slow, vehement tirade.

"Why, you cussed snake! Trailin' me after I slipped you fifty bucks! Ain't that a fine how-de-do! Took to camp by a shriveled little pea pod who ain't got sense

117

enough to play straight!"

"Listen, sonny," broke in Cruze mildly, "I'm an old codger, an' I seen lots of men hittin' the back trail, but you shore are the most criminal careless. Blame yourself for bein' ketched. Curse sech times when men don't know how to take keer of themselves no more. In my day it'd been a terrible fool who told another man where he aimed to hole up fer night like you told me. Nor would a fella be reckoned with much brains if he picketed hisself an' horse in sech an exposed place overnight. Whyn't you git back in the thicket there where nobody'd stumble over you?"

"Yeah," sneered the youth. "Ain't you a sweet old toad to lecture me? I reckon you changed your mind about the money, huh? Figgered the reward as bein' useful, huh? Well, I'll kick in. Two hundred bucks is what I'll pay fer the privilege of bein' shet of that cussed talk."

"Saddle an' mount," directed Cruze laconically. He added another indictment. "An' I'd like to've seen anybody snuck up on one of the old-timers while he was sleepin'. We could hear a bobcat sneeze two miles off. Sech times as is nowadays!"

It was full day when the fugitive took the return trail with Old Man Cruze following closely behind. And it was almost night again when Cruze brought his prisoner up to the sheriff's office at Tule Lake and confronted Sheriff Emmons.

"Here," said Cruze sadly, "is the fellah you want. I reckon I lied to you last night. He was hidin' in my barn." And in ten brief words he confessed his own complicity, at the same time bringing forth the fifty dollars he had taken from the fugitive. "I shore wouldn't have done it, only I needed that fifty mighty bad. I reckon I can take my medicine without any sweetenin', though."

The sheriff said nothing at that precise moment. He motioned the fugitive from the saddle and searched him, bringing forth from various pockets the stolen bank notes. "All here," he said, counting them. "But what caused you to change your mind, Cruze, after you fooled us?"

"Why," said Cruze reflectively, "it didn't seem's I could look a man in the face any more and tell him to go jump in the lake. An' it sort of interfered with my sleep."

Emmons grinned. "I reckon that's rock-bound honesty. You couldn't be crooked. Say, there's a reward you get, anyhow."

"No, sir!" said Cruze. "Me take a reward after this boy plays into my hands like he did? Shucks, that'd be worse'n takin' his money."

The sheriff thought for a moment. "Say, Cruze, how'd you like to be my jailer here? It ain't a hard job. Pays sixty a month an' found. Got to have somebody straight like you."

Old Man Cruze's face turned brighter. "Sheriff, you're on. Can I borrow my first month's wages?"

"Reckon so. What'd you want 'em for?"

"None of your cursed business!" shouted Old Man Cruze, feeling the returning surge of his normal spirits.

VII

"PRAIRIE YULETIDE"

It was Christmas once more. Old man Budd stared out at the snow-crusted jack pines and tried to find the Bend-Klamath Road. It was completely covered by the driving storm. It was good to be inside the store, hovering over the iron-jacket stove which showed red hot around the edges. A man had no business to be abroad in the pine flats and prairie of Central Oregon today. Budd toasted his huge body by the fire and tried to be thankful, yet he could not seem to get himself into the festive spirit. The holiday mood eluded him. *It was pretty lonesome away out in this half way house to creation,* he thought. As far as it being Christmas, well, he didn't find it different from any other day. The warped old boards of the store didn't keep out the wind any better. There wasn't any better draft in the chimney. The rats didn't seem to make any less noise in his garret.

"Spendin' Christmas alone," he muttered aloud. "Ain't it a sweet note for an old codger like me to be here without a soul to talk with? Dave Budd, it's the last Christmas you get stuck like this."

He stopped his soliloquy and made for the door. He had heard the distressful clatter of the mail stage's horn. When he got to the porch, he saw young Slim Bullit abandon the stage in the middle of the road and waddle toward shelter. Budd pulled him up to the porch and into the house. "Slim, ain't you got no better sense than to drive on a day like this?"

The young fellow slid out of his mittens. "Say, it's cold! Budd, gimme a package of cigarettes. Got a cuppa coffee handy? You darn tootin', I'm making the drive today! Say, that bus is plumb loaded to the guards with Christmas presents, and I gotta get 'em through."

"Christmas," snorted Budd. "Reminds me how old I'm gettin'." He poured out a cup of inky-looking coffee and passed it to the young driver. "Was a time when I liked to be alone. 'Tain't the same now. Need company."

The driver downed the cup of coffee and became convulsive. "Gosh, what you put in that stuff, lye or blue vitriol? Shore is gonna keep me warm. Well, gotta hit the skids now. Long ways to Klamath."

"Durn fool," said Budd. "Stay here until the storm stops. It's plumb dangerous this a-way."

"Nope. U. S. mail has gotta go." He dived out into the whirling snow and ran for his motorized mail stage. He cranked it up and jumped inside. Budd saw the wheels skid, buck the rapidly forming drift, and the mail stage go down the road, swaying drunkenly from side to side. In a moment he was out of sight.

It made Budd all the more restless. He tramped around the stove, and the boards creaked dismally under his heavy frame. "Dang it! Old hermit Budd. Christmas and nuthin' but yore own ugly mug to look at."

Of a sudden he cruised behind the counter and picked up a well-worn notebook wherein was listed the charge account of nearly every homesteader within a range of fifty miles. Budd liked to call these people his flock; he knew

121

everyone well enough to give them fatherly advice. He shared their troubles.

In good seasons he collected his bills. In bad years he asked for nothing and extended their credit far down into the red margin. He thumbed the pages over, critically casting up the individual bills.

Billy Dentler, now, had made a great fight and nearly cleared off his obligations. On the next page was Mary Cappell's rendering — a list rather long. She was fighting it alone. Old man Budd sighed. *I give her credit fer a lot of gumption, but I wish she didn't have so much vinegar in her tone when she talks to me.* Fact was, adversity had only raised this middle-aged woman's temper. It had been only a careless word with the jovial Budd, but in consequence Miss Mary Cappell had given him a piece of her mind. The only human being within fifty miles that wouldn't speak to an old codger of a storekeeper. Budd, mourning, perused the pages. *The gal's got too much false pride.*

He dropped the book and stared in heavy disfavor at the row upon row of canned goods that ran in serried ranks along the shelves. *That stuff ain't no good up there. Ought to be in people's stomachs. I reckon right now there's families out there in the cussed wind an' snow who'd feel a mite more cheerful for a can of pork an' beans. Jest snowed under an' facin' a fair to middlin' New Year.*

The bright idea struck him like a falling roof. Budd was not a man given to bright ideas; his thoughts moved usually in a sort of elephantine majesty. So it was only the more dazzling and brilliant to have this bright and happy scheme spring full born into being. *By Jeeminy! If that young sliver of a Bullit can buck snow, so can I! Santy Claus Budd! Well, by golly!* He lost his moroseness in a moment. He forged around the stove two or three times, chuckling and

122

slapping his sides in a kind of glee. *Santy Claus Budd! Guess I'm fat enough to make two er three Saint Nicks.*

Yes, sir, it was a wonderful scheme. Just pile a lot of that truck in the buggy and start out to visit some of the snow-bound people on the prairie — playing Santa Claus. Put a little cheer into a darkening Christmas Day. Transfer those gaudy-colored cans to where they'd be of more use. Perhaps he would find someone on the long road who needed company as badly as he needed it. Trade misery, he reflected happily.

He got busy right away. Taking out several empty boxes, he began to pack into them a shrewd assortment of stuff. Tomatoes and beans — the homesteader's mainstay — apricots and peaches, spuds, tobacco for the men, and — rummaging through the glass jars on the counter — horehound and peppermint candies for the women and kids. The further he progressed on this philanthropic chore, the merrier did he turn. By and by he had four or five boxes well loaded. He stared at them with a childish glee, then went out to the barn to hitch the buggy.

"You pore hoss," he commiserated. "Ain't no kind of Christmas for you. But you'll shore like yore oats when you git home."

He drove to the front and packed in the boxes. By now the spirit of the thing was infusing him with all sorts of ideas. "Old Santy Claus Budd," he murmured. "Got to have some jinglin' bells, that's certain." So he went back to the barn, fished out three old cowbells, and tied them together. Then another, more sentimental, emotion moved him. He took the axe and fought his way to the edge of the jack pines. Somewhere in the white and blinding mist he found a little tree, standing no higher than his waist, a scrubby, runty little seedling, to be sure, yet with its green branches

123

symmetrically tapering from bottom to top. He cut it down and lugged it to the buggy.

He had the tree. It was something more important than canned goods or jingling bells — symbol of peace and good will, of Christmas and a thousand intertwined memories. Under its spell Budd made one more trip to the store, this time for two tallow candles. Then he wrapped and tied a blanket around his horse's body, pulled up his own fur collar, and tightly wound the robe about his feet. "Git along, Toby. Gosh, this is goin' to be a rip-snortin' Christmas!"

He turned off from the Bend-Klamath Road and climbed over the hummocks and the drifts of the road that led through the jack pines to the prairie beyond. The horse tugged at his burden, slipped, and stumbled. The wind whistled through the forest, fretted at the buggy, and whirled down the ice-edged pellets of snow. Budd did not mind. He was thinking of his youth in a far-away Pennsylvania town. The sleigh bells would be echoing pleasantly up and down the roads now, and the church bells would be tolling. It reminded him, vaguely, of a carol he had as a boy sung under the neighboring windows. He cleared his rusty throat and tried a bar:

Christmas time, happy time . . . .

"No, you danged fool, don't try to sing. It ain't yore strong point."

After a half hour's travel he found himself beyond the pines. Through the white mist he saw a light cheerfully winking out of Billy Dentler's house. A well-filled house, that one: the Dentlers were young, but they had a brood of four. Budd chuckled and drove right up to the door. He pulled out the cowbells and shook them with his heavy arm.

They made a great dingle-dongle. To this jovial man's un-critical ears they created a sweet, harmonious music. A set of dogs ran around the house and howled. The door opened, and the family stood there, looking at him.

"Old Santy Claus Budd come to roost!" bellowed the dis-penser of good will. "I left the sleigh home! One of the rein-deer got a spavin comin' over the moon, and I had to put Toby in the harness. Jest as well, jest as well! Here's some-thin', folks, to keep the stomach full and the blood warm! Ain't it wonderful weather?"

He cruised into the house, a great hulk of a man covered with snow, and bringing with him a heartiness and a kind-liness as big as all the prairie. His round, paunchy face was whipped as red as Saint Nick's himself, and his eyes were beaming when he slid the precious sticks of hore-hound into the chubby, clutching fingers of the children. They shouted in glee. Mrs. Dentler cried and kissed him, while the bronzed young fellow who bore the brunt of the struggle in the battle for land and shelter pounded Budd on the back. "Take off your coat, draw up to the fire. Just in time for supper."

"Santy Claus stay fer supper?" cried Budd. "No, sir, I can't. Got to reach a heap of folks before the bag runs out. Shucks, folks, you're plumb too happy for an old-timer like me to come in. Christmas is jest for the family to enjoy." He backed out and tucked himself into the lap robe. "Go along, Toby. Ain't it a great Christmas?"

So in turn he dispensed his gifts along the widely sepa-rated line of homesteaders' shanties on the prairie — the Christoffersons, Ralph and Grace Olmstead, Nick Carteret, the Hunters, Jim and Mary, Pete Farrell and his houseful of folks, the Tabors, the Simpsons, and Old Man Cruze. One by one he flung the empty boxes in the snow. The little supply of horehound dwindled to two sticks, and only a few cans of food rattled in the bottom of the buggy. But the pine Christmas tree still stuck its tip in the back of his neck, and the candles nestled in his pocket. He had found no place yet to put that tree where it was really needed.

"All them houses were plumb sufficient to themselves," he muttered a little sadly. "Man an' wife and kids. A little to eat, and a fire to warm by. What more can anybody ask? Of course, they all wanted me to stay. But somewhere in these parts they ought to be some one who's plumb lonesome like me. Christmas tree, shore looks like I'll have to pack you back to the store an' set you up in the kitchen."

The road made a right-angle turn. Toby, the ever faithful, turned sharply in the snow. The buggy dropped perilously on one side and struck the bottom of an old irrigation ditch. "Up an' comin', hoss," said Budd. "Pull out like a good boy." The horse pulled. The right wheel cramped suddenly. There was a splintering of wood and a crash. The wheel buckled under, and the body of the buggy canted on its side.

Budd slid unceremoniously to the ground, heaved himself up, and looked at the wreckage. There had been a deep, narrow furrow in that ditch which, covered by the snow, had pinched the wheel as it swung outward; a little strain on the hub, added to Budd's two hundred and twenty-five pounds of bulk, did the rest. The storekeeper brushed the snow from his shoulders and looked around. It was growing quite dark, and the force of the storm, though not stronger, made a greater impression on the man and beast alike. Cruze's place was three miles back. The next and nearest place. . . .

Budd's face was rueful. "Toby, hoss, if my eyes ain't wrong that leetle light off to the right is Miz Mary Cappell's light. And, gosh, she don't like us for sour apples."

It was a fact. Ever since Budd's last unfortunate remark to Mary Cappell — some good-natured, brusque sentence, no doubt — that lady had made it more than plain that she cared less than nothing for his company. Still, the situation was not promising. Out in the open prairie a bitter wind bit into the flesh like needles. There was a useless buggy and a long journey back to Old Man Cruze's. Budd sighed in resignation and unhitched the horse. *Reckon this is goin' to be unpleasant but necessary.*

He gathered up the last of the Christmas gifts in a box and urged the horse onward. Then he stopped, dropped the reins, and went back. *Darned if I leave this tree after luggin' it plumb from home.* So he hoisted it on his shoulder and again aimed for Mary Cappell's.

He left the patient horse and advanced to the door. It took just a little reflection to knock on that door. He heard a plain "Come in," sighed again, and pushed open the portal.

"Miz Cappell, I'm shore sorry to intrude. Busted my buggy. My hoss and I'd certainly appreciate shelter."

He made a strange sight, standing on the threshold, covered with snow, and a face that was cherry red; one big arm cuddled the box of provisions, the Christmas tree slung over his shoulder. The woman had some reason for the silence she maintained during the first awkward moments of his entry. Had Budd been a sensitive man he would have felt it more keenly than the storm. The plain truth is that he had his attention on other things.

He saw Mary Cappell pretty clearly at that particular time, a medium-sized woman not far beyond the forty milestone, still carrying the rather even and good-looking features of her youth. She had elected to battle this country alone and, not being particularly successful, had nailed

127

down her guns, summoned her pride, and gone on short rations rather than run up a bigger grocery bill at Budd's. The single room of the tar-papered homesteader's house was as cozy as it was possible to make it. There were chintz curtains on the windows and cupboards, magazine pictures on the walls, and little paper doilies on the two tables. But — and this was the object of Budd's shrewd glance — there was mighty little oil in the dimmed lamp, not much wood in the wood box, and a scant row of sacks and cans in the cupboard.

"What did you say, Miz Cappell," ventured Budd by way of gentle reminder that he had asked for admission.

"I don't suppose I could refuse you in such weather," said Mary Cappell in no kindly tone. She held herself tightly together and her head high.

Budd was not so dense as to miss the undercurrent of that remark. He promptly turned around. "Oh, no, Miz Cappell, I ain't wishin' to intrude on nobody. I'll jest mosey back to Old Man Cruze's."

"Oh, stop that nonsense," she answered impatiently. "Of course you'll stay. I'd be heartless to drive a dog out in this weather. Put down all that stuff and take off your coat. And, if you don't mind, leave the shrubbery outside."

Budd went out into the night, grinning to himself. *Wasn't she a tart creature, though? All the courage in the world, but much too much of false pride. This,* he communed, leading the horse to the barn, *was going to be a plumb interestin' evening.* He took off the harness, sought vainly for a little hay, and returned to the house. The lamp wick, he noticed, was turned higher, and she had just filled the stove with wood.

"Are you hungry?" she asked. Budd, thinking again of those bare shelves, hastily said, "No." His big frame was

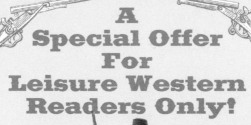

Get Four Books Totally FREE* –
A Value between $16 and $20

Tear here and mail your FREE* book card today!

PLEASE RUSH
MY FOUR FREE*
BOOKS TO ME
RIGHT AWAY!

LeisureWestern Book Club
P.O. Box 6613
Edison, NJ 08818-6613

really in need of fuel. He dragged a chair to the fire and hovered over it.

"Awful cold evenin', ain't it?" he ventured.

"Yes," answered Mary Cappell tersely. There the conversation lagged. The wind whined around the corners of the shack, and the fire glowed in the grate. Time passed heavily laden with silence. The woman was most determinedly looking at the walls. Budd, leaning far over, repressed a grin. His eyes beamed.

"Ma'am," he said hesitantly, "I been playin' a leetle game tonight. Santy Claus you might call it. Been comin' down the road with a few presents for all the people I know hereabouts. Jest a leetle Christmas present for the folks. I'd take it mighty kindly, Miz Cappell, if you'd accept what's in that box as the season's offerin's from old man Budd."

She bounced out of her chair, and her eyes sparkled with ire. "Mister Budd, you don't have to remind me I owe you money! When I am able, I shall pay you every red cent, with interest. Meanwhile, it's . . . it's insulting of you to come here and hint about it!"

It took Budd full in the sails. His mouth gaped. "Why . . . !" Then the natural dignity of the man came to the surface. "Now, ma'am, you don't really think that," he said gently. "I'd be a pore sort to come around collectin' bills at Christmas time . . . or even *hinting*."

She was not to be appeased that easily, although the edge had gone from her anger. "I know I owe you money. Don't worry, you'll get it."

"Wish you'd stop thinkin' about money on a night like this," he said plaintively. "I ain't. Shucks, ma'am, every man, jack, and baby owes me money in these parts. Part of the gamble of homesteadin'. *You* don't owe me nothin' compared to some. I ain't worryin'. My store's open to all, any time, all the time, regardless. People got to live."

"Nevertheless," she said, "I know what you're thinking. You're thinking a woman is foolish for trying to homestead alone. I *know* you think it. You as much as said so the last time I came to your store. A very cruel, uncalled-for remark. I had thought you my best friend. That showed me otherwise. I'll teach you people different before I'm through with this prairie!"

"Never said you was foolish," Budd stoutly asserted.

"You as much as said so. A very cruel remark."

Budd searched his memory. *What remark had he made?* Soon he was grinning like a Cheshire cat. The woman stormed at him. "Are you laughing at me?"

"Haw! No, ma'am, not at you. Was it the thing I said about it bein' a scandalous waste for a woman to be single when there was plenty of eligible men around?"

"I do!"

"Shucks, you needn't take that to heart. An old feller's joke."

"It didn't sound so to me. I'll show you whether a woman can win her way or not!"

Budd became stern. High time to pull in the reins. "See here, now, Mary Cappell, you an' me was gettin' along real handsome until you figgered I'd made that break. You're a plumb spirited woman and full of ginger. But you got too dang much false pride, an' it's high time someone told you. Got to take things as they come in this country. If you don't, all the pride'll be knocked from your body by old man Adversity. It's a tough struggle, an' you got to be a little meek about facin' the prairie. An' when people joke, you oughtn't turn up your nose 'cause it sounds a mite crude. We're all bed-rock hereabouts, all strugglin' to make things go. If we sound like we wasn't quite polite, it's our privilege.

We don't get much chance to practice humor, an' mebbe we ain't so good at it. Now you be decent an' civil."

She was silent and, Budd saw forlornly, not altogether convinced. He got up from his chair, went to the door, and opened it enough to pull in the Christmas tree.

"What are you doing?" she asked.

He grinned a little apologetically. "Carried this thing all the way from home, thinkin' I might find some place it'd come in handy. Got a hammer 'n' some nails?"

He tacked the base of the tree to the floor and pulled out the two candles. "I figgered we'd jest sort of light the tree up. Make it more like Christmas." Taking his pocketknife, he cut the candles in small lengths, dug out the wick and fashioned a point. He put all the pieces on the table and lighted them with a taper from the stove. Then, gravely performing a ceremony, he took the first candle to the tree. "Jest to remember folks we ought to remember. This one I'll put on the top where it'll burn plumb bright."

"And who is it for?"

He stared at it solemnly, unwinkingly. "Mary Budd . . . my wife . . . died when we was both pretty young."

"Oh." Then, after some time: "The next one will go right below it, Mister Budd."

He fastened it to the tip of the limb. *There was, after all, a streak of delicacy in this great, bulky creature. He asked no questions, never attempted to pry.* Standing back, he gave it the same solemn respect. "To someone," he said, "someone you loved."

"Yes," she answered quietly. "To someone."

He put three or four of the candles in his bear-like paw. "That's for those we ought to remember. Makes us a little sad, mebbe, when we oughtn't to be sad. Christmas was made for people to enjoy. So I reckon we'll just stick these

131

in roundabout for to light everything up." One by one he disposed of them. "Now," he said, "ain't that plumb pretty to look at?"

"If I've said things that were too harsh," she ventured, "I'm sorry. It's . . . it's hard on the nerves to live all alone."

"Haw, don't I know it?" He slapped his big hands together. "Ain't natcheral for people to live alone. Guess I'm a great, big, galumtious sort of fellow. Sometimes makes you think of a steam shovel, mebbe."

They stood rather close together, looking at the glittering tree. The fire popped merrily in the hearth and a warmth and comfort invaded Dave Budd's being. It was plumb nice to be here. He felt at home, felt rested. The tree had done its work after all. He had found one soul as lonely as his own.

Perhaps he had not turned the knob of the door tightly enough. A great gust of wind slatted on the roof and tore around the corners with a gasping sound. A finger of that wind rattled the door, gave it a huge push, and flung it open. The thing banged up against the wall with a sharp crack. It was so unexpected that the woman, nerves tight and uneasy from so much living alone, jumped quickly, turned, and found herself right squarely placed in Budd's arms.

He looked down at her in huge surprise. "Why, say, Mary, you're awful pretty now!" And, in the manner of gay blades the world over, he put his arms about her gently, stooped a little, and kissed her.

After all, she was a woman. The kiss seemed not unwelcome, for she made no move to draw her head away. Thus they stood, two middle-aged people embarked on romance, going about it somewhat stiffly, it is true, but nevertheless repeating the ancient story. Budd's hand was awkwardly hanging over her shoulder, and he had failed to meet her lips squarely. It made no difference. They stood still until the woman, shivering, drew away. "I'm cold, Dave."

He cruised across the room and slammed the door. "Mary, supposin' you open a can of these beans here and put on a leetle coffee. Come to think of it, I'm hungry as seven boiled owls. Christmas! Ain't this the greatest Christmas you ever had?"

RED KNIVES

A Frontier Story

Ernest Haycox preferred reading history, memoirs, and first-hand accounts to reading Western or frontier fiction. In 1924, while he was writing fiction for *Western Story Magazine*, living in the East allowed him to make an intensive study of the Revolutionary War. Haycox's long novelette, "Red Knives," first appeared in *The Frontier* (4/25) and in "The Trading Post" for that issue Haycox commented that " 'Red Knives' was the result of some research for a historical book . . . . At the time the book was the important thing, but as I read through all the chronicles of what these early pioneers had done the idea of a story came along and wouldn't be denied. For every man struck down by a Shawnee lance or Huron war hatchet there were others to go on, a little grimmer of purpose, a little more determined to see the land beyond the hill and the plain beyond the river. It would be hard, in looking through the history of advancing civilizations, to find another group of men so individualistic in temperament, so buoyant, or stoical." Jim Girty, a major character in this story, is portrayed even more darkly by Zane Grey in the second novel of his Ohio Valley trilogy, SPIRIT OF THE BORDER (Burt, 1906). "Red Knives" appears here for the first time since its magazine publication and is an interesting contrast with "Burnt Creek," which dates from the same period. One story deals with the early days of the frontier, the other with its closing days, but both provide the vivid characters and values forged by that uniquely American experience.

I

"TO DETROIT"

George Rogers Clark was making his last camp on the Ohio, and the four weary companies of buckskin militia stretched their legs at the end of a hard day. The flame of the squad fires illumined the dark water of the river and outlined the thicket of the unknown back country, while the men drowsed before the grateful heat, sitting cross-legged. A monotone of talk broke the rustle of the wind and the lap of the water. A sentry emerged from the woods for a moment to survey the clearing and plunged out of sight.

"Jet Bonnett, dum ye, whar's thet twist of 'baccy I guv ye yeste'day?" a throaty voice called from one fire to the other. "I'm done fer a chaw, danged if I ain't, now." A milder voice answered, and the peaceful drone went on. Near the foot of the encampment some Tennessean chanted softly the Seminole corn ritual.

By the fires came a tall, lean man who stopped momentarily at each blaze to scan its circle of men. The light revealed a tanned, aristocratic face marked above all else with lines of arrogance and sullen humor which seemed to intensify with each fire the man inspected. At last, near the end of the line, he found the object of his search and broke into an impatient exclamation.

"Cheves!"

"Yes?" A figure rose to sitting posture.

"Why don't you stay by your own fire? Been trailin' you like a puppy dog. Clark wants to see you right off."

A chuckle swept the circle, and a massive-shouldered, bearded fellow gravely rebuked the messenger.

" 'Pears like you ain't been doin' nawthin' but grouse this hull trip. Kind of spilin' fer fight. Ef I was Cheves, danged if I moughtn't risk a fall with ye, Danny Parmenter."

Cheves rose and came from the fire. "Thanks," he said, walking toward the head of the camp.

Parmenter shifted his feet, cast a swift glance of anger at the bearded fellow, and hurried after his man. Striding up the roughly formed street, they appeared typical sons of the Old Dominion who in that year of 1778, during the Revolutionary War, had cast their lot in the newer country west of the Blue Ridge. Both showed lean and wiry frames beneath the buckskin, and both possessed the sensitive features and proud carriage of native Virginians. Cheves was the more solidly built. He swung along with the gliding step of an experienced woodsman, while his bronzed face, molded by hard adventure, lacked any line of petty spite.

In the darkness between fires Parmenter began to grumble again. "General sends for you pretty often! Seems like you stand mighty close to him. Policy for you to make up, eh? Sending me out to fetch you like an Indian trailer! Damn but that's fine! There's some things I can't stand in a man, Cheves, an' toadyin' is one of them! Lickspittle!"

"Wouldn't get so steamed up. Ain't to help you," Cheves drawled in response to this irritable attack.

"Don't you use that patronizin' way on me!" Parmenter turned, furious. "All I been doin' lately, seems like, is flunkyin' between you and Clark. I didn't join for that, and I won't stand it any longer." He stopped and pulled at Cheves's jacket. "Put up your fists and we'll have it out."

But Cheves broke away in a gust of impatience. "Don't be a fool! You've been an idiot ever since we left Wheeling. If Clark had sent me to look for you, I'd have done it and kept my mouth shut. Take what comes to you."

They strode on, but soon Cheves spoke again. "I don't know what you came on this expedition for . . . but I'm mighty tired of being ragged. I don't want any more of it. We can't get along, so just keep away from me. I'd have killed you long ago if it wasn't for a reason."

"You needn't use her for an excuse," Parmenter sneered. "I don't hide behind her skirt. I'm not afraid of you!" An incredible harshness, a vitriolic bitterness tainted his next words. "You don't win all the good things in this world. You didn't get her! She's seen through you. Hear that? She's mine . . . promised to me!"

"All right." Weariness filled Cheves's voice. "All right. Lower your voice, man. If she's promised you, then be satisfied. Now shut up."

The other subsided, yet for a man who had conquered a rival he seemed to lack any trace of generosity. His success appeared only to have sharpened his hatred, and he would have continued the quarrel had they not arrived at the largest fire. Around it were four men — Clark and three captains of the party, Helms, Harrod, and Bowman. Clark was broiling a chunk of deer meat over the coals while the other officers shared a faded and creased map in which they found great interest.

"Here he is," grunted Parmenter.

"You want me, sir?" asked Cheves. The discipline between men and officers in this brigade was of the rudest sort. No officer commanded, save by the downright merit within him, and no man followed unless urged by confidence and respect. The tall Virginian stood at attention only because he held a full measure of loyalty to the stern figure in front. It was a good soldier honoring a good soldier.

"All right, Parmenter. Won't need you any more." Clark nodded.

Parmenter's mouth cursed. He scowled at Cheves and flung himself away.

Clark shrugged a burly shoulder. "That lad's spoiling fast," he commented. "Here, Helms, you finish this meat for me. Sit down, Cheves."

Captain Bowman glanced toward the rear. Directly back of them the water maples and osier bunched to form a thick bit of wood, with the underbrush winding around the tree trunks. Clark caught his captain's eye and nodded.

"I know," he agreed. "Trees have ears, but this is as safe a place as we'll ever find. Hand me the map, Bowman.

"Now, Cheves, the brigade is leaving the river at this point. Can't go down the Ohio farther without some British ranger or French voyageur seein' us. Soon as they did, immediately Kaskaskia would be warned . . . which would ruin my surprise party. I've decided to cut straight across country from here. It's five days' march. Hope to take the enemy completely off guard.

"But capturin' Kaskaskia's only a part of the campaign. I'm plannin' other things . . . and I've *got* to know what Hamilton is doing in Detroit. Last I heard he was to bring some companies of regulars down to Vincennes as a part of the reinforcements to this country. They may be on the way now. I've got to know. And I've got to know what he plans to do this fall and winter. He's been distributing red-handled scalping knives right and left. But how many tribes

142

has he got under his thumb? How many war parties will go out this fall? How many men are in the Detroit garrison? And are the French habitants contented or rebellious? A lot depends on that last, Cheves. And, most important, how many rangers are in the whole lake region? They stir up more danger than anybody else. You see what the job is, Cheves?" He leaned forward and tapped the Virginian's knee. "I want you to go to Detroit and find out these things."

"Yes, sir," said Cheves.

"Good!" Clark leaned back. "Now look at this map. Take a good impression of it in your mind. It's all we know of the trail between here and Detroit. This was Croghan's route in 1765 when the Kickapoos and Mascoutines carried him off to Fort Ouiatanon. It's seventy-five miles from here north to Vincennes. Two hundred and fifty to the bend of the Wabash that's by the Twigtwee villages. After that, I don't know. You'll be forced to stay off the Wabash most of the time, and you'll have to circle Vincennes and Ouiatanon. After that you'll be in Ottawa and Twigtwee country along the Maumee. Beyond these are the Pottawotomies and the Wyandotes, and they're the worst Indians on the border."

At this remark Harrod, veteran of a thousand Kentucky fights, raised his voice. "There ain't a friendly or neutral Injun the hull way," he declared. "Travel light an' fast. Don't light many fires or shoot much game."

"When you get to Detroit, play the part of an independent trader and use your head," Clark advised. "That's why I picked you. Find out what I've got to know and come right back. Pull out tonight. Tell the boys you're off on a small scouting party."

The wind threw a sudden puff of air into the clearing; the fire blazed higher and veered sidewise. At the same moment the distinct snapping of a twig came from behind them. Bowman whirled as though bitten by a snake, and the lines of his face turned suddenly savage.

"I knew it!" he ripped out.

"Maybe it's the wind," suggested Helms.

"Wind doesn't crack twigs with that sound," said Clark, shaking his head. "Stay fast, Bowman. Don't shoot. Won't do to scare up excitement now. But there's spies in this outfit! I've known it since we left Wheeling. I think that slew-nosed Sartaine is one of them."

"Wish I could ketch him at it," muttered Bowman.

"Get your outfit," continued Clark to Cheves. "Travel fast. When you return, I'll be at Kaskaskia, or I won't be alive." The slate-gray eyes caught fire, and the stubborn, long-jawed face lightened to the flare of his ambition. "Good luck!"

Cheves strode down the line of fires. Half way Parmenter intercepted him.

"What's up?" he growled.

"Nothin'," said Cheves, speaking loudly enough for the adjoining group to hear. "Just goin' on a little scoutin' trip."

Parmenter's eyes sought the other man's face and slowly the blood crept into them and his mouth curled back after the fashion of a vicious horse. "Damn you!" he breathed, "I'll not stand that!" and before Cheves could jerk away a flat palm had struck him on the cheek with a report loud enough for all men at the nearby fire to hear.

It dazed Cheves for a bit. After that, he moved forward. "I've stood plenty," he said. "You've picked a fight."

He moved into action quietly. A straight-armed jab threw Parmenter's head back, and before he could parry another blow caught him on the temple. But Cheves left an opening, and Parmenter's fist found it, leaving a crimson streak.

Both fought in silence, with their whole hearts. There was no avoiding punishment. Each tried to batter the other into submission. Parmenter's grimaced face mirrored quite plainly his purpose to injure or maim without scruple. Cheves caught him on the mouth, and he grinned through the hurt of it — grinned and seemed to slip, twisting his body, raising a knee and driving it full into his opponent's stomach. Cheves saw it barely in time, jumped sidewise like a cat, and took the blow on his hip. That trick thoroughly warmed him. A wild anger sent him forward, taking punishment unheeded and battering down Parmenter's guard weakly to his hips. With a kind of sob the latter met the final blow on the chin and slid to earth like a dummy relieved of props.

Cheves stood over him, angrier and angrier. "When will you learn to fight fair? Next time we fight, bucko, I'll kill you! I'm tired of using my fists, too. Remember that."

Parmenter raised his head, wiping away the blood, immeasurable rage in his eyes.

"All right," he answered, almost in a monotone. "I'll take that challenge. Anything goes, my friend."

Cheves turned on his heel and went the length of the clearing to get his equipment. Around the waist of his hunting shirt went the leather belt holding shot pouch, powder horn, game bag, provision pouch, and hunting knife. Last of all he picked up the long-barreled gun and his broad-brimmed hat.

"I'm off for a little cruise," he said. "Dan, you take care of the blanket. I can't pack it." He turned away from the fire and strode along the edge of the brush to the opening of a deer run. At this point he stopped to survey the clearing. Clark was busy with his venison, and the captains studied at the ancient map, but farther down the clearing a more

sinister sight caught his eye. Parmenter had gone to his
fire. A short compact figure slid out of the dark and gestured
to him. The two met on the edge of the light and, as the
second man turned, the Virginian saw him to be the slew-
nosed Sartaine. Both turned from the clearing and disappeared.

Cheves squared himself and plunged through the brush.
His only guides were the North Star, hanging over his right
shoulder, and a mental picture of Croghan's map.

It was Dan Fellows, wrapping Cheves's blanket around
him for extra comfort, who explained the sudden quarrel
to his companions. "Me now, I've watched them two families
. . . Cheves and Parmenter . . . since a boy. They've allus
fought. Once in a while a black 'un breaks out in the Parmenter strain. This Danny's like that."

"You-all know 'em?" The circle paid him attention.

"Yep." The speaker crushed some leaf tobacco in his pipe
and lit it with a flaring brand. "Cheves's blood is good. My
folks run with them many a generation. These two young
bucks always scrapped. Fought and kicked since they was
knee high to a grasshopper. And always it was a case of
Parmenter tryin' to git unfair advantage. There's a wild
cast in his eyes.

"Lately they've fought on account of a mighty sweet girl,
for the two bucks have run nip an' tuck with her judgin'.
But it seems like she don't know her own mind when it
comes to men, which ain't strange. Anyhow, it goes along
like that until the night there's a great fight atween 'em
and, at dawn next day, there was a duel. I snuck up and
saw that duel from beyond some willows. Me and another
Virginia man, both with guns, to see there warn't any foul
play ag'in' Dick Cheves. Way to fight is ball an' ball, God

146

helpin' the best man.

"Well, He did. There was two shots all bunched of a sudden an' Parmenter's gun dropped from his arm an' he fell. Next thing was unexpected. Cheves had turned an' was walkin' to his horse. Afore anybody could say Sam Bass, Parmenter had licked another little gun from his coat an' taken a fresh shot. Didn't hit Cheves, by Jo! Dick didn't even turn until he got a-horse. Then he speaks up in right smart voice like this, 'Danny,' he said, 'if it warn't for one thing, I'd sure kill you.' And then he rides on."

The circle hung on every word. Only one man of the crowd saw Parmenter and the guide slip back to their fire, gather their guns and belts and hurry again to the shadows — only Fellows saw it, from the corner of his eye. Unhurried he finished the tale.

" 'Twas the next day an' I was standing with Dick when he gits a note from the Ralston plantation . . . that was the girl's name . . . brought by a nigger. Dick's face just went ter black when he read it. All he said was, 'Dan, I'm goin' away.' Well, I just ketched me a horse an' here we are. 'Twas later in the trip as you boys know that Parmenter joined. Knowin' what I do, I guess none of you saw what I did. But there's one less man comin' back from this party, darn me now if he ain't."

A gust of rage roughened his voice. He drew on his belt and kicked away the blankets.

"Jed Bonnett, you keep these things," Fellows commanded — and strode, rifle a-cradle, into the shadows, following Sartaine and Parmenter over the same trail Cheves had taken a short half hour before.

II

"AMBUSH"

In the afternoon three days later, stubbled and sweat-smeared of face, Cheves was on the far end of his great circle around Vincennes with the broad river sparkling at him through the meshwork of the trees. The day had begun full and warm, but as the sun started down westward the heat, sullenly stifling since the Virginian had started his solitary trip, gathered into clouds. Flat and detonating claps of thunder broke in the sky, and by four or five o'clock all light was gone. A patter of rain fell on the leaves, and Cheves raised a fold of his hunting shirt to cover the powder horn.

Passing Vincennes was a nerve-tightening affair, for here were gathered the Piankeshaw Indians, and here centered the power of the British on the lower reaches of the Wabash. By rough calculation he had detoured the town at a distance of ten miles, but even at that interval the traces of scouting parties were plainly visible. He had passed five trails leading to the old settlement, and each bore the marks of recent travel.

Once at noon of the day before he had gone off trail to a thicket and was munching jerked venison when a silent file of ten Indians hurried by. Their bodies, bare to the waist, were daubed with yellow and red pigments, and from each hip was slung the belt with its burden of powder horn, shot pouch, knife, and tomahawk. Three warriors carried each a scalp dangling from the tomahawk. Cheves gritted his teeth. Those scalps meant slaughtered American backwoodsmen.

That night he forded a creek, swam a river, and camped deep in a tangle of grape vines. The patter on the leaves broke to a swift torrent, and in the darkness Cheves had difficulty in finding his way. Once a crack of brush sent him off the path, but it was only the falling of a tree. Again, the waving, sighing saplings so resembled advancing people in the darkness and drizzle that he abandoned the path for a hundred yards or more.

He took note of every forest sign, for he had learned two days ago that someone hung to his trail. In the dark of one night there had been the swish of brush, and only yesterday he had seen tracks of an Indian party doubling back around him. It looked as if a general alarm of his presence had reached Vincennes through some spy in Clark's outfit.

The rain increased its fury, and the bushes bent and twisted across the trail so that in the semi-darkness he could scarcely push his way on. The path had become a small waterway, and he was wet to the skin. But the physical discomfort didn't matter. Such a storm erased the marks of his trail and allowed him relaxed vigilance.

A curve shut off his view and some sleeping monitor, plus the cloak of the storm, let him forge ahead without reconnaissance. When he again faced the straight path, it was to find a bowed figure in buckskin rapidly advancing. The latter saw Cheves immediately and threw up his arm. The Virginian swore, but it was too late to take cover. Coming to a halt, he dropped the butt of his gun and waited.

"How," returned Cheves. He placed the man instantly as

149

one of the many British rangers abroad in the forest who went from tribe to tribe and from fort to fort. No other man would march through the woods so carelessly.

"Hell of a day for travelin'," offered the ranger. "Where from?"

"Vincennes," Cheves answered after a rapid estimate.

"So? Was there two days ago an' didn't see you."

"Just come in from Kaskaskia. In a hurry to reach Ouiatanon."

The ranger took a sudden interest, shaking the water from his dripping face. "What's up?"

"Spanish at Saint Louis tryin' to stir the Kickapoos against us. There's somethin' in the wind, and it ain't for our health."

The ranger cursed the Spanish volubly. "Never did trust any of 'em further'n I could throw a bull by the tail. I'm all for wipin' 'em off the Mississippi. Never any peace in the Illinois country till we do."

"Where you from this time?" inquired Cheves.

"Ouiatanon. Hell's a-poppin'. Couple hundred Saukee renegs broke away from their people an' won't have nothin' to do with the other Nations. Killed some Twigtwee bucks and are headin' this way now. Wouldn't be surprised if they was right on my heels." The thought made him cast a sharp glance about. "I'm on my way to get the Piankeshaws to cut 'em off. Can't have 'em buckin' British authority. Bad example. You'd better keep an eye skinned. No tellin' what they'd do to a ranger."

"How're the other Nations?"

"Fine as prime fur. Scalpin' party goes out every week from Detroit. Make it all hair, I say. Sooner we kill Americans off the better it'll be. If you're for Ouiatanon, hang to the Wabash an' the bottoms. Bone dry elsewhere. But you'd better watch for them Sauks."

Cheves picked up his gun. "Well, I've got to move. So long."

"So long. Tell Abbott I got through."

The bend separated them, and once more Cheves ploughed through the rain. He swore bitterly. It was an unfortunate meeting in the most dangerous of places. The ranger would soon enough find he had been duped, and Vincennes was but twelve miles back. Cheves was going to be vigorously pursued.

From any viewpoint his position was precarious. The storm would cover his traces for a while but, when the rain stopped, he would leave a trail that any savage in North America could follow. There was only one expedient left, and he adopted it as soon as the idea occurred. Grasping the rifle tighter, he broke into a dog trot. The water splashed over his head, but it made him only a little more miserably cold.

On and on he ran, slipping and sliding, picking a way where the brush had fallen across the path, gaining speed where drier ground permitted it. The gray light faded before a tempestuous night; the way grew less and less discernible and finally was altogether blotted out. The dog trot slowed to a snail's pace. The trail was worse than anything Cheves had ever experienced. The wind howled savagely, and the rain poured down until the trace became a torrent, and he no longer could pick his direction. It was utterly black. Time seemed remote. A thousand demons howled, and the bitter cold cut through to the bone. In such a state he fought his way on until the expense of energy was greater than the progress made. At that point he turned into deeper brush and, hollowing out a rest among the vines, crouched down and spent the night.

At break of day he was up and on again. He had gained during the night, he knew, but would lose by day, for the

Piankeshaws could trace him by a hundred short cuts with the common adeptness of all woodland tribes. Toward noon the wind fell off, and the rain abated. By mid-afternoon the sun forced its way through the dreary clouds, and shortly the earth was a vast rising mass of steam. To Cheves it was a great comfort, drying and warming his soaked body, but with that comfort came a new necessity. He must leave the trail and seek the forest where his footprints would not be so plainly revealed.

He was on the point of turning off when, from directly ahead of him, there came rolling through the forest the report of a gun, followed by a series of short, bouncing crashes. Cheves drew up, nerves on edge. It sounded like a hunter — possibly from Vincennes. But no, a hunter from the Fort would have small necessity of traveling so far afield for game. Perhaps, then, it was some independent British trapper.

The Virginian was about to step into the brush when a stir from behind whirled him about. He stopped, half turned. Twenty yards away stood a half-naked, paint-daubed Indian buck. Out of the corner of his eye Cheves saw another advance from the brush in front. He was trapped! For a moment the idea of resistance surged over him. A step and a shot and he would have at least one of them. But the idea passed swiftly. That rifle report meant a larger party nearby. He lowered his gun and threw up a hand in token of peace.

The Indians closed in, rifles advanced. The foremost one uttered a monosyllable grunt and jerked away the Virginian's rifle. He was given a push and turned down the trail. Thus marching, they went through an open glade, turned off the trail to deeper forest and, after ten minutes' weaving, came to a clearing of some eighty or more yards across.

In the center were several small fires around which were gathered a war party numbering fifty or sixty young braves.

Cheves was shoved into the middle of the encampment toward an Indian who, by physical fitness and bearing, seemed to be the chief. He was fully three inches taller than any other man in the clearing save Cheves. His chest was broad and deep, and his face carried the bitter lines of discontent which only accentuated his authoritative bearing. He heard the speech of his scout, nodded his head, and suddenly sprang forward with a savage gesture. "Breetish?" he demanded.

Instantly it came to Cheves that these were not Piankeshaws. This party was a detachment of the renegade Saukee people. So, in commingled relief and consternation, he simulated a deep disgust, wrinkling his nose.

"No . . . no!" He switched to French which once had been the universal tongue of the forest: *"Je suis americain."*

The chief was puzzled. "Eh?" he grunted.

Cheves tried another word, one commonly used to describe Americans around the Ohio and Mississippi villages. "Not British. I Bostonnais."

The circle around him moved in recognition of the word and broke into voluble conversation. Then the chief made another of his swift moves, thrusting forward his hand and ripping back the Virginian's hunting shirt. Beyond the tanned V was white skin. The chief ran his thumb over it, shuffled his fingers through Cheves's black hair, stared at his eyes, tweaked his nose, and finally fell to examining his apparel with minutest scrutiny. His fingers tested everything before he muttered something that sounded to the Virginian like acceptance. "Bostonnais," he grunted, and the circle dubiously nodded.

At that moment a scout ran into the glade and threw out

a guttural warning. The men about the central fire sprang up. There ensued a rapid parley, with the scout swinging his arms in a wide circle toward Vincennes. Another scout ran in from a different angle and made a quick report. Cheves, watching closely, saw some new turn of event had disturbed the Indians. The tall chief chanted a brief word, and the clearing became animated. The scouts slipped back into the brush. Even as the Virginian wondered, the main body shuffled into single file, with himself among them, and went quietly down to the overgrown trace. There they followed it, away from Vincennes.

Away from Vincennes was toward Detroit! Cheves relaxed. Their destination he did not know, but any destination to the north meant the closer approach of his own goal. So, for the time being, he could float with the tide, secure from ambush. When the Saukee trail forked away from Detroit, then must he commit himself to a different policy. Not before.

All night they traveled as if sorely pressed by an enemy to the rear. Cheves decided the ranger he had met had succeeded in calling out the Piankeshaws in such large numbers as to repulse the Sauks. Once in the small hours a ripple of warning passed down the file, and it halted off the trail for a moment. They resumed march in complete silence, each man slipping forward as the figure ahead dropped out of sight. There was nothing to disturb the swift shuffle of moccasined feet save the rhythmic breathing of Cheves's immediate neighbors.

At daybreak they camped in another secluded grove and Cheves, dead tired from forty-eight hours of constant travel, fell to a troubled sleep that seemed to last only a moment. Again they were up and on.

There was, Cheves saw, an undercurrent of uneasiness

in the column. Scouts went off on the dog trot and came rushing back later with brief reports, to go off again on the run. Thus far the trail had led away from the Wabash, but the new day's march had only been started when the party, apparently because of news brought by a scout, slanted northwesterly, gaining the stream again. At the same time the pace quickened, and Cheves's aching muscles cried for relief. But he dared not falter. In such a situation a white man's scalp was much easier to carry than his body.

They reached the Wabash at noon, plunged across, rifles held arm high, and climbed the farther bank. Topping the ridge, Cheves saw a long undulating plain, smiling under the afternoon sun, luxuriant in vines and hemp grass. The forest was behind; they were entering a new country with a new dress. Ahead was the suggestion of the Illinois River blending with the indefinite mists of the distance, and at that moment Cheves knew they were turning away from the road to Detroit.

Set as he was on this definite goal, the turn of fortune gave him a bitter taste of defeat. It had never been in his nature to accept defeat calmly and now, lightning quick, his thoughts turned to escape. But the Indians were already far beyond the river, crossing the hot flat land, and there was no possible avenue by which he might get clear in daylight. The nearest route to safety was through a thousand yards of open country exposed to fifty rifles. When night came, he might break away and run back for the river, but not before. So he accustomed himself to the swifter pace and said nothing.

The uneasiness seemed to grow stronger. Cheves could feel it in the braves about him and, when night came and they camped in a small copse, an increased number of scouts and sentries was sent out. No fires were lit, and a somber silence sat upon every coppered face. Cheves shared the sense of impending trouble. It was nothing definite, but rather an aura caught from these nomadic men who read their destiny in the leaves and smelled it in each puff of the wind. Some disturbing sign had warned them, and now they were straining every muscle to reach a secure haven.

With this foreboding Cheves dropped to a fitful slumber in the protection of a thicket, waking from time to time as warriors arrived and departed. On each waking it seemed the tension had increased and that he was the sole sleeper. He did not know at what hour of the night a rough word brought him up. His guide slipped by the trees, coming to a deeper tangle of the brush, and here stopped. Cheves dropped a hand to his belt and felt for his hunting knife. All about he saw the darker shadows of the Sauks, seeming in station for a definite attack.

Though he was prepared for this attack, the fierce, sudden gust of rifle fire surprised him. In a general way he thought the storm would break from northeastward, but the attackers were cleverer than that. So quietly as to be without opposition they had encircled the wood and now poured fire from all sides. The leaves pattered and brushed as from a heavy rain. Cheves, unarmed, threw himself flat on the ground. There was no safer place in that doomed wood, and the Virginian knew it to be doomed after the first volley. For, from the sound, fully five hundred rifles were speaking. It seemed only a matter of time before the renegades were annihilated, and Cheves took thought of his own chance to escape. Presently his guide, finding himself too deep in the thicket to be of any aid, left Cheves and crawled toward the firing. It was the last Cheves saw of him, or of any of the Sauks, alive.

The engagement settled to a stubborn rattle and patter of shots, with the occasional war cry catching and going around the attacking ranks. There was no answer. The renegades preserved grim silence, doing damage while they could. For a half hour it continued this way, dying down, flaring up, and at last settling to a deceptive calm. It seemed to Cheves as if all the fighters were holding their breath, waiting for the last act of a bloody drama.

It came presently, heralded by a full concerted war-whoop from five hundred throats, a lusty baying, a throaty snarl, a feverish yelping, which turned the Virginian's blood to ice. Then the attack closed in, rifles cracking.

The Virginian could mark each successive advance, could hear, almost, each individual battle, so strategically located was he. As the assault beat back the first line of defense, the ring narrowed and its edge came nearer to the covert where he rested. The last defiant cry of the defeated going down before knife or club, the last death rattle, the grunts and labored breathings of hand-to-hand conflicts — all mingled to form the welter of massacre.

No sound of mercy was given or of pity asked. Grim and stark and relentless. And above all this the Virginian heard, of a sudden, commands in a broad Celtic brogue.

"At 'em, me pretties! No mercy for the renegs! Bring me back sixty scalps! Hunt 'em down and stemp 'em out! I want topknots! No more renegs in this territory! Rum an' wampum, boys! Oh, ye red, murtherin' divvils, grind 'em out an' bring me the hair!"

III

"OUIATANON"

It was so unexpected! One moment the entire woods reverberated with sounds of death, with the gurgle and snarl of human throats uttering exclamations of anger and fear, with blows given and blows taken, with the noise of a surging, vindictive advance toward the heart of the brush. So furious was it that the Virginian had given up hope, resolving only to account well for himself in the last mortal struggle. Then it was all changed. The raucous, commanding voice of the Irishman was the respite of a sure death sentence.

"After 'em, my children! No prisoners! Bring in the hair! Go on through the woods! Get every mother's son!"

He came directly toward the covert, a heavy, aggressive body knocking the brush aside, fighting, swearing furious black oaths, and chanting the shibboleth of frontier war: "No prisoners! Bring in the hair!"

Cheves crouched, ready to spring. The last bush parted and the dark figure bulked dimly to view.

"Any of them damn' renegs here?" he bellowed.

The Virginian, slightly to the rear of the Irishman, catapulted forward, pinioned his victim by the arms and threw him to earth. They rolled over and over, the surprised man heaving and kicking. His rifle fell aside.

"Shut up," breathed Cheves. "I'm a ranger . . . got caught by these Saukees. Easy, easy! Call off your dogs!"

"Holy mither, ye were onexpected!" exploded the Irishman. "Walked right into your arms, I did. I'm a blind fool! If 'twere an Injun, my top piece would be airin' now." The thought of his position enraged him. "All right, man, ye needn't hang on so tight. Leggo, or I'll be forced to gouge." Cheves laughed and released his grip. The Irishman got up, still swearing. "A damn' oncivilized way o' shtoppin' a man! Who might ye be an' whare did ye get them gorilla arms?"

"Ben Carstairs, Kaskaskia. Who are you?"

"Jim Girty," growled the Irishman.

The fighting had died out. Now and again a rifle shot or war-whoop reached the two, but the skirmish was practically over. Already fires were burning on the plain and the Indians, cooling from the fever of killing, numbered their slain and counted scalps.

"Well," said Girty, "let's get out of this. Stay by me while I set 'em right. It's a ticklish business when Injuns are in heat. I was too damned careless! If it had been a Saukee, now!"

They passed into the clearing together, and Girty threw out a guttural word here and there. Cheves found himself the focus of glittering, blood-shot eyes but with his companion felt reasonably safe. What interested him most was the Irishman's stature. He was a short man with barrel-like shoulders, jet black hair, and a beard which seemed to cover every exposed bit of skin. Above it were mournful, suspicious eyes which, like those of the Sauk renegade chief, sought every detail of Cheves's apparel.

"Ye're a long, lean scantlin' of a man," he grumbled, "but

I take off my cap to those arms. Now what's your story?

Cheves sat by the fire and told the same tale he had in
vented for the ranger near Vincennes. Its effect was muck
the same.

Girty slapped a legging and cursed fluently in three
tongues. "Those hellish Spaniards! Never saw a good 'un
an' never expect to. I've told Hamilton many a time he
should go south an' wipe 'em out. By an' by there'll be hell
a-poppin' an' more dirty work for the likes of you an' me
Arragh! Hamilton's weak-kneed, and he don't use his head
What sort of man is that?"

The Indians gathered about the huge central fire on the
plain and were uttering a low rhythmic chant which ebbed
and flowed in celebration of victory. Girty swayed with the
chant.

"What sort of man is that?" he repeated. "It's dog eat dog
out here. Many a time my scalp's teetered because some
Tennessean cuddled his rifle too close. Raise hell with 'em
I say. When I plug one, I say: 'Girty, that adds another
day to your life.' Darn me if I don't."

"Why worry?" asked Cheves. "We've got things sewed tight.
Although I do hear there's Shawnees near the falls
waverin'."

Girty turned his head and looked fully at Cheves, the black
eyes dilating like those of a cat. "Ye talk mighty like a Virginian. I've heard that drawl afore."

"Man, you would, too, if you lived in Southern country.'

"How come ye be a British agent, then?"

"A man's politics, Girty, don't always bear looking into.'

Girth nodded. Yet like an animal who has smelled the
taint in the wind he could not be immediately quieted.
"Whare's your papers if you're from Kaskaskia? Rocheblave'd be sendin' some on to Detroit."

160

"Saukees got 'em and put 'em in the fire. It's all in my head."

Again Girty nodded. "Well, ye may be right," he admitted. "I've no cause to pick at a man's politics. Maybe I'm over shy. Niver met a man I'd trust save me brother, Simon. The trail does that."

The dance of victory was over, with a final shout and leap and insult at the Saukee gods.

" 'Tis a hard tomorrow and I think I'll sleep," said Girty. "We're goin' on to Weetanon where there'll be a party for Detroit." He fell asleep almost instantly.

Cheves remained awake longer, thinking over his next move. Clark had advised him to assume the rôle of independent trader but that had not seemed to promise as much information as he could pick up while masquerading as a British ranger. If he should meet anybody from Kaskaskia in Detroit, he could clear himself by posing as a new arrival in the Northwest, having come by the way of the Ohio, or he might say he was a special agent through from Tennessee, or that he had made a long circle at the behest of Haldimand, Lieutenant Governor of Canada. By these means he could gain inside councils. It meant a far more dangerous rôle, and it demanded swifter action. Already the ranger he had met near Vincennes constituted an awkward obstacle. He must get his information quickly and pull out. With that decision he fell asleep, utterly exhausted.

They were on the trail again in the gray of morning, pushing northeastward. Midnight brought them to Ouiatanon. Girty, impatient and overbearing, found the Detroit party gone on. He tore around the stockade like a madman, roaring curses.

Girty and Cheves slept that night in a far part of the fort and, relieved of watchfulness, they slept deep, not hearing the quiet entry of another party. Before daylight Girty was up, growling at Cheves that it was time to be on their way.

The newcomers were stretched on the hard ground of the court. Cheves, looking at them, saw only the blur of a white face raise up and turn toward him. No word was said. The man dropped back to his blanket again. Cheves followed Girty beyond the fort wall. The sentry banged shut the door and thrust home the bolt. On trail once again.

Thus far did Cheves and Parmenter miss each other at Ouiatanon, for it was the latter who had raised and stared, unknowingly, at the two men passing out of the fort not ten feet from him.

Up the long narrowing bend of the Wabash Girty hurried, following the river as it slanted eastward. Two days' march brought the rangers to the main column in the Twigtwee country. It was rougher going now, but the lure of the capital drew them on and instilled tired legs with renewed vigor. They crossed the Maumee portage, borrowed Pottawatomie canoes, and floated down the river to the lake. Fifty miles across open water brought them within sight of the gray, heavy palisades of Detroit town.

IV

"DETROIT TOWN"

The canoes brought up at the King's Wharf, a structure built of heavy logs split in half and covered by planking adzed smooth. Gray and weather worn, it stood solidly in the river. For nearly eighty years it had seen the departure of the fur brigades into the North and had witnessed them come sweeping back, singing their lusty free songs of river and wine, with the gunwales of their craft slipping low to the weight of hundreds of bales of priceless fur gathered west and north of Michillimackinac. The party ascended the embankment, went through the huge timbered door, and were within the town.

Detroit had started with a small stockade by the river. Each additional house and each additional alley stretched the walls until now the town inside the palisades contained about sixty houses and more than two thousand people, mostly French-Canadian. Outside the palisades the Frenchmen had long, narrow farms extending back from the river. It was natural that Detroit should start with a large water frontage and taper as it proceeded toward the forest, with the houses giving way to a large parade ground beyond which was the fort. There was scant regularity to the crooked alleys. The palisades could be entered by gates at the east and west and also at the two wharfs, King's and Merchants'.

Girty led the party single-file through the alleys. Small, low-hanging houses made of logs and rough board fronted the street. Cheves caught sight of piled counters and shelves, while at intervals the proprietors came to the doors and threw effusive greetings at him. They passed a wine shop, and Girty suppressed a bolt.

"You keep them whistles dry ontil we reach the fort!" he growled.

Winding and twisting, they crossed the parade ground worn hard by many tramping feet and arrived at the fort gate. The fort formed a part of the town wall, yet was itself palisaded from Detroit by a bastioned barrier. A sentry challenged the party.

"Hell, I'm Jim Girty!" answered the agent. Restraint of any kind angered him. "Party from Weetanon. Put down that stabber an' let us by!"

They passed into the yard, flanked by officers' quarters, barracks, and general store rooms. Girty seemed to know his way, striding across the square and through a doorway where Cheves, entering, found himself in a guard room. A lieutenant rose as they entered.

"Hello, Girty. You're back early. What luck?"

"Found 'em and took hair," the agent reported, drawing a significant hand across his neck.

The officer slapped the table. "Good! The governor will want to hear that right off." Girty nodded. The officer turned to Cheves. "Don't believe I know you," he said, a professional mask dropping across his face.

"Carstairs is my name," said Cheves, "from Kaskaskia."

"Lieutenant Eltinge," explained Girty to the Virginian. The two shook hands.

"From Kaskaskia?" Interest thawed the lieutenant. "Been looking for word from there for more than six months. Place might have been sacked for all we know. What's up?"

No news from Kaskaskia for a half year! The talkative young subaltern had unwittingly taken a great load from the Virginian's mind. He was safe until dispatches did arrive from that distant outpost.

"Bad news," he returned. "I had dispatches."

"Saukees got him," interrupted Girty. "Was headin' him straight for the Illinoy when I come up." He grew restless. "Go in and tell the governor we're here, will you?"

The lieutenant, checked in his gossip, rose with reluctance and disappeared through the door.

"He's harmless," said Girty, ranging the small room. "Not snobbish like most of 'em. Got a lot of book learnin', I hear. Hell of a lot of good it's doin' him here!"

Cheves was preoccupied with the coming interview. Luck had played with him so far, save in one instance. The thing that would most establish his position was the corroborative testimony of Girty, a trusted agent. And Girty had a good tale to report. He had pumped and cross-questioned the Virginian all along the Maumee River until finally he confessed himself satisfied.

"It sounded fishy at first," he told Cheves. "I know most rangers hereabouts, that's what got me. Can't take anybody on their face. If I'd been convinced you was Virginian, you wouldn't ha' lived five minutes." And the Irishman's sullen eyes flashed with a diabolical humor.

The masquerading had been far easier than Cheves had dared to expect. *Too easy,* he thought.

Eltinge came out. "Go right in," he directed, holding open the door. "Governor's very anxious to see you both. Mind stopping on your way out, Carstairs, for a little chat? Been trying to get down to that country on brigade for a year."

Cheves assented and passed down a dark corridor. At places store rooms broke the hallway like bayous in a creek, and they opened and closed three different doors before coming to the entrance of the governor's office. Girty strode boldly through.

"Back again," he announced gruffly.

The very contrast of the place astounded Cheves, unused as he was to seeing luxury in any western building. Coming from undressed timber and split puncheons, he now stood in what was undoubtedly the finest, most pretentious room in the west country. The stained walls were covered with furs and an incalculable array of Indian blankets, beadwork, and weapons. Immense polar and grizzly bear hides covered the floor. Around two walls ran a shelf of books four tiers high. A couch held place in one corner, draped by a silver fox robe. In the center stood a mahogany desk, from behind which the governor had but recently risen.

As for Hamilton, Cheves found him to be one of those indeterminate persons who seem never to possess a striking characteristic by which they may be remembered. Medium in build, tending to corpulence, no great amount of expression on his face in repose, but showing traces of latent nervous excitability, hair graying, possessing an English shopkeeper's features — he seemed, of all men, to be the least fit for governing his wild dominion and the least capable of carrying out a ruthless frontier war. And yet he was doing just that. He was the man whose name spelled anathema to every border settler.

"Glad to see you, Girty," he said in a short, hurried voice.

Cheves introduced himself. Girty broke through formalities in his restless way and delivered his news. Hamilton's eyes lit with animation.

"You got them all, Girty? Good . . . very, very good! Now we sha'n't be bothered by insurrection for a while. It must have been an affair."

" 'Twas!" replied the ranger in a sudden flash of pride. "Wish to God you'd do the same with the Americans. Saw half a dozen prisoners in the yard. Prisoners ain't no good. Use the knife. That'll make 'em cringe!"

The governor's face set with determination. "You can't scalp a helpless man, Girty."

"Better if you did," growled the agent.

"Damn it, man!" exploded Hamilton. "I won't have my hands dipped outright in blood. The world calls me murderer as it is. Understand?" He saw dissent in the ranger's face and turned impatiently to Cheves. "Now, sir, tell me of Kaskaskia. Where are you from? I haven't met you before."

"From my Lord Carleton. I had some documents for you, but the Saukees got them."

"Carleton . . . Carleton! What has he to do with you?"

"I came by way of New York, toured the Pennsylvania country, got to Fort Pitt and enlisted in a flat-boat company down the Ohio as far as the falls. From there I went to the Holston country. Strayed into Saint Louis as an independent trader and then made my way to Kaskaskia," Cheves explained.

"What's the news from east of the mountains? I never hear a thing. No dispatches from New York for a month."

"The rebel, Washington, has reached the end of his tether."

"Ah, they grow weak!" Hamilton exulted. "Now Kaskaskia?"

Cheves unfolded his perfected tale of intrigue and plot — of Spanish designs, of a thousand details which kept the governor on the edge of his chair. Cheves played the man for double purposes. Above all he must get the governor's confidence and secure an exchange of vital news. What were Hamilton's designs on the far southern corner of the Illinois triangle? What schemes were they harboring against Ohio and the Pennsylvania frontier? Of late there had been whispers of a great Indian uprising. What truth to it? And above all things — what of Detroit's vulnerability? So Cheves spread his web of words. He cherished the wild plan of working Hamilton to a state where a detachment of troops might be sent down to Kaskaskia from Detroit, thus weakening the main garrison. He, Cheves, would go along, run ahead to warn Clark, and ambush them. Detroit would be wide open then.

When he had finished, Hamilton leaned back and closed his eyes. For a long period he seemed to be thinking. Of a sudden he startled Cheves by observing: "Carstairs, you sound like a Virginian."

Cheves forced a smile and turned to Girty.

"Your same suspicion," he said and was further alarmed to see the sudden hardening, the sudden freshening of suspicion, in the ranger's sullen face.

"Damned if I didn't think so, Governor. But he's got a good yarn."

"It's nothing, perhaps," said the governor. "That's all, Carstairs. Stay in the fort until I get my correspondence ready for return. Girty, I've got something for you."

Cheves acknowledged the dismissal and went down the hall. He would have given much to have overheard the rest of Hamilton's talk to Girty. At the door he found Eltinge shuffling disinterestedly through a book. He dropped it quickly.

"Ah, back to chat with me," the British officer welcomed. "Have a real Virginian cigar. Pretty rare nowadays. I've a friend who smuggles them through. Let's take a turn about the yard."

The smoke was a luxury and Cheves said so.

"I'll get you a handful after a bit," rejoined Eltinge. "Wanted to talk with you. Minute I heard your voice I spotted another University man. I think I'm the only Oxford chap west of Montreal. I get very tired hearing jargon. What's your school?"

"William and Mary's," answered Cheves truthfully. It was a ticklish business, this mixing of truth and fiction, but it served his purpose, and he saw by Eltinge's face that he had established another contact within the circle he most needed to move during the next few days.

Eltinge launched a storm of questions, and Cheves began a description of the Ohio country which lasted for many turns about the yard. A bugle call brought the stroll to a halt.

"First mess call," said Eltinge. "Come to my quarters and we'll clean up. You're my guest at officers' table tonight. Anybody arranged to bunk you. No? I'll attend to it."

A second call drew them to an inner part of the fort where Cheves was admitted to a low, heavily raftered room lit by innumerable candles. A blazing fireplace dominated the scene, and in the center of the chamber was a long table around which some ten officers were gathered. Eltinge directed Cheves to a seat.

"Gentlemen, Mister Carstairs, on the King's business from Kaskaskia," he announced.

After that the Virginian found himself busy detailing his tour for the officers' entertainment. When the meal was over, he left the hall and returned to the open court.

"I believe I'll take a swing around the town," he told Eltinge. "It looks interesting."

"Would go along were I not on guard," Eltinge replied. "But be a little careful. We don't have entire harmony in Detroit. Too many French-Canadians . . . and there's a small group of American sympathizers we can't lay our fingers on. Three weeks ago a ranger who'd just come in from Little Miames disappeared, and we never did find him. So watch the dark alleys."

The Virginian strolled through the main gate as the late twilight faded into dark. Winking lights gleamed across the parade ground over which he walked, gradually approaching the mouth of a narrow alley. Somewhere a bell tinkled, sounding clear and full in the quiet evening air. To Cheves it was blessed relaxation after the weary travel. Here for a brief time he might loiter.

The alley enveloped him with its darker shadows. Once he flattened against the wall to permit a horse and cart to pass. The driver, probably late in his return home, urged the weary animal forward with unwonted grunts. The outfit creaked and clattered into the night. Cheves went on and came to an intersection, then drifted aimlessly to a new alley, absorbing the sounds and sights and vagrant smells of this far-famed western capital. Sounds of violins came from many houses. Windows of dressed oilskins drawn taut over frames let out yellow shafts of dim light. The door of a wine shop opened suddenly in the street and Cheves walked in, seating himself at a vacant table. The low-ceilinged room was filled with smoke and the babble of many men. A buxom girl of twenty or so came up for his order.

"W'at you 'ave?"

"A glass of port," returned Cheves.

He was aware of being keenly inspected by the men of the place. A natural thing, he decided, for here were typical Frenchmen, while he was labeled from head to foot an An-

170

glo-Saxon. Well, let them inspect. He did not care. Perfect serenity pervaded him this one evening. Surely he could drop his guard for a short time.

He did not see four men slip quietly from the door, for his eyes were fixed on the glint of light through the dull red color of his wine. It was excellent port and felt tremendously good on the flat of his tongue. After the second glass he paid his bill and walked out.

At first it was utterly dark and he stood in the middle of the street, arms slightly forward for protection, while his eyes became accustomed to the night. His ears, always sharp and attentive, caught a scraping of feet nearby. For a moment he thought of Eltinge's warning, but his guard was relaxed and he could not bring himself to realize danger. He groped forward.

It was absolutely dark. Only the faint lights through the oilskin windows guided him. The alleys gave way to another intersection, broader and lighter. He paused, deciding to return to the fort. It was useless to grope through the town. He would see it under the better light of day. Turning, he reëntered the alley.

Behind the wine shop he heard the scraping of feet for a second time, now closer by. He could not disregard this, and instinct threw him against a wall. Two shadowed figures advanced through the blackness and stopped before him. Cheves could not distinguish their faces.

"Pardon, *m'sieur,* but is it that you know the way to King's Wharf?" one of the men requested. "We 'ave just come in by *bateaux.* Thees town is strange."

"I think it's down this alley," returned Cheves.

He turned unsuspectingly to point the way. It was a fatal move. In some manner two men had slipped along the wall behind him. When he turned, they were upon him. A club came down on his head with the force of a ton of lead. A streak of pain and red light shot through his brain. Falling forward, he had this last thought, too late to help him: *Ambushed again!* Oblivion closed over him.

V

"OUTSIDE THE STOCKADE"

The awakening of Cheves was by far the most painful event of his life. A thumping headache was his memento of the attack, and his whole body caught up and repeated the throb. A musty smell filled his nostrils, and he seemed to be tossing back and forth in space. He tried to wet his lips and then was aware of being gagged. As his senses flooded back, he determined to rip off that impediment but, when he moved his arms, he found them trussed to his body. A kick of the feet revealed them likewise bound.

"Ehu, ehu," came a tobacco-cracked voice. *"Nom du nom, allez vite."*

The grunt of the cartwheels, the grumble of the driver —and he, Richard Cheves, bound on some unknown journey beneath a pile of straw. The cart hit a rut and climbed out with a jar; the pain became too great, and the Virginian dropped away to a far land, hearing the stentorian cry of a sentry: "Halt there!"

The next thing he experienced was the teetering of the cart on a dirt road and the *plock, plock* of the horse's feet. A fresher air filtered through the straw and his head felt immeasurably better. If he might only relieve his chafed wrists of the rope and his cramped mouth of the gag. . . .

"Get on, François, prod that beast! We can't be all night on the road!" a second man said.

"Eh? W'at you t'ink dat horse can do?" responded the gruff voice. Cheves recognized it now as belonging to the same man who had passed him in the cart earlier that night. "He ees no race horse. W'at you t'ink?"

"I know, I know. But prod him along." The second voice was that of an Anglo-Saxon; Cheves could not be mistaken about that. "We've got to get under cover before some sort of general alarm goes out."

"By gar, dat's right," assented a third voice. "Dat sentry, he look ver' close on us w'en we pass by dis time. I t'ink mebbe he got suspicions of men w'at travel by de night time. Speak to dat animal, François."

Thus encouraged, the driver lustily cursed the horse in fluent Gallic patois, using tongue, hands, and feet to express his purpose. The animal must have long been acclimated to its driver, for Cheves could feel no appreciable difference in the gait. At last the old man grew angry, and the Virginian heard him climb off the vehicle, run ahead in his clumsy sabots, and strike the horse on the withers. The cart gave a quick jump forward.

"That's it, François. Prod him along. Work that animal more and give him less oats. He's overfed and lazy."

It was becoming insufferable on the bottom of the awkward contrivance. Cheves could endure it no longer and, summoning the whole of his energy, he gave a desperate heave and raised up. The hay cascaded about him, and the blessed star-spangled sky broke clearly overhead. Simultaneously the two men remaining on the cart turned about.

"Hah, de fish he 'ave flopped," observed the younger Frenchman. His face broke into a sardonic grin.

Cheves was not so much interested in him as in the other

man, a young, clean-cut fellow evidently not over twenty-five, dressed in homespun which fit snugly over a compact, muscular frame. His not unhandsome face, plainly visible in the clear starlit night, surveyed Cheves with a somber noncommittal gaze.

"You have a heavy clout, Pierre," he observed. "More than you needed to!"

"Bah!" said the younger Frenchman in disgust. "Dees Engleesh 'ave ver' strong heads. No t'ing can bodder dem. Eet was just a little tap *d'amour*."

"We're not midnight assassins," the leader frowned, surveying the Virginian's face carefully. "You look dashed uncomfortable there, my friend. Also you appear to have some kind of intelligence. Most British rangers don't," he continued. "Now, if I take off that gag, will you promise to keep your mouth shut. On your honor?"

Cheves nodded vigorously.

"No!" said Pierre. "Don't take no trust in any of dem killers!"

"I have your promise?" persisted the other man.

Cheves again nodded his head. Pierre gave a sigh of disapproval and turned away. His partner moved forward and relieved the Virginian with a few deft turns of the bandanna. The latter could not have said a word at that moment if he had so desired. His jaw muscles were half paralyzed. Carefully he twisted his mouth to lessen the pain, wetting bruised lips and tentatively biting them lightly to massage back the blood.

"Better, isn't it?" asked the man in homespun.

Cheves nodded, essaying a half inaudible, "Thanks."

The road they were following kept close to the river, winding through sandy fields and many orchards. Whitewashed houses and barns showed in the distance along the route, resembling so many sheeted ghosts marching across the countryside. A mile or more behind the cart Cheves made out the palisades of Detroit. Suddenly the horse turned off the main river road and went along a ruttier, less traveled way.

"You'll have to lie down," was the curt order.

Cheves obeyed promptly. He had no mind to be obstinate now; it was futile, and moreover he had given his word. For another quarter hour he watched the sky, while the cart jostled and bumped through an unusually large orchard. The outlines of a barn showed over the sideboards, and finally the elderly Frenchman trudging by his horse gave a brief grunt. The cart stopped; the men dismounted, and Cheves waited the next move.

A few whispered words reached him; the head of the cart dropped as the horse was unhitched and led away. Pierre crawled over the sideboard and cut the rope with a swift slash.

"Climb out, *m'sieur,* but don' try to run off," he directed. A long-barreled, unwieldy pistol appeared from beneath his coat.

It required some effort for the Virginian to reach the ground. He stamped his legs and swung his long-fettered arms to restore circulation. The exercise set his head to throbbing more painfully, and he desisted. Running a hand over his face and head, he was surprised to find the amount of blood caked there. The blunt weapon had cut the scalp badly, and the furrow lay open to the touch of his finger. A gust of anger swept him, and he turned to Pierre.

"I'd like to have an even break with you some time with my fists, my friend," he said. "I think I'd pay you back for this."

A sardonic grin was the reply. "Any time, *m'sieur*," the Frenchman promised.

"That's enough of that," the leader of the party cut in. "Shut up, Pierre. As for you, Mister British Ranger, you're devilish lucky to get off with a plain blow." For the first time Cheves heard heat and bitterness creep into the voice. "Your cursed cut-throat Indians use scalping knives. I guess you shouldn't be bellyachin' over a little tap. All right, bring him along, Pierre."

An orderly pathway bordered by whitewashed stones led from the barn to a house sitting amidst a grove of trees. They came by this house, went to the rear, and opened a trap door to the cellar.

"Step down," Cheves was invited. "At the foot of the steps you'll find yourself between two bins. Go straight ahead ten paces or so and there'll be a roll of tarpaulin. That'll be your bed for the night, Mister British Ranger. I wouldn't bother about looking for ways to get out. There's no windows and only two doors. The one up to the kitchen is locked. This one will be also. I suspect that Pierre or François will be nearby most of the night. Both are good shots."

Cheves accepted the situation without a word of protest. Throughout his whole life he had pursued one plan of action: be a good Indian until the breaks of luck came. If none came, then there would still be plenty of time left for desperate action. He had emerged victorious from many a straitened and grim situation by this method. Just now his muscles hardly obeyed his will, and in his enfeebled condition he eagerly embraced the opportunity for rest. Slowly he descended, bending his head to pass the sill. The doors closed over him and a hasp fell audibly on a staple lock. It was pitch dark.

Following directions, he crept along a dirt floor, hands

touching parallel bins. He found an apple in one and took it. Farther on, his foot struck the tarpaulin and he knelt down to smooth out a fold of the stiff, tar-scented fabric, making a rough bed. Into this he crept, and dragged a lap of it over him as best he could, munching the apple. Finally he fell into a fitful sleep, miserable and cold, and with this one thought haunting him: his pursuers were doubtless nearing the city. The messenger from Kaskaskia might come in at any moment — and here he shook and shivered in a dank cellar while his chances in Detroit grew thinner and more desperate.

VI

"THE SURPRISE"

He did not see dawn come, but the shuffling of feet overhead heralded breakfast and the new day. After a while heavier steps tramped across the floor; a scraping of chairs and feet ensued. It all whetted the Virginian's appetite and made him sorely conscious of his hurts. Yet, for all the buffeting he'd received, he found himself clear of head and lacking only some kind of food to be stout and fit for service. He rose and groped to the apple bin. Apples helped, but it was hot tea he needed to thaw out the cramped muscles.

A trap door opened from above. "Come up," a voice commanded.

A shaft of yellow candle light revealed the way. He got through and stood in the kitchen. The two Frenchmen of the night before were there and in addition a buxom mulatto presided over the kettles hung on the hearth.

Pierre held the same clumsy pistol. With it he motioned toward the kitchen table, where Cheves sat down without a word and ate what came before him. The meal performed wonders for him, restoring his strength and refurbishing his self respect. This latter quality had fluttered low in the night. Now again he could wait with smiling confidence for his turn in the swift, uncertain passage of events. Meanwhile he had figured out for himself one puzzle. These Frenchmen were probably servants of the young leaders — not servants in the usual sense, however, inasmuch as the man had allowed them considerable freedom of speech. A closer bond of interest held them together, and that bond, Cheves guessed, was a common hatred of the British. Well, they had gone to a lot of trouble and hazarded their lives to kidnap a Virginian who wanted nothing so much as to be back inside the walls where he might do some good to their common cause.

But did he dare tell of his true identity? A thousand prying ears might overhear and carry the news to town. There might be counter spies. Would they believe him? He doubted it.

He drank the last of the third hot cup of tea and leaned back. That was a signal for François, who had watched him like a cat, to disappear through a door. Presently he returned and directed at Cheves the single word: "Come!"

The Virginian followed with alacrity, for he hoped now that he might get to the core of this mystery. A hallway opened into a large, well-furnished living room. The breakfast table had been recently abandoned and drawn aside, the dishes still on it, while two men sat before a fireplace and smoked morning pipes. Cheves, giving first a casual glance to the younger, knew him as the leader of the previous night. Then he turned his eyes to the elder and received a great shock.

The man had risen and stood supporting his spare, bent frame on the back of a chair. His white unpowdered hair, his blue-gray eyes, his thin aquiline nose, his whole proud, redoubtable carriage — Cheves recognized them all in one astonished wave of joy and relief.

"Colonel Ralston!" he exclaimed.

180

"Richard Cheves! I'm not mistaken, by gad!" The man fumbled for his spectacles. "My old eyes have been going back on me, Dick. Come here, man, and let me see you! Hardly knew you under all that gore," Ralston continued angrily. "That slugger, Pierre, came near bashing in your skull. I shall have to cane him, by gad! You've hardened, Dick . . . I see it! But you're Richard Cheves, of Cheves's Courthouse, Virginia. Three years since I've seen you. By gad, it's a wonderful thing to see your own kind after mixing with the 'breeds and puddin' eaters!" Of a sudden the old man's fingers dug into Cheves's arm. "What are you doin' in that British garrison and movin' around through the country with James Girty?" he asked fiercely. "Don't tell me you're a turncoat. I'll not believe that of a Virginian."

"I imagine, Colonel, we are both playing the same game, after the same ends," Cheves retorted shrewdly. "You went to a lot of trouble to catch one of your own fowls."

"Best catching John has done for a long while," said Ralston. "Dick, let me introduce John Harkness. I think we two are the only white American men left in Detroit." His voice grew sad. "They've weeded us out mighty fast. Were I not such an old and rickety and helpless-looking fellow, I think my turn would have come long ago. But they don't suspect me."

"How did you know I was with Girty?" queried Cheves.

"News travels fast," replied Ralston, sitting down. "I know more about Hamilton's business than he does himself." His eyes snapped with a quick fire. "I've got an organization that'll drain his little well dry some of these days. Oh, if I only had force to back up my information! Information my men get from right under his nose. We know every last one of his precious secrets. That bit of a dishrag, Hamilton! Pah! And that lumbering, barbarous, conceited Dejean!

They can't down us, no matter how many men they line up against the wall or export from the country. They haven't been able to discover the leak yet. We've been too clever."

"I heard you did away with a ranger a short while ago," Cheves remarked.

Ralston smiled gently. "We play for high stakes, Dick. Can't always be too nice about the means. But a little gold found this fellow's heart. We didn't have to go farther. He's alive and safe and a good many hundred miles from here."

"Do you think it wise to tell so much," Harkness broke in quickly. "It may be that he. . . ."

"What? Doubt a Virginian I've known since he was born?" said Ralston with irritation. "Why, I'd trust him with my life, as I do right now." He sighed. "Dick, if only I had something to strengthen my hand," he sighed, and turned to Cheves with a fresh interest. "You've come from the Illinois country. Tell me, what's goin' on down there? A bit of gossip came out from the Pennsylvania settlements last spring about George Rogers Clark going down the Ohio for some purpose. What's it mean? What'd he do?"

"That," returned Cheves, very soberly, "is why I'm here."

Excitement caught both men at once. "What for? Why?" queried Ralston, throwing the questions after each other. "I've heard mutterings and whispers and guesses and all manner of things come out of the lower country, but never any definite fact I could base hopes on. What is it?"

"I left Clark at Massac, seventy-five miles from Kaskaskia. He told me I should find him there, or that I should find him dead. He has a mind to take Detroit, if ever a fair chance comes. That's why I'm here, to find what Hamilton's plans are."

It seemed as though twenty years dropped from the colonel in the single jubilant gesture of his hand. "By gad, I can help then! My work hasn't been for nothing. My coming here was of use." He got up and strode around the room. "You've come for facts? I can give you nearly all you'll want. We'll scourge 'em out of the country! Did I tell you why I came here? All because, two years ago, Washington rode over from his winter camp and met me at Chester in the Red Lion Tavern . . . a few miles out of Philadelphia, that is . . . and asked me to come. He only said a word or so, but it uprooted me from Virginia and sent me here to do what I could. I worked a long line of alleged English connections, got into New York, rode into the Provinces as a loyalist and came here. I'll always remember one thing Washington said. 'It's possible that nothing may come of the venture, sir,' he warned me. 'But someone must be in Detroit, for it may be that a force can get through. Then we shall need your information.' That's the thing which has heartened me to the task. And now it's to be used!"

"Well," returned Cheves, "it may come to pass. I've come eight hundred miles, and I've suffered a few times on the way. But that's no matter. If we can get hold of the Illinois forts and Detroit, that will be the end of the British in the Northwest."

Gray dawn had given away to the first approaches of the sun. Another fair day came, with its burden resting heavier on these men. They sat, each inspecting the other, hope struggling to overcome the odds of fear and sad experience. Throughout the talk one great question had been uppermost in Cheves's mind, and only pride kept him from asking it. He hoped that the colonel himself would let slip what he was most anxious to know.

"It would be months before Clark could get here," mused Ralston. "That would mean a fall campaign, snow, and privation, I'm afraid."

"You don't know Clark," returned Cheves, his mind only half on the conversation, for he was recalling the bitter memory of an ill-starred day when a duel and a note from a girl blotted out his dreams of happiness. Well, all that was now behind him forever. Doubtless she was managing the Ralston plantation, after the manner of the Virginia women, while her father struggled here in Detroit. Waiting at home with her heart set on that dog, Parmenter. An unreasoning wave of fear and jealousy ran through Cheves at the thought. No matter. As long as she chose to doubt him unjustly, he would never try to correct the error.

A light step sounded behind him, a door closed. He turned and on the instant had jerked himself out of the chair, standing very erect, ice and fire running through him. There stood Katherine Ralston. She had come from upstairs and was but recently risen; sleep still clung to the lids of her eyes, and the lusty blood of day had not yet filled her cheeks. But beyond all that she was beautiful. Yes, she was beautiful! Cheves, looking at her with a kind of pride-ridden, hungry despair, knew that whatever came in the years to follow he could not scourge the sweet vision of her from his heart. So he stood, irresolute, wishing he were gone, wishing he had the courage to take her into his arms, wishing he had not so much pride, wishing he had more.

For her part, a moment's inspection of this strange, bearded, blood-smeared man had not revealed his identity but, when he made the short bow and she saw the curl and color of his hair and recognized the mannerism of his movement, she knew. The flush of blood stained her cheeks, and a hand went up toward her heart. A dark mass of hair, done up in a loose knot, set off the sweet oval of her face, on which many contrasting emotions mingled —

a high courage, pride, sympathy, and a sudden concern. Her father rose, his voice trembling just a bit as he spoke.

"Katherine," he said, "do you recognize our visitor? The Lord never brought us a more welcome one."

She extended her hand.

"Richard, I . . . we are glad to see you here." The tone of the greeting, low and sweet, went to his heart like the barb of a Shawnee lance. With a remnant of old-fashioned courtesy, he took her hand and bent over it.

"I am glad to be here," he stammered.

She gave him a quick gasp. "What have they done to you! Your head!"

"Oh, that confounded Pierre!" Ralston's voice filled with anger. "John, you must watch that always. I've told you many a time there's no need for undue violence. We are not common sluggers, Dick. I hope you'll pardon us for the heavy blow."

Cheves laughed, and found himself surprised at the lift of his spirit.

"I've endured worse things," he replied.

Harkness flushed. He had been an interested spectator of this scene, his eyes seeking first the girl's face, then Cheves's. Now he turned to the window.

"It's as the colonel says," he explained shortly. "A fortune of war. How was I to know?"

" 'Tis nothing," assured Cheves.

Katherine turned to the kitchen. "Richard, come with me," she directed. "We must fix that cut before it gets worse."

Cheves followed her out, with the unsmiling eyes of Harkness staring at them both. By the time the Virginian got to the kitchen, she had already filled a basin with hot water from the tea kettle. From some small closet she drew tattered bits of linen and cotton cloth, ripping these into regular strips.

"Sit in that chair," she commanded. "All night with your head in the cold. What a savage, unkind country this is . . . even with men like my father and John. I wish I had known!"

His heart jumped at that and, the next moment, sank. After all, she would have felt the same pity toward the worst, most degraded man in the Northwest. His face drew tighter.

"Do I hurt you?" she asked.

"No. I was thinking of other things."

She sponged the last of the caked blood into the pan and began wrapping the bandages about his head.

"You are always thinking of something far off, Richard. It has always been that way." A trace of sadness came to her words. "Am I so depressing as all that?"

Depressing! Good Lord! Cheves thought. "I was only thinking," he replied aloud, "of why you did this for me since I am what you believe me to be . . . what another man said I was. Why do you do it?"

"Let's not quarrel again, Dick. Time changes so many things. So many, many things." She started to say something else but stopped. Cheves, wrapped in his own thoughts, struggling with his own desire to utter his grievance, did not note the implication of the unspoken words.

"Time!" he said bitterly. "Time doesn't do a thing save score the old wounds deeper. Never tell me that time softens anything. I've sat awake a hundred nights, trying to puzzle things out . . . and can't."

"Dick . . . ," — her voice fell low — "there isn't so much to puzzle over."

"Parmenter," he broke in. "You believed him, let him paw around your sympathies, and never listened to a word from me."

"Richard, you never came to explain! What was I to think?

186

I saw you knock him down like a street bully. The next day you nearly killed him in a duel. I heard people whisper. Nobody told me a thing. I grew angry at what you had done to him and wrote you that note . . . and you never came back! Oh, that was the thing which hurt me so much! You never came back to explain! I would have listened!"

The mulatto had left the kitchen long before. They were alone, fighting out the battle so very, very old, stumbling across new facts that seemed to change the whole face of the quarrel, trying desperately to be fair, to tell all without hurting, trying to keep pride from spoiling everything again.

"And then Parmenter came to you, and you believed all he said . . . that I was a bully and a liar," Cheves charged.

"For a while, Dick, just for a while. Then I knew him better and sent him away, to tell you to come back. And you didn't come!"

"Sent him away?" Cheves turned swiftly.

She nodded, eyes clear and brilliant. "To tell you to come back."

He took a deep breath. "He never told me that. When I saw him at Wheeling, a year ago, he never told me that. He said you had promised to marry him, after the war. He came down the Ohio with me from Fort Pitt . . . and told me you had promised him. . . ." A great overwhelming weight seemed to be slipping from Cheves, and a new hope came in its stead. "Oh, what a mess I made of it!" he groaned. "I didn't know."

"Time . . . time does so much," she said wistfully. "Richard, while you were gone, I found . . . I found . . . ," and again she failed to say the thing within her. But now he heard the pause, sprang up, and came closer.

"Found what?" he insisted.

She summoned her courage, keeping her eyes upon him

in the mute hope that he might not misunderstand. "That there never was any man, Dick, save you. It doesn't matter now, I guess. But whatever happened, I didn't care what you had done. There never was a place in my heart for Danny Parmenter."

She was in his arms the next moment, crying in small, stifled sobs. As he kissed her, she whispered, "It has been so long."

The mulatto's footsteps drew them apart.

"We had better go back to Dad now," she said, and in the hallway she leaned up to him and whispered, "you queer, dear man! Never leave me like that again. Don't you understand a woman?"

VII

"A LIE FOR VENGEANCE"

Night, and the whitewashed farmhouse again bulked vaguely through the soft summer night. Within Cheves was ready to start on a return trip to the town.

"It will not be difficult," he reassured Colonel Ralston. "I'll find a way. By the river, I think."

They had spent the day exchanging notes. Cheves told of the events beyond the Alleghenies. Ralston revealed a store of strategical secrets concerning Detroit. Privately, to Katherine, the Virginian had disclosed the main items of his western pilgrimages since they had quarreled, but one thing he did keep from her — the full extent of Parmenter's defection. If she did not know the depths of that gentleman's character, Cheves decided, then he would not tell her.

"Be careful of the river's undertow," warned the colonel. "If you swim around the stockade, stay close to the shore. It's a dangerous river. I wish," he continued regretfully, "you'd stay here and let my agents get what little you need to know now. It's risky for you to be inside those walls. My men'll know as soon as any decision is made. You can start back to Clark from here. Won't be the danger of running into the real Kaskaskia messenger then."

But the thought of hiding out from danger, the thought

of shirking first-hand sources, was distasteful to Cheves, and he shook his head. "I'd best do this myself. You've told me things that will make Clark everlastingly grateful," he insisted. "Now I must go and see with my own eyes and hear with my own ears."

"Very well," sighed Ralston, "but above all things remember Detroit is weak. Only a handful guard it. A hundred determined men could take it easily, with a little surprise. And once it's taken, there'll be no more Indian raids on the frontier."

Cheves rose and shook Ralston's hand. He only nodded to Harkness who stood nearby, for some inexplicable and mutual dislike animated these two men and edged their words.

"You, sir," said Cheves, "I wish luck, and I hope you'll keep these people from danger."

"I will," Harkness nodded shortly.

Cheves turned to the door and found Katherine Ralston there, waiting for him. Together they stepped out into the night and walked down the pathway, past the barn. Midway they came upon the two Frenchmen who stepped from their path and touched a hand to their caps. Next moment they had disappeared into the night. Katherine shivered and gripped Cheves's arm more closely.

"Oh, Dick, this is a cold, cold, deceiving place in which to live. I'm not sure . . . not sure," she whispered.

"Not sure of what?"

"Many queer things happen, Dick. One never knows who is a friend and who is not. Many things have happened to make me distrust even those men. And I sometimes find John looking at me with a queer stare that makes my blood run cold. It's like having a knife forever at your throat."

A wild impulse swept Cheves to turn and tell this lovable

girl he would not go back to the town, that he would stay here and fend for her, be some comfort to her in a grim and suspicious country. He smothered that impulse with a savage, silent reproach. There was work to do. He had followed his duty through a thousand weary miles and must continue on until that duty was done.

"I wish," he said gently, "that I could stay. I can't though."

She held his arm and forced a brave little laugh. "Oh, it's just that I get terribly nervous. It's all right, Dick. Nothing's wrong, and I wouldn't keep you back. That would be selfish. But some day, some day. . . ."

"Yes," he said.

They had got by the barn. Suddenly she turned and drew him off the path to a nearby tree.

"I can't help feeling strange, Dick. Do you see this rock?" It sat at the foot of the tree, just small enough to move with some effort. "Well, if anything should happen . . . if something should go wrong . . . I'll leave a little note under it for you. Remember."

"What do you expect to go wrong?" Cheves asked.

"I don't know! I wish I did. There's just two people in the world I can trust, father and you. The country seems to breed suspicion into my bones. There's things I feel but can't understand. But it's just womanish fancy, I guess. You mustn't worry about it, Dick."

He stood, looking ahead at a winking light which came from a farmhouse, a half mile distant.

"I'll come back on my way south," he promised. "I'll see you again. And as long as I live. . . ."

He turned and kissed her, held her for a moment, then with a whispered word started down the pathway. A soft "good bye" reached him as the darkness blotted out the outline of the barn.

His path was much the same as that by which he had come, following a rutty byway through an orchard, turning and twisting a dozen times in its course to the larger river road. Setting foot on this broader, more substantial highway, he struck directly toward Detroit town, paralleling the river.

A world of doubt and misgiving rose to worry him on the trip down that dark and silent road. After all, Ralston was an old man, while Katherine was a woman, lovely and appealing and because of that a greater bait for some ruthless individual in this land of physical force. About these two people were doubtful henchmen. Perhaps — spies.

Cheves, inured to the frontier, trusted no one until reason for trust had been evidenced. And now he doubted Harkness. True, he was forced to admit that jealousy perhaps played a part but, setting that aside, he could not read sincerity or loyalty into that somber face. He gritted his teeth. More of this reasoning and he'd turn back. Resolutely he banished it.

The sudden shuffle of advancing feet threw him off the road and flat on his stomach — a file of six Indians went by. He got up and resumed his journey, shortly to make out the wall. Now he left the road and struck diagonally across a meadow, touched with the solid bulk of the wall and followed it down a hundred yards to the river bank. The heavy logs marched on out into the water for a dozen feet or more.

The boil and eddy of the midstream current came clearly to his ears, the backwash rolled up and lapped against the shore. He went to the bank's edge and tried to discern his path, but all he might see was the stockade wall marching out into the murky water and losing itself in the night. He knew that once beyond the wall he had to swim four

192

or five hundred yards before reaching King's Wharf — that was the total sum of his knowledge. Well, there was nothing to do but go ahead.

He stripped off his hunting shirt and ripped the bandage from his head. When he was found, it must not be apparent that he had received any care. He waded forward into the cold water, walked off a bench of the river's bed, and struck out. A sudden swirl of the eddy carried him against the wall, and he guided himself by treading and edging along the upright logs.

He was past them, was caught up by the current and carried along swiftly down the frontage of the town. The question now became where, in the black night, was the dock? He felt the water set sharply from shore and, for fear of being carried into the stream, began to swim to land, making as little noise as possible. Somewhere, within the palisades, he heard the distinct challenge of a sentry.

Another abrupt swirl of outsetting water hit him in the face, and he found himself striving to keep going ahead. It was the devil's own current, he decided, making in a dozen ways at once. This would not do. He could not gain the wharf in this fashion. Kicking over, he headed still farther in and at last had the satisfaction of reaching quiet water again.

He heard the soft ripple of the current against some solid object and, reaching out, came upon the blessed bulk of a pier log. The water flattened him against it, and there he rested while recovering his breath. It was well for him that a knot in the log formed his anchor, for directly above came the abrupt challenge of a protesting voice.

"Eh, Antone, I t'ink you are crazy," it protested. "De current, he make strange noises out dere tonight. Swish, swish, he say. I t'ink we will not get anyt'ing by startin'

193

in de black of de night."

A voluble stream of French answered this. Would that lazy son of good-for-nothing father never stop grumbling? There was a living to be made; the night was the time for making it. Would he have the whole town knowing where they were bent?

"By gar, I t'ink yes. Best some fallow know w'ere we go. Den, w'en a log heet us, dere will be help. I t'ink some day we pile up. De night, eet is for sleep."

Also, replied the other, the night was for energetic men of business who knew what they were about. Let sluggards sleep.

A third figure clumped methodically out upon the planking. "Well, when're you night birds a-goin' to get off?" it demanded. "Won't keep this gate open no longer. If the patrol'd see me, I'd have a hell of a time explainin'."

"Be of patience, *mon vieux*. Does not the silver chink pleasantly in your pocket?"

The light of the watchman's lantern cast a faint glow upon the water. Cheves flattened the more against the pier log, but he did see, by the same dim rays of light, a ladder nailed against the neighboring pier log. To this was fastened a canoe, and down the ladder descended a Frenchman, then his partner. Cheves swam to the far side of his covert and watched a few lusty strokes carry the canoe into the stream and out of sight. The watchman mumbled a mild curse and turned about to go back across the wharf.

His departure called for swift action. Two strokes brought Cheves to the ladder, and he was up on the dock in time to see the lantern shine midway in the gate. He ran forward, his moccasined feet making no noise. Some worry must have delayed the watchman, for he had stopped, back to the river, and was staring at the ground, idly swinging the lantern.

194

"Too dangerous," he whispered.

An instant later Cheves slipped one lean arm about the man's neck, snatched the lantern away with the other, and sent it hurtling through the air. The small flame went out as it fell. The best the victim could do was thresh the air futilely with his arms. Cheves clung on until he felt the body grow limp. At that signal he loosened his grip, turned away, and ran across the road into an alley leading toward the fort. The watchman would be all right in another ten minutes, he guessed. He disliked this pussyfoot manner of fighting, but no other way suited his needs. For the watchman, in fear of revealing his own guilt, would never report the entrance of a man through the gate.

By the time he had reached the fort and sent up a call he had worked out his tale for Hamilton. After a parley with the sentry, the guard brought Lieutenant Eltinge to the gate. The latter was visibly upset to see the Virginian again.

"Good Lord," he sputtered. "We thought you were dead . . . gone the same route our other ranger went."

"I nearly did," replied Cheves. They walked to Eltinge's quarters, where Cheves stripped while Eltinge rummaged his chest and found a tight fit in pants and hunting shirt.

"Get you fresh clothes from the commissary in the morning," he promised. "What happened?" He was all eagerness, pathetic almost in his desire to hear a story of adventure. "Where were you? Fort's been in an uproar ever since you disappeared."

"Let me see Hamilton," returned Cheves. "Right away. I've got important news."

Eltinge very reluctantly led the Virginian to the guard room, from whence he disappeared into the long hallway. He was shortly back. "Broke into a big meeting, but they're

195

on needles to see you. Go in," he requested.

Again Cheves, nerves taut and wary and face schooled to a fair degree of impassivity, approached Hamilton's quarters. The door stood open, and they were all watching him as he entered — the governor behind his desk, Girty to one side, his bearded face a mask, two officers of the post, and a great, gross-featured hulk of a man who overflowed the largest chair in the room.

"Well?" said Hamilton impatiently. "What happened to you?"

Standing there before a battery of half-hostile eyes, Cheves told them of his capture in the dark street, of his ride through town, of a complete circuit of the palisades (at that point began the fabrication), of being thrown in a dungeon, of being tortured by a band of men, of finally, on this evening, being given the water trial. He had strangled and suffered, and he was now filled with gallons of pure Detroit River water. But he had not told, and the last thing he remembered was unconsciousness. When he woke, it was to find himself in the dark alleys of Detroit again.

They finally rained questions on him, yet to all he was indefinite and vague. The clout on the head had fuddled his brain; he could not identify the men or the house. His sense of direction was lost by the eternal switching and turning.

"I couldn't locate it in a thousand years," he protested.

He felt a growing tension in the atmosphere as he proceeded, as if some new and portentous event were approaching, as if each man were weighing some decisive question in his mind. It was Girty, the hostile and implacable Girty, who finally leaned forward, face still a mask.

"Carstairs, I'm damned ef you ain't a slippery sort of flea," he growled. "Ye're too slick fer me. I cain't trip you up, but

196

I tell you this" — and here his face broke into a blaze of suspicion — "you ain't no Englishman, and yez ain't fer us! Ye're a domned, murtherin' traitor, that's what ye be!"

The Virginian thrust his forefinger almost into Girty's face. "Come out to the square, and I'll beat that statement out of you," he raved.

The governor toyed with a quill and looked frankly puzzled. The two officers were like wooden statues. It was the grotesque fellow in the huge chair who opened a cavernous mouth to growl out in a dead bass voice: "Girty, what's your evidence?"

"Ain't got none," snapped the ranger. "But there's been too many things I can't explain. I tell you he ain't fer us, and I'm of the idee he should be in the guard house. There's somethin' new afoot, I tell you. Captured, be damned!"

At this outright accusation, Hamilton came to one of his rare, abrupt decisions. The quill snapped between his fingers.

"That's enough ragging, gentlemen. We'll not get anywhere by this method. Foley," he asked one of the officers, "will you go out and bring in the new messenger from Kaskaskia?"

The word struck Cheves like a blow from a cudgel. Here he was, trapped! He had tarried too long.

The officer left the room, forgetting to close the door, and the Virginian wished wistfully that it were clear and that the way beyond it were clear. He heard the governor talking.

"New messenger came in late this evening, very tired, and with two runners from Vincennes. Gave him a bit of time to rest. We'll soon settle this question."

It was but a scant five minutes that the officer was gone, yet it seemed like an hour to Cheves. Girty's eyes, glinting from behind the tangled black beard never left the Virginian's face. Hamilton leaned back in his chair and stared at the ceiling, seeming bored by it all. The fellow in the large chair shifted his immense paunch from time to time and emitted strange whistling sounds of annoyance from his mouth.

Footsteps sounded in the hall. Cheves, still standing with his face to the governor, heard the officer and his charge enter the room and stop, yet he did not turn, choosing to retain his attitude of immobility and indifference as long as he might. Hamilton lowered his gaze from the ceiling.

"You were brought in to settle a slight difficulty," he said, addressing the newcomer. "Could you identify the gentleman in front of you?" He motioned for Cheves to turn.

The latter swung on his heel. The new messenger was Parmenter! It was a straitened, weather-worn edition of the man with whom Cheves had come down the Ohio. The long chase had drained his physical vigor until there was left only a shell of a body, within which burned a consuming fire. The fire was there, no doubt of that. Cheves saw the black eyes of the man snap and light with the ineradicable passion of hatred. Then, as suddenly as they had lit, so quickly did a veil of courtesy, a screen of polite recognition conceal the man's real feelings.

Cheves waited for the exposure. His mind covered a hundred details in the moment's silence. What would be Parmenter's concealment if he revealed Cheves? What was Parmenter's real status? And how had he managed to come as the accredited messenger from Kaskaskia, bringing with him two 'breeds from Vincennes?

"Well, do ye know him?" the irritable voice of Girty broke in.

"Yes," replied Parmenter, "I know him."

"Who is he?" insisted the ranger, the rancor of a long suppressed suspicion rendering him furious. Cheves waited for the final word.

"Messenger from Kaskaskia," announced Parmenter laconically. His sharp eyes sought the features of his fellow Virginian. The taint of mockery found its way to his face.

"What's his name, damn ye!" roared Girty, fast losing control of himself.

Here, thought Cheves, Parmenter must reach his rope's end.

"We are not exactly the best of friends, if you please, though we have known each other under many circumstances," Parmenter returned. "His name is Carstairs."

Utterly amazed, Cheves was attracted by a sound to the rear and turned in time to see Girty shut his mouth with an abrupt, vindictive snap. Hamilton had secured himself another pen and was chewing its point.

"That seems to clarify things, does it not, Girty!" he remarked curtly. "Now will both you gentlemen be kind enough to leave us? Foley, go along and show Parmenter quarters. Come back as soon as you're finished."

VIII

"BENEATH THE PAULIN"

Within the privacy of quarters Cheves essayed to untangle the twisted skein of events. Where had Parmenter gotten his knowledge of Cheves's pseudonym and rôle? How had he managed to get into the confidence of the Vincennes habitants and rangers? An obvious answer to this last was that Parmenter was as capable at masquerading as he. More so, in fact, Cheves decided grimly, since he now languished under a cloud of suspicion while Parmenter was unquestionably accepted at face value.

"Of course!" he said aloud to himself. "I should have known it sooner. He got my name when he followed the same trail from Ouiatanon. So much for that mystery."

Parmenter would lie. He could do nothing else. He would only succeed in compromising himself by trying to expose his fellow Virginian and the same applied to himself, Cheves knew. They were both in very much the same boat, their fates irretrievably mingled whether or not they willed it so. Cheves, looking up to the dark ceiling from bed, gave a short, hard laugh.

"Danny boy, we'll have a talk in the morning. 'Twill be to the point, likewise." And with that Cheves made an effort to dismiss the whole thing from his mind and go to sleep.

He did see Parmenter in the morning. The fort square was teeming with life when he left the mess after breakfast. Swarthy *coureurs* crossed and recrossed the square, now and then a more indolent habitant mixing in with the crowd. A few soldiers performed the detail work of policing. Girty strode toward the gate with a file of men behind him. And out in the center of all this life Cheves met Parmenter. By accident, it seemed, yet it was not accident, for Cheves had been maneuvering some time to get his man in this position. He came up from Parmenter's rear.

"Well, Danny?" he whispered.

Parmenter whirled around, his eyes startled, then he caught hold of himself.

"Thought I might stab you in the back, or somethin' like that, eh?" queried Cheves. "That's your way, not mine. When I get ready, 'twill be fairly and squarely."

Parmenter thrust his hands nearer the weapons in his belt. Alertness hardened his eyes.

"What's your idea in followin' me eight hundred miles and tryin' to do me up?" Cheves continued. "Who gave you permission to leave the expedition?"

"You ought to know without bein' told," growled Parmenter. The thought of his grievances began to inflame his morose soul and set his nerves to dancing and jumping with rage. "I've stood all I'm a-goin' to! I ain't makin' no bones about it either. One way or another, I'm after you, and I'll get you. 'Twouldn't do me any good if they found you out here and shot you. I want to do that with my own hands. One way or another, Cheves, I'm a-goin' to hurt you so bad you'll never get over it. Take warnin' now!"

"Thanks for the warnin'," returned Cheves, hard and dry. "Knife and knife it's to be? Very well, I can watch out for myself."

It was a queer thing, these men facing each other with the similitude of friendship in their eyes and the anger of death in their hearts, with a half dozen Britishers looking on, unaware of the significance of the tableau.

"Let me say this," remarked Cheves. "I've held off many times from hurtin' you when cause was given me. You're from Virginia and so am I. But I can't disregard it any longer. It's your life or mine, and I've work to do. Next time we fight I shall kill you."

The coldness and deliberate finality of this tone seemed to quench, in a measure, the other's anger. Bereft of that, Parmenter's face seemed only thoroughly weak and vicious, capable of any crime.

"One thing more," continued Cheves. "You'll be questioned about Kaskaskia by Hamilton. Tell him the story I did." And he gave, in a brief phrase or two, the message he had given the governor. "Best to hang together on that much of it," he added, "or neither of us will accomplish our designs. Both be shot for nothin', then." And with that he walked off.

He saw Eltinge wave a hand from the guard room, and a moment later the lieutenant had come up.

"Let's take a turn about the parade," he suggested. "Must have fresh air and exercise. I'd give a hundred pounds if I might go north with the next fur brigade. It's a silly state of affairs, is it not, when a man comes seven thousand miles to have a bit of adventure and then finds himself in a job like that of a clerk in a London counting house."

They went through the gate. It was another warm day in Detroit town. The sun fell across the hard packed earth of the parade ground and blended its warmth with the breeze coming off the river. A scattering of blanketed Indians were sitting against the fort wall, wrapped to the

202

ears. A larger number of them than he had previously seen, Cheves thought. Eltinge offered a cigar to Cheves and lit another himself.

"Look at me," said the lieutenant with ill-concealed bitterness. "I might as well be a London hack driver for all the West and North I've seen. King and duty! King and duty! Damn, I've had my share of king and duty! I want active service. Now you," he said, taking a vigorous pull on the cigar, "are seeing things. I'd give five hundred pounds to be in your boots right now. More than that. Give all I had to have come down the Ohio and up the Wabash. Man! Think of it!"

It was a rather amazing outburst for a phlegmatic Englishman to make, Cheves reflected. Now, *he* would give nearly anything he possessed to be out of his boots and into those of Eltinge — for the brief time in which he might come closer to the heart of the fort and learn a certain indispensable secret which was all that held him back. He needed desperately to get that secret and clear out. No telling when the real Kaskaskia coureur might turn up.

"University man, with a backwoods training! Lord, what a life you're having," Eltinge began afresh. "Me, a-rusting in this infernal village. And now Hamilton's figuring on a fresh expedition south, and I can't go along."

Cheves came to a sudden alert attention and flicked the ashes from the cigar. "No fun in a scalping expedition," he said casually. "That's bloody work. If he were going south to Vincennes with regulars, it would be different."

"That's what it's to be. Girty and Hamilton and Dejean had a long powwow over it last night. Tonight they're having another. Isn't just decided yet. But the governor has his heart set on it."

Dejean! Ralston's contemptuous, bitter description of the

man occurred to Cheves. Dejean, then, was the fat, gross figure in the large chair. So they contemplated an expedition southward toward Clark? Here was the secret for which he had tarried so long. But he must find more about it.

"Of course," he said in an off-hand manner, "it will be slow and cumbersome with regular troops. It will have to be a small detachment if they expect to make time."

"It will be," returned Eltinge confidently. "Why, Carstairs, we've hardly enough men to keep this garrison. A good strong force of Americans coming up some night could nearly wipe us out. It's ticklish to think of. And now they want to weaken us further by taking a wild chase down the Wabash to the Illinois country. Let 'em take care of themselves down there. Detroit's the queen of the Northwest, just as Cadillac said it was sixty years ago. Lose Detroit and we lose the whole country. Yet I'd give anything to go along!"

"Girty ought to be due to go to the border settlements pretty soon with a war party," Cheves offered as a mild comment, trying another tack. "Time they were sending some old-hand ranger out. We don't know what's taking place east of the Scioto any more."

"You know," and the young lieutenant said this in a very hesitating way, "I am not wholly in favor of letting Indians help us fight our quarrels. It isn't exactly in the blood of Englishmen to fight in that fashion."

They had made their detour and were back within the gate again.

"Duty once more," continued Eltinge bitterly. "Garrison duty!"

"Your turn will come," said Cheves, trying to console him. With that they parted, the lieutenant headed for the guard room.

And so will mine, Cheves thought, going back through the open gate. Tonight they were to hold a council in the governor's room again? Through some means he must hear what they had to say. Time was getting short, and the strands of inevitable exposure seemed to draw tighter about him. Clark, eight hundred miles away, waited to hear his report.

For the best part of the afternoon he wandered around the village and sat on a stringer of King's Wharf, watching the canoes furrow up and down the river. There was in him a great desire to see Katherine Ralston.

Night came and the hurried forms of men sliding through the door of the guard room, heading for the council chamber. Cheves, loafing in a dark corner of the fort, saw them enter, one by one, counting them until he had reached six. After that no more went through. Now, if he could get past the guard room, he felt secure in his concealment for the hall leading to the governor's room opened out at intervals into storerooms, and it so happened that the door of the council chamber abutted upon just such a storeroom. Bales of goods, trading trinkets, and other items of barter were stored there. It would be no great job to find concealment once he reached the place.

He crept along the wall, in the shadows, toward the entrance to the guard room. A sentry paused on the corner bastion twenty feet above but did not see him. A door opened from officers' quarters, and a pale dim candle light seeped out as a man emerged, buttoned a jacket, and closed the door behind him. Cheves flattened against the wall and kept still. The officer cut across the court toward the guard room; the door opened and another similarly thin wave of light flickered. The officer hesitated on the threshold. Cheves was only a scant thirty feet from him.

"Hey, O'Malley," called the officer softly. "Come out and have a bit of fresh air. It's my turn now, but I'm cursed if I want to go in there yet. Let's walk a bit. I've a bottle of Medford rum that might int'rest you."

The offer drew the officer of the guard out into the night, leaving the guard room door open. This was the thrice golden opportunity for which Cheves looked. He ran softly forward, crossed the threshold, and went swiftly through the room, got into the hallway, and closed the inner door behind him.

He went perhaps twenty feet down the dark passageway before striking another door, opened and closed it behind him, and continued on, being now in a sudden bayou of the hall wherein were barrels of lead shot from the Illinois country and the mines of the Wisconsin area. He slid through another door and came at last to the room of supplies, beyond which was the governor's chamber. It was perfectly black and that was protection for him. He got closer to the door, beneath which streamed a thin line of light and through which came the undertone of speech — heavy, irritated, passionate speech. Girty talking again!

But Cheves had yet to provide safety for himself. He crept back from the door and felt about with hands and feet, coming in contact with a heavy, tarred canvas paulin such as were used to cover canoe loads in wet weather. It was jammed between other bales of goods. By much fumbling labor, he straightened it in such a fashion that he might crawl under, still between the bales. It was protection of a sort. Then he crept back to the door.

The voice now audible was that of Dejean. Cheves recognized the heavy, dull tones.

". . . Evidence not good enough, Girty," he was saying.

"I'd line him up against the wall and shoot him if we had the least scrap of evidence. There is none."

"Gentlemen, keep to the topic." It was the impatient voice of Hamilton. "Can we spare that many soldiers from our garrison to strengthen the southern forts?"

"I say no," Dejean voted. "We can't weaken Detroit. What's the danger in the south? I've heard of none. Let them fend for themselves. No great damage done if they fall from Indian attacks. Detroit must be kept strong. Why, a force of a hundred Americans or four or five hundred savages could wipe us off the map if they had the chance of surprise and weak defense. We're criminally weak! Damn the commandant at Montreal that he can't send us another company."

"Hark!" said Girty.

Cheves caught the shuffle of a foot. He sprang for the paulin and got beneath it. The next moment the door was jerked open and light flooded out, reaching vaguely back to the pile of bales. Cheves guessed, rather than saw, that Girty stood peering across the threshold.

"Oh, come back here," growled Dejean.

After a bit the door closed. Cheves waited another good ten minutes before venturing back to his post.

"Weakness it may be, but I'm responsible for the whole country," Hamilton was arguing. "Detroit's in no danger." His voice fell to calmer tones, and Cheves lost a part of it. Then it rose again. "Detroit's in no danger while the southern forts are abominably weak."

A silence, then argument, then rebuttal. It was a long while before he could again catch the threads of conversation. When he did, it was to note a new and strangely familiar voice. Then a quick, near paralyzing shock of concern and surprise struck him as he heard the name of Ralston mentioned.

"What have you found?" It was Hamilton who put the question. "Isn't Ralston one of them? Wasn't he responsible for that last ranger's disappearance? — Isn't he a rebel? You've been working with them for two months now and haven't given me a jot of information. Haven't you found anything?"

"I haven't found anything yet, sir." It was only by the questioning silence of the room that Cheves was able to hear the slow, cold, deliberate answer. "No cause for you to take them in. No proof of anything whatsoever. They've tended to their business."

At that point Cheves recognized the voice as belonging to John Harkness, the lieutenant and right hand man of Colonel Ralston.

"Must be that girl. She's been influencing you. Damned strange about that family! That's why I gave you the job this spring. And you haven't found a thing. It's hardly believable."

"Didn't I manage to put your fingers on the rest of the malcontents? Haven't we got them nearly all weeded out? Haven't I done good work, sir?" The cold voice rose to a metallic, angry pitch.

"Yes," replied the governor. "You've done such good work that this singular ineffectiveness of yours recently doesn't seem right. And I'm morally certain the Ralstons are the most dangerous enemies we've got here in Detroit."

"I have found nothing, sir," replied John Harkness obstinately. "But I've got my eyes on another man, within this fort. Give me three days and I shall turn him over to you."

"Who is he?"

"I beg not to be asked that until I can bring him to you with the proof."

Again the talk fell to a long jumble of questions and answers, and Cheves felt that the conference was drawing to a close. It was just as well. He had heard all he could assimilate. This revelation of the duplicity of Harkness left his mind racing along a new path. Harkness, then, was a British intelligence officer and as such had been responsible for the Americans deported and executed around Detroit town.

Yet why had he lied thus to his commandant, reporting that he knew of no subversive acts on the part of the Ralstons, when he was the full confidant of all of the colonel's plans? In the mind of Cheves there was a swift answer to this. The Lord bless Katherine Ralston. She had turned a British officer off the straight path of his duty. Hamilton had made a shrewder surmise than he knew.

A general stir and scraping of chairs forced Cheves back beneath the paulin. The doors opened, and the officers marched out one by one, retreating down the hall to the guard room. Again Cheves took a swift and dangerous chance. Crawling out from concealment, he followed the last man at the interval of a room's length. The gloom of the passageway made this possible. When he came to the guard room, both inner and outer doors stood open, and the chamber itself was empty. He saw, through the vista thus formed, the small group disappear in the direction of officers' quarters, swallowed up in the night. He stepped into the guard room, closed the inner door behind him, and walked slowly out into the court, to come face to face with the lieutenant of the guard who advanced out of the night.

The latter appeared a bit flustered, as though caught off his post.

"Pardon," said Cheves. "I came by here thinking to find Lieutenant Eltinge."

"Oh. Dare say you'll find him in quarters." The officer got within the guard room and unceremoniously closed the door on Cheves.

IX

"MAELSTROM"

The lieutenant was not in quarters which was just as well, for Cheves had a great amount of thinking to do and wanted nothing so much as time and solitude. He helped himself to one of Eltinge's cigars and settled in a camp chair.

His mission in Detroit was ended. He had secured the essential knowledge that a company of men was being dispatched south. Likewise, he had secured a hundred other tag ends of information for which Clark thirsted. It had been an unusually successful trip, and there was no further reason for postponing departure.

No reason? Frankness asserted itself. There were Katherine Ralston and her father, two very good reasons for tarrying. These people lived on the rim of a crater, sheltered only by the efforts of a man who had betrayed his duty. And Harkness, to bolster up his difficult position, had dangled the prospects of another victim before Hamilton's covetous eyes. That victim was to be Cheves.

Yet how could Harkness incriminate him without involving the Ralstons? He did not see. A recollection of the hard-bitten face and the direct, unfriendly eyes of the Englishman left him with the conviction that here was a man to deal with. Very dangerous and with unknown sources of power in reserve. The fact that he now played a double game made him only the more dangerous. He was no callow youth, but a desperate, grown soldier, playing the grimmest rôle of all.

There was also Parmenter to contend with. There was Girty sulking about, waiting only for the slightest misstep. Above all, the real messenger from Kaskaskia must shortly be on his way. That meant inevitable exposure. In all, the situation had become too badly tangled for one man to forecast.

The promptings of his conscience impelled him to pick up the pistol and holster lying on the cot and start immediately southward, while an inner feeling of loyalty, mingled with some other emotion he did not care to analyze, rose to combat the first impulse. And there he sat, undecided and distressed, trying not to think of the dismal future for the Ralstons which seemed to him inevitable.

He rose and went out, and the fresh air made him feel better. After all, was it not his duty to remain and see the war council? Some new factor might develop which would be highly important for Clark to know. Ah, there was a solution! He recognized immediately that it was but a subterfuge, that he sought now to deceive himself. This genuinely distressed him.

The tramp of a sentry, twenty feet above, echoed evenly down. The night was serene, the sky luminous with stars, and the moon riding high behind a passing net of clouds. He had come by the closed main gate, drawing full on the fragrant remnant of the Virginia cigar, the tip of which glowed in the night. Turning a corner, he started down the north side of the court, locked in the struggle which has oppressed men since the beginning of time. It wore on him worse than the combined hardships of his journey.

The roar of a pistol filled the court and thundered around the stockade. The bullet thudded into a nearby log, not a foot from Cheves's head. It was as if a breath of air had been expelled against his face. He jerked back and stood on tiptoe at the same time as he heard the crack of the sentry's musket changing positions from shoulder to charge.

"Who's there?" bawled the guard from the bastion top.

That bullet had come from officers' quarters, Cheves swiftly noted. By chance his head had been turned that way, and he had seen the red finger of flame. It was from the room next to his own, he thought. The door of the guard room jerked open and the lieutenant ran out; at the same time men popped from quarters. Cheves, eyes still riveted on the point from which the bullet had come, saw a door open and a man slip out and mingle with the other approaching figures.

"What's up?" called the lieutenant to the sentry.

"A shot, sir, man in the court alone."

"What's the matter?" the officer called, seeing Cheves.

"It's nothin'," returned Cheves laconically. "Probably someone cleaning his gun after dark. No damage. Just a bit more lead in the stockade."

"Very strange. Did you notice the direction it came from?"

"Not at all. Was just goin' along with me head in the air, thinkin' of other things. It's nothin' at all, Lieutenant." He scanned the circle and found, as he expected, Parmenter. The moon slid hastily out to a clearer sky, and Cheves got a better view of his fellow Virginian. The face was drawn to an expression of veiled unconcern, but the restless, bitter eyes, they were the sole testimony Cheves asked. He turned away from the small group. "It's nothin'," he repeated with impatience. "Have none of you heard a pistol shot before?"

212

He made for quarters and once there got quickly to bed. The struggle had been briefly terminated. He would stay now.

He woke to a day of sullen and fitful contrasts. A gathering haze blanketed the town and the wind, toward mid-morning, died away, leaving a murky sun and a torrid fog to torture and bake the inhabitants. It was insufferable within the fort. Even the stolid Indians, now cluttering up the court, suffered visibly, sweat rolling down daubed faces. Yet they clung to their dignity and suffered rather than cast the swathing blankets from their bodies. Dressed for ceremony in a white man's fort, they must so remain.

Cheves endured it as long as he could then left the fort and started for the river. There, at least, he would find cool water. He crossed the parade and was almost suffocated by the waves of heat reflected from the packed earth. It made his head swim and he was glad to gain the partial protection of a narrow alley. A short way down the cool interior of a wine shop drew him in; it was some relief. He ordered a glass of port and sipped it in grateful leisure. On the point of going and continuing his journey river-ward, he saw Eltinge and motioned for him to enter.

"Gad, this is insufferable!" panted the lieutenant, well-nigh dazed. "Nothing like it since I've been here. We're due for a heat storm soon enough. Sooner the better. I'm near done for." He wiped a vagrant trickle of sweat from his forehead.

"I'm headed for the river," vouchsafed Cheves. "Come along. We'll have some comfort there."

The girl came up, but Eltinge shook his head.

"*Non, merci,* no liquor on a day like this. To the river?

213

Not a bad idea. Probably find most of the town there. Well, let's go. I've got to be back at three o'clock. My turn of guard again. I hope the storm breaks by then."

They passed out and continued down the alley. At the first intersection they came upon an old Frenchman, bent and rickety, hobbling along. His mouth hung wide open, and fear was visibly stamped on his wrinkled face.

"Mon Dieu!" he gasped as they went by him, and immediately thereafter clapped a hand to his heart.

A woman ran down the street, got hold of the fellow's hand, and led him back to a house.

"Be somebody dead before this is over," panted Eltinge. "Never a thing like it before, in my time."

Even then, as Cheves surveyed the eastern skyline, he saw a black mass of clouds forming up.

"Won't be long," he said and was aware of a tension in his body. He had come near to shouting that last phrase and was vaguely surprised at himself.

Eltinge gave him a curious glance. A small group of men were bunched up at the next intersection and seemed to be busy over a prostrate form in the roadway.

"Hello," said Eltinge. "Somebody's gone under. I knew it."

He turned toward the group, and Cheves followed. The Frenchmen parted as the Englishman came up, revealing Danny Parmenter kneeling in the center. Pillowed on his thigh was the white, drawn face of Colonel Ralston.

"What's the trouble?" demanded Eltinge, assuming authority.

Parmenter looked up and saw them. A brief flicker of excitement animated his face as he recognized Cheves.

"Old gentleman here went under to the heat," he responded. "Just happened along as he toppled over."

"I thought so," said Eltinge.

Cheves nodded impassively. "It would be wise to get the man out of the sun," he offered in a noncommittal manner. "Come on, Eltinge, let's get to the river before we melt."

Parmenter shot him another quick, triumphant glance and turned back to his charge. Willing Frenchmen gave him aid, and they picked up the colonel and headed for the nearest wine shop.

"Cold-blooded chap, aren't you?" said Eltinge in a kind of admiration. "Life doesn't seem worth a plugged ha'penny to you rangers."

"Ain't time to worry about it," responded the Virginian. "Trouble enough to keep your own skin." Internally he boiled.

Here was an unfortunate circumstance! Parmenter would know soon enough of the Ralston residence. Ah, there was an opportunity for injury, and Parmenter would see it in a flash. Trust his diabolic treachery. Why hadn't he killed the man before and saved all this untold accumulation of animus and certain misfortune? If harm came to the Ralstons — then Parmenter should pay.

They went through the gate and walked out upon the puncheons of King's Wharf. No townspeople were there. They had gone to the beaches on both sides of the stockade, where they might swim.

"Just seeing water makes me feel better," remarked Eltinge. "Gad, I never want to be as hot as this again."

"Just as bad as this in the Illinois country sometimes," offered Cheves, leading the way to a seat on a stringer within the small shade afforded by the wall. "When you have to cut through the prairie covered with hemp and grape, it's pretty bad. Heat stays in the tangle, and a man swelters till he's like raw beefsteak."

"That's different. You're out doing something. Here you

215

just sit passive. Might as well be a huckster in Whitechapel."

The black cloud soared out of the eastward at a tremendous pace. A half hour ago it had been only a suggestion. Now its ragged edges swept the sky. Far off came the tremor and report of thunder.

"Storm's about due," said Eltinge, twisting his neck in acute misery. "There's the wind."

The sun was blotted out in the space of a minute. The mass rushed on, first showing the gray-shot edges, then appeared the solid opaque center. A quick wind struck them. In five minutes it grew perceptibly cooler. Cheves saw the people on the beaches come out of the water and begin a general hurried movement toward town. Came a crash and rumble of thunder, and the reverberating roll of the echo. A strong gust of wind hit them, wind cold enough to be comfortable.

"I think we'd better go back," said Eltinge, a trace of nervousness in his voice. "I'm not used to this. We'll be rained on shortly."

" 'Twill be worse than that," assented Cheves. They got up and returned through the gate.

It was but mid-afternoon, yet from the darkness it might have been twilight. The whole sky was filled with black, twisting clouds. A patter of rain struck the dusty alley.

"Here she comes!"

A root-like flame of lightning flashed and disappeared and then came the roar and tumult of the ensuing thunder crash, rolling and booming like the cataclysmic fall of mountains. The wind sharpened, and the rain came in larger drops. The two men hurried up the alley, being met and passed by sober-faced inhabitants. One man shouted out a phrase of unintelligible French to them from an open door then slammed it behind him. A candle light appeared through

216

a window and was, the next moment, snuffed out.

They crossed the parade in driving rain and went through the gate as a huge clap of thunder shook the earth and deafened their hearing. It was black night. The storm took on a deeper, more sinister note as the two men gained the shelter of their room.

Eltinge tarried only long enough to put on a dry tunic and buckle on a pistol.

"My turn at guard," he said and went out the door, leaving Cheves alone.

The things that fate accomplished! What was he to do in the face of this last dilemma, Cheves thought rapidly. By this time, in all likelihood, Danny Parmenter had wormed his insinuating way into the graces of the Ralstons. Oh, why hadn't he told the whole story of the man's defection to them? He supposed that wouldn't have been possible. He could not have done it and still kept his self respect. Yet how much easier it would have made his own position here in a hostile land. Now he must rack his brains and forestall the man's trickery, for Parmenter had sworn to hurt him until he would die of the pain. Well, here was the chance: Parmenter confiding to the Ralstons, duping them under the guise of friendship and old acquaintance, weaving his own designs into their fears.

How was he to prevent this? Better to have shot the man down in cold blood than to imagine all the injury he could do now. Cheves grew angrier and more gloomy. The tremendous onslaught of the storm outside, the crash and roll of the thunder, the drive of the rain against the door, the shriek of the wind, the whole fierce and resentful tempo seemed to communicate its surge and animus to him. He got up and paced across the small quarters, unable to stem the slowly rising rage. It was a cold, implacable rage such

217

as he had experienced but once before in his life, and that on the occasion of a particularly bloody border massacre. He had gone into the woods, at the head of an avenging Kentucky company, in just such a mood.

Of a sudden he reached out for a belt and pistol, strapped it around him, then struggled into a great coat. Time had come to use ball and shot. Here, at last, one strand of the tangled skein must be cut in twain. As he put on a cape and started for the door, a sinister chill of apprehension invaded him. Things went wrongly, he knew, at the Ralston place.

He did not open the door. It was pushed wide before him under the impetus of a newcomer's hand and the drive of the storm which streaked across the small room snuffed out the candle.

"Pardon," said a cold voice. "Didn't mean to create such a disturbance."

The door closed, and Cheves fumbled to relight the candle. When once again it guttered and flared, illuminating the room, the Virginian turned to identify this sudden visitor. It was John Harkness who leaned against the door, one hand to the knob. Bundled up as the Englishman was, Cheves made out only the slit of the thin, restrained mouth, the arrogant nose, and the harsh eyes.

"Take a chair," said Cheves.

Harkness shook his head and stared at the Virginian. Internal excitement of some sort began to work at his face.

"What can I do for you?" asked Cheves, impatience cropping up. He had work to do.

"Going out?"

"I thought to." Perhaps this man had come upon an errand of capture. Cheves hunched his body to loosen the great coat and render the pistol and holster more accessible.

218

Harkness noted this movement and shook his head. At the same time he unbuttoned his coat to reveal an identical service weapon.

"That's what I've come for," he said, with a significant stab of a forefinger.

"I don't understand," said Cheves.

"You and I . . . got to settle this . . . out of court." The words came in a sketchy phrase or two, lacking coherence. Harkness seemed to realize it and suddenly jerked up his head. "Here," he began afresh, "there's no use in beating around the bush. You and I've got to fight this out. One man goes under. Understand?"

"Only a part of it."

"I'll tell you more, then. Last night I turned around to look back when I got out of the conference. Was half way across the court when I looked. Saw you coming out of the guard room. You overheard that conference."

Cheves nodded. Little good to deny it. Moreover, this man had some other plan up his sleeve.

"Well," said Harkness, raising his chin to a higher, more stubborn level. "You know the part I play then." Here bitterness asserted itself. "I guess you might call me a traitor or a renegade. But you know the reason!"

Cheves inclined his head.

"A soldier has no right to fall in love," continued Harkness. "Damn it all, a high-bred woman has no right in this country. What was I to do? She doesn't stand the ghost of a show if her father is discovered. I've done the best I could, by both sides. Now you come and, damn your soul, she likes you! Oh, I saw that. Well, I've not perjured myself, and eaten dirt, and lost my self respect just to have you step in. I've done these things for a certain reward, and I shall have it. I'm desperate now. You'll have to fight me. One of us goes under!"

Cheves straightened. Here was a plain and simple call to duel. He bowed ceremoniously.

"I'm at your service, sir, at any time," he replied courteously.

"Now!" Harkness closed his mouth with a snap. "We'll have it out, while all this infernal racket is going on. I warn you, I'm a dead shot, and I don't mean you shall cheat me."

"I have always been able to care for myself," Cheves observed, buttoning his coat. "Will you lead the way?"

They went out. The dead-black center of the storm clouds had passed over, but the light was grime colored and the rain was blinding. The thunder boomed and rolled; now and then a dart of lightning streaked across the heavens and ended in a fury of noise that stunned the earth. Harkness led the way through a corridor of the fort, traversed the mess hall past several storerooms, and stopped at the end of a blind passageway. Here was a small and heavily bolted door. Harkness shot back the draws and opened the barrier. It led out behind the fort, beyond the stockade, on the far end and wooded side of the town.

"One man only comes back through here," said Harkness on the threshold. He was forced to raise his voice to a higher pitch. "Things . . . well enough . . . you hadn't stepped in! Ralstons weren't doing any damage. Did my duty. Won't put my head in a noose to be cheated."

"It's quite a natural thought," observed Cheves. "I was on the verge of going out to do myself a little justice when you stepped in."

They advanced toward a grove of trees with the wind and the rain driving them along. A racketing clap of thunder shivered the ground. Not far off was the crash of falling limbs.

"Lightning strikes close," said Cheves. But the wind snatched the words from his mouth, and his companion, hearing only a faint sound of the voice, turned to catch what had been said.

Cheves shook his head. They went on. Funny, the Virginian mused, he could not find it in his heart to be angry at his challenger. The way of life got a man into positions from which he could not extricate himself by diplomacy. The only alternative then was to close the mind and the heart and fight it out. And Harkness, become ensnared in the tangle of a double rôle, had soldier-like elected to cut the mess squarely and cleanly in twain, falling back at last upon the simplest code he knew. Cheves admired him for this.

There came a diminution of the storm, and Cheves was aware that they had penetrated to the heart of a grove of oak, the branches of which were fending off in part the attacks of the storm.

"Remember, I'm a dead shot," Harkness warned, facing about. "Want to give you an even chance, but I'm going to kill you. Take your choice of positions."

The light, such as it was, broke slantwise through an opening of the oaks and fell on the north side of the glade. Cheves, by a sweep of the hand, elected the south side. It forced Harkness to stand in the small bit of light thus being more exposed, while Cheves stood in comparative darkness and was the harder to see.

"Leave top coats on, pistols beneath them to keep powder dry," said Harkness, reciting the conditions of the duel. "I'll walk over there, turn, and face you. When I turn, begin to count three, like this." He spaced three counts. "Fire when you've pronounced three. Is that satisfactory?"

Cheves nodded, walked to the spot of his choice, and turned.

"I'll wait here for you," he said.

Harkness tarried, seeming to have lost for the moment his usual decisive manner. "Damn it, man, you've forced this. No other way!"

"I'm not complaining."

"Can't be both of us. One has to get out of the way. I'll leave your body here. Some wood gatherer will pick it up in a day or so."

Cheves drew the gun from its holster and held it beneath his coat. Lacking free play, he unbuttoned the top of the garment.

"I'm ready," he said.

"You're not afraid," Harkness remarked, staring at the Virginian a moment with compressed lips. He walked a step, exclaimed, "Ready," and began a methodical advance toward his chosen place.

A shaft of lightning flashed across the sky and clearly revealed the scene. The earth jarred, and the world went black, leaving Cheves half blinded from the glare. A dozen streaks of red danced before his eyes. Nerves taut, he peered ahead and saw the dim form of Harkness halt, back turned. The Virginian got a firmer grip on his gun and waited.

Glare caught him, too, he thought. Then the Englishman swung, slow and careful, on his heel. Cheves saw his face lift in signal, the white standing out against the surrounding black. At that the Virginian began to count, dragging each syllable to create the proper pause.

He had not uttered "three" when the world rocked again and a larger, more blinding flash came and went, playing havoc with his vision.

"Three!" he shouted — and held his fire.

He could not see, and he would not waste his shot. Yet the etiquette of the situation demanded that he stand there,

222

immovable, and take the other's fire. Across the space came, after what seemed a life-long passage of time, a shout.

"I can't see!"

In answer Cheves returned a similar cry.

When at last his pupils began to distinguish objects on the far side of the glade, he noted that Harkness had folded his arms and was showing his back. A surge of admiration invaded Cheves. The man had plenty of courage. He waited until clearer eyed and sent over a second shout. At this Harkness wheeled and again jerked up his head. Again Cheves began the slow, monotonous count. At "three" he raised the pistol from its security, extended it, and took up the trigger's slack. He saw that Harkness came up slower, and he withheld final pressure until the man's gun was nearly horizontal. Then he fired.

He saw the flame from the answering gun, heard the echo of the answering shot, but felt no impact of bullet. His mind, coolly detached, seeming remote from excitement, decided that he had not been hit, and in an impersonal way he was glad it had been decided. Lifting back the flap of his coat, he replaced the pistol and advanced across the glade.

Harkness had fallen and now struggled to remain up on one elbow, but he was too far gone. The elbow slipped, and his head fell to the ground. The Virginian drew out a handkerchief.

"Where?" he asked.

Harkness stabbed a futile finger at his chest. Cheves started to open the tunic but was stopped by a sudden access of strength from the other man.

"Get away," he growled. A species of surprise flitted across his face. The quick energy ebbed away. "I'm done up. Get away."

When next the Virginian thrust his hand across the stained chest, the heart had stopped its labor. Cheves rose, retraced the way through the glade, and came upon the rear door. Getting within the fort once again, he shot the bolts and half ran down the passageway, wanting only to be out of this angle of the fort unwitnessed.

It seemed that the whole military population had gathered in the square, not under arms now standing any formation but milling and shifting from place to place, congregating into small groups, breaking up, and reforming. A high excitement was stamped on each face. Cheves halted on the edge of the crowd and sought to catch the tag ends of conversation that came up to him on the wind.

"Come down the Ohio, crossed seventy-five miles of Illinois prairie land, and surprised Rocheblave after dark. Kaskaskia's fallen!"

Cheves waited to hear no more. The thing feared had come to pass. Clark had struck, and the real messenger from Kaskaskia had come. Now he must get out.

His first thought was of the rear door. Turning, he strode toward the entrance to the mess room, whence he had just come. An officer bumped sharply against him and stared into his face, to break into a quick cry: "Eh, Carstairs? There you are! Stop!"

He had caught the Virginian on the shoulder. Cheves tore loose and broke into a run, but it seemed a dozen men sprang up on the instant. The shout went up: "Here's the spy!" and was born on fifty tongues at once. Confusion and riot! With the whole garrison pressing toward him, five feet to the mess room door, if he could only make it and stem the rush for a moment. He cast one swift glance behind and saw the rage-swollen face of Girty glaring at him. Then he turned and knocked the only remaining man out of his path with the butt of his gun, leaping ahead. No time for parley nor subterfuge. Get on! Fight it out!

A blow on the head felled him, senseless, to the hard earth of the court.

X

"THE BENEFIT OF LEARNING"

The fort prison, Cheves had learned earlier, was below ground, being truly a foul, dank, and oppressive kind of residence. This was the description of Eltinge: "You know," he had once confided to Cheves, "there's a lot of inhumanity in the world, and I'm sorry to see so much of it on the English side of the fence. That prison, now, it's abominable." And here it was that Cheves found himself.

A chilly drought of air swept diagonally across it, from one unseen vent to another. It was this drought, added to a moist yet hard earth, that brought him back to reality, aching of head, sore of limb. Yet the bludgeon-stroke had been more stunning than dangerous. He felt gingerly over his face and hair and found no blood. The old cut held fast under the strain. The sum total of this last accident was a huge, pounding pain over the eyes.

Acute discomfort brought him to his feet. There was one small beam of smudgy light coming from a corner grating, high up. It was the sort of window built not to admit light but to tantalize some light-hungry prisoner, and from appearances it was built level with the surface of the ground. The current of air did not come from that direction, so evidently there were other openings of a kind in this dreary

226

dungeon. Well, he might find some more comfortable spot to rest than here in the center of this black pit. He began a slow tour forward.

His arm, stretched ahead to fend against accidents, struck a log wall, wet to the touch. At another point when his fingers came in contact with a small, slimy body, it sent an unpleasant shock through him. Probably a snail. It was well that no illuminating light revealed the whole nastiness of this place. His foot struck softer material. Reaching down with inquisitive fingers, he felt a thick, wet fabric which parted under the stress of a gentle pull. Once, he decided, it had been a blanket.

By now he had come to the unknown source of air. As far as he could determine, it was simply a small tunnel, entering at the bottom of the prison area and going back and upward to the surface. It was too small, his foot determined, for any effort at escape. Continuing on, he arrived beneath the window, some ten feet above his head. His exploring fingers seeking everywhere found small gouged niches in the logs, ascending at intervals of a foot. Some poor lost soul previously jailed had tried to attain freedom. The Virginian thrust a toe in a lower aperture and found a finger hold farther up. A small excitement stirred in him and gave zest to the discovery. A bare chance, here, for escape. His groping fingers found a higher niche, and he drew himself up.

He had climbed four feet perhaps, each succeeding hole becoming smaller and more untenable, when his hand found only the unbroken surface of a log. This, then, was the end of the attempt at freedom; the man had given up. Poor devil! Doubtless gone under and now an unknown bit of wreckage in an unknown grave. The Virginian let himself down, reluctantly, and continued his explorations.

Opposite the window the log wall left off to admit a heavy, spiked, and bolted door, solid save for a small aperture some six inches square. Some blacksmith had spent many laborious hours in fashioning that impregnable barrier. Well, nothing to do save seek the least uncomfortable spot and play 'possum.

As far as he could determine, the foot of the door was as good a place as any, so there he sat and stared into the dark. He had not rested five minutes before coming to a characteristic and irrevocable decision: he would again stake his future on one last desperate fling of chance. As events now stood, he saw but one future, that of being lined up against the outer wall of the fort and shot. It seemed inevitable. If such were the outlook, no possible risk he might take could be either rash or wholly past hope. Born and bred to the idea of loyalty, he believed in the fulfillment of whatever mission entrusted to him. Here, at the low ebb of personal fortune, he did not so much choose the idea of overpowering the jailer from a hasty temperament as from the hard shove of his clear, ruthless logic. He had failed to escape, and he carried a precious knowledge that his chief needed. Now he must atone for that failure.

The light gradually merged with the inner shadows until at last there was no light. At some point in the evening he slept. The hard, damp ground caused his slumber to be fitful. Once a rat crawled its lethargic way across his hand, and again the current of air momentarily shifted its course and brought him a fresher stench. But his final wakening was due to a steady advance of footsteps down the hall and the scrape of a key in the prison door. On the instant he had sprung up, fully alive, mind racing over the coming struggle. A quick blow on the temple, or a swift arm about the throat, and after that it would not be so difficult to find his way down the passage to the small rear door of the fort. His body curved and his muscles became hard, predatory cords. The door swung back. An arm thrust through a smoking lantern. Behind it Cheves saw the troubled face of Lieutenant Eltinge. Cheves relaxed, and his hands fell to his sides.

"Carstairs," called Eltinge softly.

"Here."

"Gad, but this is a foul place to put a white man," grumbled the officer. "Inhuman!" He supported a bundle in one hand. This he gave to Cheves, stepped within the prison vault, and closed the heavy door behind him. "Something to eat here," he said. "Hurry! Get after it!"

He put the lantern on the ground. Cheves knelt and unwrapped the cloth and found a piece of meat, a loaf of black bread, and a bottle of wine. He wasted no time but fell to them immediately. The events of the last few hours had famished him.

The lieutenant looked on, clucked his tongue, sighed, and ended by striding back and forth from the lantern's light to the farther gloom and back again, casting troubled glances at the Virginian, sighing, and resuming the march. Once he forced the door back and looked down the passage. He watched the Virginian swallow the last of the wine with mingled sadness and admiration on his fair, boyish face. It was easy to see that he fought with tempting devils and that the older man came near supplying the image of a resourceful, fearless Western god in his young, adventure-craving heart.

"You'll be lined up and shot!" he blurted out finally. "Lined up and shot like a common criminal!"

Cheves silently cursed him for entering the vault out of friendliness. How could he go on with his plan when a man approached him on honor?

"Shot like an ordinary criminal! Isn't as if you were an illiterate ranger. There's enough of them to spare. But a university man! Shot! Oh, that's impossible! We can't afford to do that. Better kill a hundred ordinary fellows!"

Eltinge spoke with the intense loyalty of class, mingled with a bitterness. Here was the major problem of his young life. Here at last he had come to grips with a stern, stark phase of the primitive and warring West. Manfully he fought through to his conclusions.

"Why didn't you leave before? Why did you wait? 'Twas a blunder. Your partner got away."

So Parmenter had slipped out. Once again a chill of apprehension and foreboding thrust its spidery fingers up Cheves's back. Something had gone wrong at the Ralston place.

"You'll not do us any hurt by escaping," Eltinge went on. "You Americans will never get Detroit. It's too far from your base, and you'd not get up this way far without our being warned in advance. So, no matter what you know about the fort and the town, it'll not help Clark." He was arguing more to himself than to Cheves.

"And whatever you know about our future movements in the southwell, that doesn't matter either. You can't stop us. We'll retake Kaskaskia shortly. You can't fight us on equal ground. We're too powerful. We've got millions to your thousands."

A long silence followed which Eltinge ended by a brief snap of his fingers. He opened and stared through the door again and listened with a warning eye turned on Cheves. Then he swung around, unbuckled his pistol belt with its shot and powder pouch, and handed it to the Virginian.

"Strap it on," he commanded.

Cheves, who had seen the processes of the man's mind go on, knew well enough what this meant.

"How will you clear yourself?" he asked, taking the belt.

"There wasn't any man of the guard available to bring down your food, so I did it. They don't think I amount to much . . . the officers don't." He laughed bitterly at this. "They think I'm just a young lad. It won't be any trouble at all to make them believe I was overpowered. 'Just boy foolishness and carelessness,' is what they'll say and let it go at that. I'll probably get a few hard words from Hamilton, and that's all. Oh, I know how I stand around here. That's why they won't let me go on expeditions. Too young! Too inexperienced!" He spat the words out with venom then came suddenly back to the business at hand and stripped off his great coat. "Let's change these. Cap, too."

The transfer was effected swiftly.

"Now listen closely," directed Eltinge. "Go straight up this corridor, take the stairs, and open the door on the first landing you reach. This avoids the mess room and puts you into another passage. Follow it down and you'll get to a door, unbolt it and you're out of the fort. Only one chance in a thousand that you'll find anyone in that passage. Nothing but stores there. At the door I've put a pouch with some food in it, jerked meat and bread."

"Eltinge," queried Cheves, "why do you take all this trouble and put yourself in so much danger?"

The young lieutenant's eyes sparkled. Here, at last, he was involved in direct adventure, and it seemed to affect him like old wine. "Because," he said briefly, "it isn't right, under any kind of war law, to shoot a good university man. There's only a few of us left in the world, and we've got to hang together. Some day, after this war's over, we'll have a few things to say about running governments. It may seem like treachery now, but we'll both be glad when we've quit fighting." It was idealism — sincere boyish idealism. Eltinge suddenly went shy. "Come, no tosh. One more thing. You'll have to mark me up. Let go with your fist and strike me in the eye. Got to leave me with some physical evidence of struggle."

Cheves said nothing; there was nothing to say. In his life he had met and encompassed a variety of strange happenings and out of this had grown a philosophy that was compounded largely of quiet acceptance when tight situations of a kind involved him. His mouth closed tighter. To save Eltinge suspense he shot a direct, hard blow at the slightly pale but entirely resolute face. It landed flush on the right eye. Eltinge clapped a hand up and staggered back. Cheves buttoned the coat and pulled down the cap.

"What time was it when you came down?" he asked.

"Ten o'clock," responded the lieutenant, still pressing his eye. "You'd better lose no time. Good luck."

"Good luck yourself," replied Cheves, and that was all.

He closed the door tightly and locked it, throwing the key in some dark recess farther on. It would take them an hour or better to find that key or to unhinge that door. Then he set out down the passage, swinging the lantern before. He went up the stairs and got through the first door, as directed. He was back, now, in the passage traversed earlier in the day. At the door he found the pouch. This he slung up, got out of the door, and closed it behind him.

Blacker than pitch, this night. Against it the lantern gave but little assurance, yet it was sufficient to keep him from breaking his neck in some unexpected ditch. Doubtless there was a guard on both of the rear corner bastions, but from experience Cheves knew they would be within the shelter of the blockhouses, evading the driving, miserable rain. Discipline, Cheves had decided earlier, was somewhat lax in the fort.

He struck out through the first grove of woods where he had fought his duel, got beyond it, and thence turned south, heading for the Ralston farm. He pronounced, as he went, a silent blessing upon Eltinge. Only a man untouched and unscarred by the hard suspicions and crafty deceits of frontier life could have done so unselfish a deed.

XI

"DAN FELLOWS"

Beyond the southwestern angle of the fort, the woods fell away for a space and the wind, coming northeasterly across the open waters of Lake St. Clair, rushed over the easy rise of the French farms in a gust of fury, bringing with it the lash and sting of rain. The lantern guttered and threatened to snuff out and Cheves, having great need of its small comfort, sheltered it beneath his great coat. Travel was tedious and difficult. Long before he had embarked upon the main road from the fort, a sweat covered his skin, while his hands and face were whipped raw.

He guessed it was near to midnight when finally he stumbled upon the side road and came through the Ralston orchard. A tentative use of the lantern revealed the pathway leading by the barn to the house. Thus he came to the small porch which fended the front door. There was no light within, but then it was long past time for bed. He stepped up and rapped strongly against the panel and waited, turning his back to the bitter wind. After an interval he rapped again, with greater force. This storm was near to drowning out all lesser noises.

But, with the passage of fifteen minutes, broken by as much effort as he could effect against the door and productive of no results, he decided to force it and go inside. The lock was not turned, and this struck him strangely enough, too, in a country where precautions were not usually overlooked. The living room was still warm with the last embers in the fireplace. His lantern showed some evidence of disorder. A book or two tumbled from the shelf to the floor. The doors to the kitchen, to the second story, and to the bedroom off the living room were wide open.

"Colonel Ralston!" This time Cheves raised his voice high enough to wake the sleepers.

And still he got no answer. In sudden impatience he walked to the bedroom. This, he was certain, belonged to the colonel. On the threshold he thrust forward the lantern and inspected the interior. The bed, neatly made, was unwrinkled and unoccupied. Here again he saw evidence of disorder, private letters, clothing, and a book or two thrown in a big heap in the center of the floor.

All the while a rising, premonitory thrust of fear had been working in the Virginian. He turned and made his way into the kitchen in a few swift strides. Again the same spectacle of wide-flung closet doors and small disorder with no human occupancy. There was left now but one other place, the second floor. Cheves was loath to go above, for that was Katherine's domain. He thrust his shoulders through the stairway door and called again.

No answer. He went up, now thoroughly aroused, and found himself in the single room which constituted the whole upper part of the house. The lantern revealed the distinct feminine touch of this room. Yet here again there spoke the same story, disorder, as though indicating sudden flight.

Sudden flight! Now why had he thought of that? Cheves turned on his steps and went below. Sudden flight! What would be the reason for their fleeing? No sooner had he asked himself that question when appeared before him the vindictive, vicious face of Danny Parmenter. Here, he was morally certain, rested the efforts of that fellow's malignant brain and cankerous heart.

"I'll hurt you so bad you'll die of the pain of it," Parmenter had threatened.

And here was the hurt. If he still doubted, Cheves told himself, he had only to remember the meeting of Parmenter and Colonel Ralston in the town that same day. The line of evidence was too strong to be overlooked. A roaring anger, a gritting, surpassing rage swept the Virginian. He was done forever with mild means. He would find that fellow and kill him, as he should have done long ago.

If they had fled, Katherine would have left some note for him under the rock beside the barn. He retraced his steps down the pathway, found the rock, and rolled it back. A white bit of paper, released of weight, skipped off in the wind. He made a wild dash and recovered it. By the lantern he read the few brief lines:

Richard:
Danny brought back Father from town, ill. He says there is great danger and that we are to leave immediately. I don't understand it all, but Father believes him. I'm afraid, Dick. John left and didn't come back. What does it mean? Something terrible seems about to happen and there's no one I can trust save you, and you haven't time to worry over us. Danny says we are going to St. Joseph's, then down the Illinois to the Mississippi, and on below to St. Louis. Oh, I wish you were here! Danny's face makes

236

me shiver. It's a terrible night to start out.
Pierre and François go with us, and I feel a
little safer. Dick, come when you can!

Katherine

Bless her! Trying to be honest about the matter and yet
not wanting to pull him away from his duty. "You haven't
time to worry over us." And Parmenter's face made her
shiver! She couldn't keep out that foreboding note. Perhaps
Cheves never suffered so much as in the next fifteen minutes, pacing the ground and puzzling out his own best course
of action.

His own trail was southward to the Maumee. The St.
Joseph's trail turned sharply westward, across the lower
end of the peninsula to the small fort which sat on the south
tip of Lake Michigan. When he left this house and started
his return journey to Kaskaskia, each step took him farther
from the St. Joseph's trail. And his plain duty, inscribed
in every argument he thrust at himself, made him tarry
no longer but to make all haste to Clark. It would be late
summer when he reached his chief with information that
might lead to an expedition northward. And if that expedition were to be successful, it must start before the fall
storms. Thus on his celerity depended a large measure of
the conquest of Detroit and the Northwest. The conquest
of a kingdom for the Americans.

It was a battle of heart and head with this loyal Virginian.
The colonel, he knew, would be so much clay in Parmenter's
hands. The two Frenchmen, very steadfast to the family,
would protect the girl as long as they were able. But once
Parmenter had the upper hand, there was no fathomable
depth to his iniquity. No man can plumb the mind of a

renegade; and Parmenter was a renegade.

Yet out of it all came one unalterable conclusion. The party did not dare to touch the British St. Joseph's. They would skirt it, gain the Illinois River, descend it to the Mississippi, and thence go down by rapid, easy stages to the Spanish town of St. Louis. Such being the route, Parmenter would hardly pick a quarrel with the men of the party until St. Louis was within striking distance. He needed such strength as he possessed too badly to do away with any of them. Posing as British he would gain through the Indian tribes without difficulty. Here, then, was Cheves's hope: to return to Kaskaskia as fast as he was able and, having completed his mission, to strike up the Mississippi and meet the party. Then he would settle with Danny Parmenter.

It was a slim, tenuous hope, and it made Cheves groan to think of what might happen on the long trail down the Illinois. Again, he repeated to himself, the heart of a renegade was unfathomable. But he had no alternative. It was a struggle of head and heart, and the head won, albeit it fairly tore him in twain to make the decision.

Now he must go. There was much territory to be put between him and Detroit town before daybreak filtered through the storm. He left the house, traversed the path and by-road, and came again to the main road, continued southward on it until it dwindled to a thin Indian trace, skirted the river, abruptly left it to plunge westward through a forest, heading ever for the broad highway of the Maumee. He went as fast as his long legs would permit, holding nothing for reserve. The lantern guttered and was extinguished; with an oath of regret he threw it away and continued on. In his heart was a heaviness which he wistfully hoped not many men might be called upon to suffer. The very light of life itself grew more drab the farther he advanced upon the plain path of duty. He wondered why his own lot never seemed to correspond to the many tales of romantic love he had heard or read, where dawn was rose shot, and life seemed an unending bliss.

Westward the course of empire. The unbending, loyal fiber of such men as Richard Cheves made that empire possible. Lesser, weak-grained men could not have done the work. He plunged on through the rioting night. Though every instinct of private and personal desire might cry out in outraged feeling, he could not change his decision. The blood of Virginia held him fast. Eight hundred miles south Clark waited, curbing his bold, impatient imagination until his messenger arrived.

Morning two days later found Cheves forging a steady way up the Maumee trail toward the portage. He did not fear being overtaken now, for he knew that only an Indian runner could keep a faster pace than the one he traveled and, since he came from the direction of Detroit and wore part British equipment, he had but little fear of any obstacle ahead. Thus he relaxed vigilance. The storm which had cloaked his escape from the British stronghold passed over, and now the wet woods steamed under the hot summer's sun.

Once, at noon, he stopped beside the river to eat. When he turned to leave again, he found himself confronted by the sudden apparition of a squad of savages advancing out of concealment. Boldly he adopted the ranger's front, threw up a hand in salutation, and waited. To enlighten them he shoved forward the British pistol and holster, with which he knew they were acquainted. They spoke in a tongue he could not understand but took to be Ottawa, since this was their country. He shook his head and tried French with futility. English was equally incomprehensible to them, and so he at last fell back upon the universal language of signs.

He was, he told them in this medium, from Detroit, going southward, and in very much of a hurry. Three gestures accomplished this much for him, hands forward and back, and a rapid moving of feet. The Big Knives were sending out war parties, and he hastened in advance to warn the lower forts. They nodded gravely, understanding much of this by implication. They also had scouts out and even now some of their chiefs were in Detroit with the white chiefs. A few ceremonious gestures, and they filed in behind him as he retook the path. For an hour they gave him company and then silently faded into the brush and were gone.

Evening brought him by an immense grove of water maple. The river shallowed up and formed a long sliding riffle which sent its wash of sound out through the surrounding territory. Through this Cheves threaded his way, going as long as there was a ray of daylight to guide him. He had come through a copse of hazel, making a horseshoe turn to go by a scarp of rock when, on looking ahead, he saw a tall bearded fellow advancing along the path. Throwing up a hand, the Virginian stopped. The amazing thing happened when the fellow got within ten yards. He had been staring at Cheves with earnest seeking on his face, and now the gaunt, black features broke into a huge smile. A cavernous mouth let out a whoop of joy.

"*Yeee-ipp!* Wal . . . Dick! Dog me, if it hain't himself! Whar in thunderation ye goin' now?"

All that Cheves, amazed, could see was a mass of whiskers and white teeth. When they got quite close, he caught the outline of the bold jaw, the steel-gray eyes, and the beak of a nose. An immediate shaft of warmth and security invaded him.

"Dan Fellows!" he cried in delight.

"Yup. What's left of him. Ain't she a hell of a country to get through?" His face darkened. "Whar's that rat, Parmenter, and his friend, Sartaine? They lit out beyint you, bent on mischief, so I jest took a chaw er baccy an' my gun an' got beyint them."

"Haven't seen Sartaine," replied Cheves. An idea struck him and left him with an expanding heart. He turned off the path and started toward the river. "We camp here."

Thereafter they were busy exchanging notes over the fire and the grub.

"Gosh a'mighty!" exclaimed Fellows in a rage when he heard of Parmenter's career in Detroit. The presence of the Ralstons amazed him, and the whole tangle left him lowering with doubt and anger. "Ef I ever see Parmenter, I'm a-goin' to kill him, s' help me. A dad-burned rat! Sartaine, he prob'ly done for along the trail somewhar's. But the Ralstons! Whut in thunder air we a-goin' to do, Dick?"

"You're goin' to start back to Clark with my information," said Cheves. "I'm turnin' off now for the Saint Joseph's trail. The Maumee parallels it right along here. I'd guess they were a day behind me, since I've been travelin' single and fast. It's a fifty-mile jump from this trail to that one. I ought to intercept them tomorrow night or the next day."

The gaunt-featured backwoodsman grew solemn. "Dick, she's a hell of a journey around Ouiatanon, an' I thought like I'd lose my hair by Vincennes. But I'll go! Whut's the larnin' I'm to take back?"

Cheves summarized it briefly, and bit by bit the sparkle returned to the elder man's eyes.

"You'll have to make a fast trip," warned Cheves. "If Clark is to come north, he'll be wanting to start before the snow flies. I'm comin' down the Mississippi with the Ralstons and without Parmenter."

Fellows's fist clenched across the fire. "Dick, don't ye take no chances," he insisted. "Shoot him like a copperhead. Don't you git any hifalutin notions about his honor. Birds don't have teeth, nuther do renegades have any Virginny spirit. I'm afeard you'll be a givin' him too much rope and fust thing he'll stab you in the back. You don't never take a hint from the tricks he's worked. Now you be foreminded and watch him close."

"I understand thoroughly," returned Cheves somberly. "Be sure you explain to Clark the reason I'm doin' this. Let's turn in now. There's hard work ahead."

Fellows sighed and shook his head, running a horny paw across the jet whiskers. "Wisht you'd let me go. Ain't never been a time but what you give him too much leeway. I'm dumned afeard." Sitting cross-legged before the fire, black and saturnine of visage, and brooding of eye, he appeared a harbinger of fate. He sighed again. "Damned Ouiatanon! Wisht they'd a-built it a hundred miles to one side of the Wabash. Took me a week to git around it. Thought I was nigh to losin' my hair, too."

The fire sank lower and the swish of the riffles lulled them to a wary sleep.

XII

"SHOWDOWN"

That night, one hundred miles to the northeast, Colonel Henry Ralston gave up his life from physical exhaustion, and Parmenter's somber eyes seemed flecked with sardonic amusement as tragedy stalked abroad for Katherine Ralston. Yet, being a thoroughbred woman, she closed her mouth tight down over the impulse to loose bitter tears and reined her horse — she rode the single plow horse that the Ralston place had boasted — to follow Parmenter and the two Frenchmen. They had buried her father in a crude, unsatisfactory way in the sandy soil of a creek bottom and weighted the grave down with rocks. This latter precaution had been the stubborn insistence of Pierre and François. Parmenter looked on and cursed them for the delay. Then it was the girl saw this man's real worth and turned away to shudder. Betwixt her and the menace of him was only the strength of the two servants. She wondered how long they would resist the cunning and trickery he displayed and, wondering, was lost in an abyss of misery. Better a thousand times imprisonment in Detroit than all the misfortune now upon them.

The trip through the storm had been a nightmare made increasingly terrible by the knowledge that her father gave up more of his small supply of vitality with each punishing step after Parmenter. And now the irony of it! With her father dead and buried, Parmenter had relaxed the pace.

"I think we can slow up a bit," he said, dropping beside her. "We're out of their track. Cheer up, my dear. Don't look so solemn. Your father was an old man. His time had come to die."

She kept her gaze straight ahead, not replying, not even wishing to notice him. Anger struggled through a dead load of grief.

"And don't pout," he added with a touch of petulance. "I'm goin' to get you out of a difficult situation. You should be grateful for that. I think, when we get to Saint Louis, you should show your appreciation in a more tangible form, my dear."

She blazed up at that, turning fairly toward him. "Danny, have you not enough courtesy to keep from calling me endearing names to which you have no right? Can't you ever be a gentleman? Must you always be using unfair means to make love?"

"Unfair?" He grew sullen on the instant. "You've never been anything but unfair to me, young lady! Didn't you play with me and then throw me over for that scoundrel, Cheves?"

"Stop! I'll not have you call him that! You don't even possess decency enough not to run a man down behind his back. I thought there never was a Virginia man who would do that."

"Don't use heroics on me. I won't stand for them. All that kind of sentiment is dead. Honor . . . decency! Pah! Those are just subterfuges you women nurse to keep a man off, until you want him. Don't try them on me."

"I wish," she said, very pale, "that Richard Cheves were here."

"That paragon of virtue! That sugar-mouthed, wooden-faced, lead soldier! You'll never see him again." Parmenter sneered with a short, contemptuous laugh. "He's one of these toadyin' general's pets and, so help me, I'll settle with him one of these days!"

The vitriolic passion in his voice startled Katherine. She squared about in the saddle, hoping that he might leave and go ahead. He had raised his voice to such a pitch that Pierre, marching fifty yards in advance, turned about and halted, a dogged expression on his face.

"Get ahead!" stormed Parmenter, swayed by his rage. "Who told you to drop back here?"

"I stay here eef I like, you unerstan'?" replied Pierre. "I don't take no talk from a fallow like you," he glowered.

Parmenter shifted a hand to his pistol. Something in the steady expression of the Frenchman halted that movement, and he finished by brushing past the man and striding along the trail.

"Pierre," breathed the girl, "stay by me."

"*Mais oui,* eef he use hees mout' too much, Pierre he weel close eet."

"I never knew," she said, more to herself than to her servant, "that he could be so violent."

"Hees eye, Pierre don' like. Dere's wan bad cast, like a wil' horse."

The trail to St. Joseph's was a thing to be hunted for and carefully kept, so thin and uncertain a trace did it make through the varied country of the lower peninsula. After leaving Detroit, they had passed a succession of hard wood groves. Now pine began to cover the ground and the trail twisted through multifold varieties of underbrush. They forded a stream shrunk the size of a creek — and here lost the way altogether.

Parmenter scouted ahead for the best part of a forenoon before finding the route, which did not help his surly disposition in the least. Once, the elder Frenchman, François, got in his path. The Virginian shoved him aside with a grunt of disgust. François hit the ground, and his wrinkled face puckered from the hurt of it. Pierre gave a shout and grabbed at his wrist. The sun glinted on the blade of his knife as he came by Parmenter's elbow.

"Don' make dat meestake no more," he growled. "You wan' t' fight, eh? *Alors,* anny time you say, den we fight."

Parmenter thrust a bloodshot glance at him and forged on. Pierre dropped back, shaking his head in manifest displeasure and sending a rapid volley of French at his partner.

The afternoon shimmered and danced under the September heat. The pace of the party slackened, each member suffering. Even the patient, slow-footed horse moved with difficulty, tongue hanging sidewise from its mouth. Pierre stalked directly ahead of Katherine, and François kept the middle ground between the young Frenchman and Parmenter. The latter's face had gone white. Obviously the man suffered in a physical way but still stronger was the goad of his temper, stinging him to fury. His initial hatred of Cheves was rendered the more intense by Katherine Ralston's contempt and Pierre's cool defiance.

Added to this was perhaps a fear that he made ill progress on the St. Joseph's trail. The signs of travel had faded into the forest carpet some distance back. He judged his way now solely by the width and accessibility of the terrain ahead. He had embarked upon this expedition with knowledge and confidence mostly assumed. Now he floundered and doubted. The rest of the party kept its own counsel and suffered in silence.

The sun fell over the horizon, and the cool of evening brought its sweet relief. They crossed a green bottom and came to a creek. Parmenter waded and kept his way. The Frenchman stopped to see that horse and rider got safely over. The animal limped patiently to the water's edge and stopped to drink. Katherine felt its flanks quiver.

"Poor Ted," she said, "he's very tired. And so am I. Why can't we stop here for the night? Perhaps we'll not find water farther on."

Pierre nodded his head and thrust up a hand for her to dismount. Thus he took the management of the party on his own shoulders. François mumbled a word of warning, to which Pierre responded by a shrug and motioned for his partner to get firewood.

Parmenter threshed back through the brush and sent out a shout across the creek. "We don't stop here. There's another mile or better to go before dark. Come along."

"We stop w'en *ma'm'selle* ees tired, *m'sieu*," replied Pierre, all softness. "Eef you wan' to go anudder mile, *allez*." He spoke in a pleasant way yet, anticipating the coming storm, squared toward the Virginian and thrust both hands to his hips.

"Be careful, Pierre," warned the girl. She raised her voice. "If you don't mind, Danny, I'd like to stop here. I'm so tired."

"I don't want to stop," yelled Parmenter, "and I'll have no half-breed tellin' me what to do! Pick up the reins of that horse, put the girl back on, and come through," he ordered.

Pierre was pleasantly obstinate. He manipulated a shrug, without letting his hands stray far from the sheath-knife. "*Ma'm'selle* is ver' tired. We rest here."

"Will you do as I say?" roared Parmenter. The pistol came to his hand.

"Never mind, Pierre," said the girl. "I'll get back on."

Pierre smiled and shook his head. His eyes never wavered from the pistol.

"We stay here, *m'sieu*," he repeated, and gathered his muscles.

The pistol came level with Parmenter's angry eyes. The Frenchman gave a prodigious leap aside and down as the report came and uttered a cry of pain. He had not been quick enough. The bullet caught him in the arm. He was up, next instant, leaping forward with the spring of an injured cat, fumbling for his knife with the left hand. Parmenter reversed his pistol and waited.

"Don't, Pierre!" cried the girl. "Don't!"

Pierre stumbled through the water, gathered himself, and sprang upon Parmenter. Katherine Ralston, looking fearfully on, saw the knife describe an arc and slash through the Virginian's tunic, saw, at the same time, the heavy pistol butt come down upon the Frenchman's head. The latter slid to the ground, leaving Parmenter above him, swaying and holding fast to a shoulder.

"The beggar slashed me," he said, then raised his head. "Now will you do as I say? Come on!" he snarled.

"No," said the girl, "I will not."

Parmenter, breathing heavily, glared at her for a full minute in a battle of wills then gave in. "All right," he yielded sullenly. He gave the prone figure a prod with his foot and recrossed the stream. "Get the wood," he ordered François.

Katherine Ralston went to the creek.

"Where you goin'?" queried Parmenter.

She refused to answer, waded the stream, and knelt beside Pierre. Parmenter sat apathetically on a log and watched her spill water on the unconscious man's face.

Presently Pierre stirred and sat up, got his bearings, and protested at her ministrations. "Eet's noddin'. *Ma'm'selle,* she should not bodder wit' me."

Despite her protests he struggled to his feet and returned across the stream. It distressed him to see her wading in the water after him, yet he did not dare to carry her over.

François nursed the fire, and Pierre made shift at supper with now and then a covert glance at Parmenter. It was plain to see that he put no trust in the other. But the Virginian scarcely stirred. The whole driving animus that rendered him active and dangerous had apparently evaporated, and he seemed only a dull, petty sort of figure, engrossed wholly in himself. A tinge of red colored one sleeve of his shirt; the knife wound was, from all appearances, only a scratch. When the time came to eat, the girl, out of the pure sympathy of her heart, motioned for him to get his share. Mechanically he obeyed. It put courage in her to see him thus, and she did dare to ask him a question that had long been troubling her.

"Danny, where are we now?" she queried.

"A little better than half way to Saint Joseph's," he replied. "And off the trail. I think we're too far south."

She had not the heart to ask more. A fresh feeling of despondency swept her. With all the misfortune of this ill-starred journey, the culminating catastrophe must come to break her small shoulders. It took the savor from the food she ate.

At that moment Richard Cheves, guided by the pistol shot, had reached the creek at a lower point and was following it upstream. That shot was the first tangible result of a heartbreaking three-day journey. A bit later he turned a bend and caught the cheerful light of the fire. Here he crossed the stream, without noise, and threaded the trees.

Fifty yards off he stopped to forewarn himself. He saw, first of all, like a sinister beacon, the hunched form of Parmenter on the log; next, he caught alternate sight of the Frenchmen as they moved about the clearing looking for firewood. And, with a stirring heart that seemed recompense enough for the toil and privation he had undergone, he saw last the small, bowed figure of Katherine Ralston looking soberly into the flames. Though he searched all parts of the clearing, he did not find Colonel Ralston, and this troubled him. Well, time to go forward, time to put a full stop to his worries and their worries. He shifted his holster and advanced to the light.

Katherine saw him first. It was wonderful to note the way her face changed from shadow to sunlight.

"Dick!" she cried.

Parmenter sprang to his feet as though stung by a scorpion and reached for his gun. It was then too late. Cheves stood in front of him.

"Easy, Danny, just a moment. You and I'll square up in just a minute," he said. Then he turned to the girl and announced simply, "I came as fast as I could, as soon as I could, Katherine."

"I knew you would." Her face echoed her words.

"Where," he said, in that same sober, granite-like tone, "is your father?"

"Dead," she whispered. "It was too hard for him."

She saw his face clearly then, as he turned toward Danny Parmenter and the fire. It was thin and fatigued from hard traveling, with lines stamped upon it that do not belong to a man of twenty-eight. The hard frontier! It was not a life for soft men and, if frontier hearts were sometimes steeled beyond human compassion, it was because inexorable forces so tempered them. She pitied Danny Parmenter.

"Well," said Cheves, "are you ready now?"

"My gun is not loaded."

"I heard it a while back," Cheves acknowledged. "Load it."

His eyes did not leave Parmenter while the operation took place.

"All right, go in front of me, Danny, straight down the creek." He turned to Katherine. "One of us will be back in a moment."

Her heart constricted until it seemed on the verge of breaking. She thought to cry out and say — "Don't! Let well enough be!" — but she knew immediately that here was a man whose mind she could not change now. So she bowed her head, lest he might see the suffering on it, and clenched her hands.

She heard the brush crack under foot and the steady tramp of deliberate steps marching to duel, receding out of hearing until all was silent. The whole world stood on tiptoe, it seemed, waiting for the one event to take place. Pierre refueled the fire and, while still kneeling, crossed himself. She found herself counting.

The roar of a pistol shot rushed through the woods. She gave a small cry and immediately suppressed it. One shot! Only one shot! One man had not even a chance to fire! Pierre sprang up, all aquiver.

"By gar, I bet Parmenter he shoot biffor de time come! Dere ees wan cast in dose eye, like a wil' horse!"

Again she found herself counting and listening, wholly numb to all other thought and sensation.

The second shot!

251

Soon she heard the methodical tramp of a man's feet, growing louder and louder until he stood on the threshold of the clearing, until he had come by the fire, until he stood before her. With a supreme effort of will she forced up her head and found there the grave, lined face of Richard Cheves looking down at her with inexpressible hope and longing and sadness.

She gave a cry and was the next moment in his arms. The whole pent-up flood of emotion broke and swept her away. She was crying, crying as though her heart were about to break. Cheves held her, saying nothing at all but fully content just to hold her.

They skirted St. Joseph's and came to the navigable Illinois. Here Cheves boldly entered an Indian village and bartered for a canoe. With it they continued down the river in long stages until the broad Mississippi met them. They paddled ever southward and one fine day sighted an American flag over Kaskaskia. Clark was there to meet them, and after attending to the girl, took Cheves to his headquarters. Fellows had come through a week previously with the vital news, but Clark wanted the information first hand and Cheves told his story from beginning to end.

Clark's aggressive, stubborn face lit. "They will come south, then, Cheves?"

"Hamilton at the head of the party," Cheves nodded.

"When will this be, do you think?"

"Between now and winter. There's but a small force in Detroit and they can't spare many men now."

"That's our opportunity!" Clark's fist smote the puncheon table. "Colonel Hamilton never will see Detroit again if he comes."

With the information Cheves had brought back from the British post, George Rogers Clark won the Northwest for a new and democratic nation. Hamilton and Dejean came south in the fall of that same year. Clark engaged them in the winter campaign across the Illinois drowned lands and took them both prisoners of war. The victory forever ended British dominion south of Detroit. Henceforth the whole broad sweep of that plain was American. The power of Detroit town had been broken by one audacious commander backed by the impatient and rugged men under him. Of that Northwestern victory Cheves performed the pioneer work that made the last great coup possible. As another result of Cheves's arduous undertaking, the Americans embarked on a system of rangers to combat the British. Throughout the Wabash land these solitary voyagers met and successfully coped with foreign representatives, stood before Indian camp fires, and told of a new authority in the land. The Long Knives — the Americans — had come to stay.

It was within the fort at Kaskaskia that Katherine Ralston and Richard Cheves were married.

"I can't leave this country," he told her. "It's a great empire. You and I have helped make it, and we've got to stay. There'll be thousands coming across the Alleghenies and down the Ohio to keep us company. Here I shall stake my claim."

"Where you go, there I shall be," she reminded him.

On the rich bottom land of the Illinois, fronting the Mississippi, they made their home.

THE END

New Hope

Ernest Haycox

New Hope combines three of Ernest Haycox's finest short novels with the interconnected stories he wrote about New Hope, a freighting town on the Missouri River in what was then Nebraska Territory. In "The Roaring Hour," Clay Travis, the new town marshal, and his fiancée, Gail, are up against the combined forces of the gambling hall owner, the sheriff controlled by him, and the local outlaw leader. A young upstart holds up a stagecoach in "The Kid from River Red" to prove his manhood and impress an outlaw. "The Hour of Fury" tells the tale of Dane Starr, who has come to town to lose his identity as a gunfighter and instead finds himself at the center of a dangerous power struggle.

___4721-7 $4.50 US/$5.50 CAN

Dorchester Publishing Co., Inc.
P.O. Box 6640
Wayne, PA 19087-8640

Please add $1.75 for shipping and handling for the first book and $.50 for each book thereafter. NY, NYC, and PA residents, please add appropriate sales tax. No cash, stamps, or C.O.D.s. All orders shipped within 6 weeks via postal service book rate. Canadian orders require $2.00 extra postage and must be paid in U.S. dollars through a U.S. banking facility.

Name_____
Address_____
City_____ State _____ Zip _____
I have enclosed $ _____ in payment for the checked book(s).
Payment <u>must</u> accompany all orders. ❑ Please send a free catalog.

ACKNOWLEDGEMENTS

"A Burnt Creek Yuletide" first appeared in Street & Smith's *Western Story Magazine* (12/20/24). Copyright © 1925 by Street & Smith Publications, Inc. Copyright © renewed 1953 by Jill Marie Haycox. Copyright © 1996 for restored material by Ernest Haycox, Jr.

"Bud Dabbles in Homesteads" first appeared in Street & Smith's *Western Story Magazine* (11/1/24). Copyright © 1924 by Street & Smith Publications, Inc. Copyright © renewed 1952 by Jill Marie Haycox. Copyright © 1996 for restored material by Ernest Haycox, Jr.

"When Money Went to His Head" first appeared in Street & Smith's *Western Story Magazine* (10/25/24). Copyright © 1924 by Street & Smith Publications, Inc. Copyright © renewed 1952 by Jill Marie Haycox. Copyright © 1996 for restored material by Ernest Haycox, Jr.

"Stubborn People" first appeared in Street & Smith's *Western Story Magazine* (12/27/24). Copyright © 1925 by Street & Smith Publications, Inc. Copyright © renewed 1953 by Jill Marie Haycox. Copyright © 1996 for restored material by Ernest Haycox, Jr.

"False Face" first appeared in Street & Smith's *Western Story Magizine* (2/13/26). Copyright © 1926 by Street & Smith Publications, Inc. Copyright © renewed 1954 by Jill Marie Haycox. Copyright © 1996 for restored material by Ernest Haycox, Jr.

"Rock-Bound Honesty" first appeared in Street & Smith's *Western Story Magazine* (6/12/26). Copyright © 1926 by Street & Smith Publications, Inc. Copyright © renewed 1954 by Jill Marie Haycox. Copyright © 1996 for restored material by Ernest Haycox, Jr.

"Prairie Yule" first appeared in Street & Smith's *Western Story Magazine* (12/19/25). Copyright © 1926 by Street Smith Publications, Inc. Copyright © renewed 1954 by Jill Marie Haycox. Copyright © 1996 for restored material by Ernest Haycox, Jr.

"Red Knives" first appeared in *The Frontier* (4/25). Copyright © 1925 by Doubleday, Page & Company, Inc. Copyright © renewed 1953 by Jill Marie Haycox. Copyright © 1996 for restored material by Ernest Haycox, Jr.